William Hope Harvey

A Tale of Two Nations

William Hope Harvey

A Tale of Two Nations

ISBN/EAN: 9783742862983

Manufactured in Europe, USA, Canada, Australia, Japa

Cover: Foto ©Andreas Hilbeck / pixelio.de

Manufactured and distributed by brebook publishing software
(www.brebook.com)

William Hope Harvey

A Tale of Two Nations

A TALE OF TWO NATIONS

BY

W. H. MARVEY

—

To the people of this age—and
ages yet to come—this book
is dedicated.

NOTE

This book was extensively advertised to appear illustrated. On its completion it was found that illustrations as designed would add so greatly to its size as to make it impracticable to illustrate it and produce a 25 cent edition. The ability to have it accessible to the general reader and the great masses of the people, was regarded as of more importance than to add to it the illustrations. It has therefore been published in its present form. The characters are so faithfully described and the scenes so graphically presented that the story needs nothing to add to its value.

It will, however, be dramatized and will appear upon the American stage in living pictures. There are three editions in print: One to be sold at 25 cents; another printed on fine paper and bound in double enamel paper cover at 50 cents, and a third on fine super-calendered paper, bound in cloth, the price of which is one dollar.

THE PUBLISHERS

A TALE OF TWO NATIONS.

CHAPTER I.

Two bankers and financial operators in London met one evening at the residence of one of them by invitation of the host, to discuss what he claimed to be a highly important matter. It was in the year 1869. The fog had hung heavily over the big metropolis all day long, and the manipulators of stocks, bonds and money, had deserted their offices early in the afternoon, to frequent the clubs, or to enjoy the luxury of their magnificent homes.

Baron Rothe, the host, was a portly, well-fed, brainy diplomat and financier. He dealt in bonds, and in bonds only, save that he was a banker and that through his bank all deals were made. The bonds he bought and sold were governments or municipals or the first issue of railway bonds. All of his collaterals were such that he could realize on them at any time in a few days. This is what he called safe financiering. If at any time he so desired, he could have raised the enormous sum of two hundred and fifty million dollars or fifty million pounds sterling, on ten days' notice. He came of a family of financiers and was an improvement on his ancestors.

His guest, Sir William T. Cline, like himself, was very wealthy, and had two brothers and a partner, each of whom enjoyed about the same amount of this world's goods as himself. His advice was the governing monitor of the four. He had planned successful money-making campaigns in Chili, Argentine, South Africa and India. He liked bonds and gave them the preference, yet sometimes dealt in stocks. His affairs were in good shape, and if his wealth and that of his partners had all been converted into money it would have made an amount greater than was that of the king of money-makers whose sumptuous library he had just entered.

Both believed in the power of money, and held in contempt any man not "solidly on his feet." The merchant and trader did not belong to their set. They were another breed of men. The merchant, no matter how great, was to them a shop keeper, and the trader, like him, traded with the common herd—with individuals—while these magnates dealt with governments and corporations. They knew they were aped by the large class of well-to-do people, and that their dictum would be accepted generally on matters of finance by this large following who only heard but to repeat.

The Baron arose to greet his friend, the former large, of medium height, and fine looking, his hair dark with streaks of gray. The latter, neither thin nor stout, in good health, smooth-shaven, looking young for his age. Both were about fifty.

"I am glad you came early," said the Baron, "for I wish to elucidate a matter to-night upon which I am not sure we shall at once agree or that you will readily admit the force of my proposition. Take a cigar—they were made especially for me in Havana." Then touching a button on the wall, a male servant responded and was told to bring some wines.

In the meantime Sir William had made himself comfortable in a large leather chair and announced that he was ready to listen to anything from discussing nitrate investments in Chili, to a new issue of government bonds by the United States.

"I wish to talk with you this evening," began the Baron, as he seated himself on a hard-bottom chair, facing Sir William, "about something bigger than bonds. Something bigger than either of us, or all of us together, have ever undertaken."

"Well," replied his guest, "I am your most attentive listener, and if what you have to say is as pleasant as your cigars, you will have a most appreciative audience."

"For more than a year," continued the Baron, as if he had not been interrupted, "I have been trying to satisfy myself as to the effect a single standard of money would have, if adopted by the whole world. I have been playing a game of chess, as it were, with myself, and studying the combinations. I know now exactly what the result will be, and that it is feasible."

"Where is the money in it for us?" asked Sir William.

"Wait till I am done, and you will not ask such an idle question. England is now, and has been since 1816, on a gold basis. All values here are measured in gold. Silver is token money; but—15½ to 1—silver is worth as much as gold. The reason is, the balance of the world is on a bimetallic basis. With them, both gold and silver are legal tender in the payment of all debts, and their mints are open to coin all that comes of both metals. The ratio in the United States is 16 to 1. In France it is 15½ to 1. The stock of silver in the world is so small, that the free and unlimited coinage of it into money, by any one large nation like France, Russia or the United States, will make a sufficient demand for it, to maintain its value, and while these conditions exist, the whole world is virtually on a bimetallic basis, and that includes us.

"So long as things go on in the way they are now going, silver and gold will continue to trot in the financial harness side by side, and our law that we have had since 1816 is a dead letter. No man will sell his silver here for less than 15½ to 1, when he can cross the channel into France and at that ratio exchange it for gold. Hence, if we want his silver to use in India, we must buy it with gold at the French ratio. If the French ratio is knocked out, then we will have the American ratio to contend with, which is 16 to 1. No one here would part with his silver for less than 16 for 1, when he could get that for it in the United States. If the United States and the principal governments of Europe adopt our law as to silver, it will double your fortune and mine. Our money will have a purchasing power twice as great as it now has.

"It will do more for England than conquests by arms, on both land and sea, could do in a thousand years. England is a creditor nation. Her greatest rival to-day is the United States. If things continue as they now promise, that great American republic will soon rival us as the creditor nation of the world. The only way to defeat this is to keep her in debt to us. From my latest advices, I am satisfied they are opening up enormous mines of gold and silver, and will soon have it in their power to achieve the object I fear, unless we take it away from them.

"If we can induce the nations I have named and the United States to demonetize silver, here is what the result will be. We will use their silver, bought at a large discount, to ship to India. India wheat and India cotton will cost us as much less than American wheat and cotton as we can depress the price of silver. It will have a double effect on their wheat and cotton. We will use their cheap silver to buy wheat and cotton in India. It will reduce the amount of actual money to the quantity of gold, and all values must shrink accordingly. The American producer must meet this competition from India, and down will come all their prices. We will destroy silver, one of the principal sources of their wealth, and with the fall in values we will destroy their balance of trade. With their wonderful recuperative powers, if they still force a balance of trade in their favor in the exchange of merchandise and commodities, we must take the balance of money in settlement away from them in interest on bonds and other loans."

"That sounds well," interjected Sir William.

"What would make the United States the dominant nation of the world," continued the host, "would be her *net* balance of trade. At the present prices for her cereals, backed with her enormous production of gold and silver, in thirty years, as I have stated, she will be richer than England, if not richer than all Europe. She will own her own debts, and all the world will be paying her tribute.

"We must destroy this balance of trade in her favor. To do it, we must demonetize her silver. It is the key to the situation. All the rest will follow."

CHAPTER II.

While the Baron was thus delivering himself, Sir William had first listened attentively and seriously; this had now changed to an incredulous smile, and his first interruption was to ask,

"Do you believe that a man can be persuaded to cut his own throat?"

'Yes," was the reply. "It is being done every day! I have considered that. In the first place let me tell you, there is not one man in a million who understands the science of money. In the whole American Congress there are probably not two men who understand it. Now, here is a five-pound note"—and as he spoke he took from his pocket a note and a silver shilling. "*It* is not money. And this silver shilling, with us, is not money. The people think they are both money. The note is a promise to pay money, and the silver piece is also by law a like promise to pay money. In each instance the money promised is gold.

'If the world is put on a gold basis, the only money will be gold—all other forms of so-called money will be promises to pay money. Paper notes and silver coin will bear the same relation to money—gold—as your checks would bear to your bank account.

"Actual money will support about so much secondary money—or rather promissory notes of the government to pay money on demand. Outside of England gold and silver are both money. We can get them to shift the position of silver from money to that of credit money, and not one in ten thousand will see wherein it makes any difference.

"Here is another proposition they cannot see. Money, and I now mean *money*, measures its value in property, and property measures its value in money. Now, they all understand that the less there is of any one kind of property for which there is a regular demand, the higher the price that property brings in the market, and when there is an over-abundance of that kind of property the less it brings in the market. But they don't understand that the less *money* there is, the higher price *it* brings.

"You cannot understand the feasibility of my plans, until you appreciate how ignorant the people are on monetary questions. I will illustrate it this way: Suppose silver was demonetized as *money*, in the United States, but was left in circulation as secondary or token money, and before and after that act there were 500 million of gold, 500 million of silver, and 500 million of paper money in circulation. The statement would be made after demonetization and accepted as the truth, *that there was as much money in circulation as there ever was.* The fact would be that before demonetization there was 1,000 million of *money*, and after demonetization there was only 500 million of *money*. In the first instance the gold and silver both would be money, and in the other case gold only would be money—the silver and paper would be promises to pay money.

"I can see now in my mind some old college professor who imagines he is a scholar in political economy, tackling this question about like my little boy would a grizzly bear."

By this time Sir William had sipped a second glass
of wine and was lighting another cigar. At the last
remark he laughed, and as he leaned back in his chair
and crossed his legs he said,

"Baron, it would be a good idea, then, to keep up
our donations to the colleges, hey? But for the life of
me, I don't see how you are going to get it through
in the United States. I could put it through the Latin
Union myself, but I am skeptical of those Yankees.
They have always been too smart for us."

"That is true," said the Baron, "in war, but not in
money matters. But it will have to be nicely managed.
This is a one man's world. One man on the finance
committee in the Senate, and one on the same committee in the House, and one hundred thousand pounds,
and the job is done. Once enacted into a law, we are
safe."

"I think you have underestimated the integrity and
sagacity of the members of the American Congress.
The proposition will be combated, it will raise a storm
throughout the republic and your agents will be powerless," said Sir William.

"But you do not understand the conditions to be
dealt with. A bill can be presented to reform the coinage laws—a bill innocent on its face. It is customary,
I find, every few years for such a bill to be put
through. This bill, on its face, would not demonetize
silver, but, as enrolled, it would. Congressmen would
vote for it under the impression of a necessity for a
revision of the coinage laws. The interlineation of a
line or the changing of a word and the bill as finally
recorded would be as we desire it. I doubt whether
it would become known for several years. You must

remember that the American people have not yet resumed specie payments, and the only money they are handling is paper money. It circulates on the confidence of the people that it will be ultimately redeemed, but they are not now handling either gold or silver. They are off their guard and this is the opportune time to strike the blow."

' "Yes, but," interposed Sir William, "when they do discover it, a cry will go up and repeal will be inevitable. The public will—"

"The public be damned. Once enacted into a law it can be maintained. Every money lender and banker in America will arraign himself on the side of the new law. Show a man how he can collect a dear dollar for a cheap dollar and he will be in favor of it every time. Patriotism will cut no figure with them. Money has no patriotism. The combined wealth of the United States will support the law. They will see the direct benefit to themselves, but they will not see the general wreck and bankruptcy that will ultimately come, pulling most of them down with it. They will bite at it, like flies do at poisoned molasses. We will set in motion arguments in favor of a single standard, and they will help us devise new ones. These arguments can be made ingenious. To repeal the law, it will require both Houses and the President to be in favor of the repeal. You can risk our friends in Wall street to take care of one of these three."

Sir William here arose and began to pace the floor. He put his hands behind him and hung his head in deep thought. The man's impulses were 'for humanity, and had his training been different he might have been a philanthropist. At last he said:

Baron, the result will be terrible.   The people will
put off the evil day by borrowing, until they cannot
borrow any more, and then there will be sad havoc.
People will go hungry.   Women and children, who
will have no conception of the cause of their suffering,
will be reduced to poverty and wretchedness.   Baron,
do you think this is right?"

He stopped, and turning round, faced his companion, and continued:

"The fall in prices, the shrinkage of industries, the
hopeless position of the debtor classes as values decline in adjusting themselves to this reduced quantity
of money—no, do not tell me that the people in a republic, where they elect their own president and legislature, will permit such a state of affairs to exist."

"Then," replied Baron Rothe, marking the effect of
his words through half closed eyelids, "England must
cease to control the commerce of the world.   All the
earth will no longer pay tribute to us.   The power of
London will be transferred to New York.   The people
who have humiliated us at every opportunity will have
new cause to rejoice.   We tried to cripple them in
their late war by dismembering the nation.   Had we
succeeded, they would have still further split up into
republics like South America, and their national suprem-
acy would have been destroyed.   But they have come
out of that danger stronger than ever, and unless my
plan is adopted, the day of our decay is fast approaching, I tell you, Sir William, it is a national necessity.

"Enough!" said Sir William.   "I will further your
plans, if you put them in shape, but I fear they are
impractical.   You may get the law passed but its
repeal is certain to follow."

"Sir William, I would not undertake it, were I not so sure of the woeful ignorance of the masses on the subject of money. When the effects of demonetization set in, they will act like a nest of rattlesnakes in dog-days when a load of shot is fired into them., They will wiggle and twist and bite each other, but will have no conception of what hurts them. They will lay it on everything but the right thing. And when they finally discover what did it, if they ever do, it will be too late; the power of money will have done its work. It will establish two classes—the rich and the poor. The first, to enjoy this world, and the other to live by waiting on the first. We must crush their manhood and independence by making them poor—they then make good servants and gentle citizens.

"Now join me in a drink to merry old England, on whose possessions the sun never sets—may she continue to encircle the world with her influence. and London remain the Capital."

And there they stood, one on each side of the table, and drank to the prosperity of their native land. The success of their scheme meant much to them personally, and more to their city and government. It meant ruin and desolation to the republic across the ocean.

They smiled, passed pleasantries, and talked of family matters. Returning to the subject later on, Sir William remarked: "Baron, you seem to have studied out every phase of this movement. Tell me how you are going to get your senator and congressman out of 'h' hole when it is discovered that the bill enrolled is not the bill that was read."

Baron Rothe replied, "I will tell you. When Congress is about to adjourn, things are done in a great

rush.   In rare instances bills are voted on without being read, an explanation of the chairman of the committee having the bill in charge being accepted.   We
must seek that opportunity.   There is another custom
among them that will also help us.   It is usual to
grant a member the right to have his   speech printed
in the record without ever having delivered it;   or of
changing it.   In this way we will have no trouble in
showing afterward that the bill, as passed, was explained to be just what it is.

"I will at once arrange for a distinguished member
of the United States Senate to visit this country, and
I am sure from an investigation I have had made as
to his desire to make money, his antecedents, and selfish disposition, we will be able to make him our easy
instrument."

With this the conference ended.   Sir William's carriage was ordered for his. return home.   It was the
beginning of a financial movement that was to encircle
the globe.   It began as was suitable, in the financial
center of the world.   Its prompting motive was self-
aggrandizement, but the memories of Bunker Hill,
Lexington and New Orleans, whetted the appetite and
made keen the desire to enter upon the herculean and
seemingly impossible undertaking.

CHAPTER III.

"Father, this card is for you."

The speaker was a young lady, tall and graceful. She was about twenty-two years of age, and her black eyes and raven hair betrayed her Semitic origin. She was dressed in a dark, fluffy material that set off her beautiful figure to advantage.

She was the daughter of Baron Rothe, and had inherited the form and features of her mother. Modest and unassuming in manner, gentle in disposition, she also possessed that rare taste in style of dress and care of person, which adds so greatly to the charms of woman.

She was standing just inside the library, where she had come to speak to her father about some trivial matter, and was in the act of going out, when a servant opened the door and presented a golden salver, on which lay a card. Removing it, and with the remark that opens this chapter, she walked over to the desk where her father sat and handed it to him.

The Baron read the inscription on the bit of pasteboard, and as his daughter turned to leave the room said:

"One moment, Edith."

And as she returned to his side, he continued slowly, without raising his eyes from the card:

"Edith, the gentleman now waiting in the reception room is a member of the United States Senate. He arrived in London yesterday, and as you see, has sought an interview with me to-day. I have reasons, important ones, for desiring to know more of the true character of this man than I may be able to glean from a short interview and I desire your assistance."

He was looking straight into her eyes now, and she, in some wonder, heard and noted his request.

"Women," he went on, "as a rule, excel in reading character, particularly of the opposite sex. At your age your mother possessed this faculty to a very remarkable degree and I never found her to be at fault. You are her daughter, very like her in all other respects, and I believe this gift is also yours. He will be shown in shortly, and after we have been together some minutes, do you find an excuse for entering the room. An introduction will enable you to notice him well and I trust you may be able to read what I desire to know. When our interview is concluded, come to me here."

She had stood silently looking down into her father's earnest face while he was speaking, and now taking the card he still held, said quietly:

"I am aware that I do possess the faculty you speak of, father, though not perhaps to an extent such as you seem to believe; but of course I will aid you if I can. I presume this is his autograph?"

It was in truth the autograph of the caller, written at his hotel just before leaving, and its plain and not too bold characters traced the name, "*John Arnold, U. S.*"

Edith Rothe held the card in her hand a moment, then laying it on the desk before her, smiled confidently into the Baron's somewhat grave face as she said:

"I will tell you all about him, papa, if he is not *too* sphinx like," and as she turned to go, he answered:

"I am sure you will. Be kind enough to tell James to show him in here."

A moment later Senator John Arnold of the United States entered the sumptuous library of the money king of Europe.

The Baron greeted his caller warmly, and with much friendliness, the reserve which usually marked his meeting with Americans being quite absent.

He offered his distinguished visitor a courteous apology for the few minutes the latter had been kept waiting, and expressed the hope that the Senator had "experienced a pleasant voyage, with no ill effects."

"Thank you," replied the Senator. "We encountered no rough weather, and as you will note, I am not of that 'build' to be readily afflicted with *mal de mer*."

The American was tall and thin, being about five feet and eleven inches in height, and weighing not to exceed 140 pounds. In contrast to the rotund Baron he appeared thinner than he really was. In his own land the Senator was known as a remarkably bright man, a lawyer by profession, and had served several terms in the United States congress; first in the lower house and later in the senate. He was one of the recognized leaders of his party, a leader of leaders, and no steps were taken toward the framing of a policy for that party without first consulting with Senator Arnold.

He had been, thus far in a small way, a successful financier, and by his party associates was generally recognized as an authority on matters of finance. He was conservative, possessed a quick and intelligent comprehension of public questions, and bankers and

business men generally of his own country had great
confidence in his judgment and discretion.

The United States congress had adjourned and the
Senator had come abroad for a period of rest and recuperation. The season was now May, and the conversation between the Baron and his guest naturally
drifted to England and its climate, now at its best.
During all, the Baron was closely studying his companion, carefully observing all he said and noting the
words and manner of the reply; yet so diplomatically
that one would have thought him anxious to entertain
only. He possessed that charm of manner given to so
few of making one feel at ease in his presence and to
lose one's self in interest in the man and what he said.
So that it was not long ere the stiffness of reserve in
the manner of the American upon meeting the richest
man in Europe, gradually melted away.

Still, the knowledge of this man's great wealth, the
evidences of which he had seen on all sides since
entering the spacious grounds, had a certain effect,
which did not wear away.

As great as the Senator had become among his fellow
Americans as a politician and statesman, he was still,
perhaps because of that very fact, greatly infected with
that curious strain in human nature that bows to wealth,
and stands uncovered and with bended knee before the
power of money, to listen to its utterances as words of
wisdom.

"Your great transcontinental railway line is nearly
completed, I notice," observed Baron Rothe. "It will
no doubt perform wonders toward peopling your vast
interior, and to facilitate trade between your eastern
and western coast countries."

"Yes," replied the Senator, "we anticipate very great and important results from this line of road. The Union Pacific and Central Pacific companies have made a junction at the city of Ogden, in Utah, and trains will soon run from Omaha to San Francisco. I have predicted a rapid growth of all that country west of the Missouri River."

"What effect will all this have upon your output of gold and silver?" inquired the Baron.

"It will assuredly greatly increase the output of those metals," answered the other. "We look to precious metal mining as one of our chief sources of wealth," he continued. "I do not think any very important developments have been made recently, and I am not advised as to the extent of what miners term 'prospecting,' but with the advent of these new lines of railway, we anticipate many new and rich discoveries of precious metals in the Rocky Mountain region."

"The Comstock Lode," the Baron asked, "continues to produce, does it not, a large amount of silver?"

"Yes," replied Senator Arnold, "but you are doubtless aware that forty per cent of the output of the Comstock mines is gold."

The Baron elevated his eyebrows slightly as though the fact were new to him, and evincing by his manner his interest in the subject, the Senator launched forth into a description of the Rocky Mountain region and the expected effect upon that region and the whole United States by the opening of the stores of precious metals.

To better illustrate a condition which obtained prior to the opening of these mines he cited an instance which had come under his personal observation, in the settle-

ment of certain matters for a client from that region.
When he had finished, the Baron remarked without any
seeming abruptness:

"I presume, Senator, your law practice takes up much
of your time?"

The query was innocent enough and was in that
calm and courteous tone, as though a polite interest in
the affairs of his visitor was its only purpose. In reality
it was the first move in the great game this money king
had set himself to play with the nation across the Atlantic.

Flattered at the evident interest in his affairs evinced
by the Baron, whose very voice assumed the tone of
compliment, the Senator said:

"A very great deal of my time, indeed too much of
it, is required by my clients, and inasmuch as my con-
stituency does me the honor to deem me worthy to
represent them at the capital, I am constrained to believe that all interests might be better subserved were I
to retire from law practice, and devote myself entirely
to affairs of the nation."

This was said with becoming modesty and as one
who knew and appreciated his own value and place in
the affairs of his country.

At this moment the rich tapestries at the end of the
room were gently put aside and the lovely face of the
Baron's dark eyed daughter appeared at the opening
as she said, advancing and courtesying slightly:

"Pardon me, father, you have the letter containing
the address of our friends, the Sommerfords, and I am
very much in need of it at once."

Which was quite true, and had been welcomed by
her as she thought of it, when considering a pretext

upon which to appear uninvited. The Senator had risen as the young lady entered the room and now stood in respectful but illy concealed admiration gazing at the beautiful girl as her father handed her the desired letter. Then with a smile he turned to his guest.

"Senator, it affords me great pleasure to present you to my daughter, Lady Edith Rothe. My dear," to the girl, "I make you acquainted with Senator Arnold, a member of the upper house of the United States congress."

The young lady bowed low and gracefully, while the American expressed his pleasure and looked his admiration.

"I hope you will like our Island home, Senator," said the girl, as she gracefully accepted the chair the American had tendered. And with his assurance that he should, the conversation glided smoothly to places and people in the British Isles, and of himself.

She looked him directly in the eyes as she talked, which the Senator found somewhat trying, though not altogether unpleasant. It has been said, "The eyes are the index to the soul," that "the eyes are windows through which one can look and see what is beyond."

Senator Arnold had never given even an idle thought to the occult. In his hard and practical nature there was no room for attention to the "isms" of the day. His life had been passed among surroundings and with a people where calculating reason was the measure of all things, and cold fact the sum and substance. Therefore he saw nothing in the eyes of this beautiful girl, but the directness of an innocent and unsophisticated nature, evincing a modest and pardonable interest in one holding a high political office in a foreign government.   It was really a subtle flattery to this American statesman, which he felt and accepted as ' quite natural, and so far as his cold nature was capable, enjoyed.

The Baron remained a passive listener, engaging in the conversation only when directly addressed, but by no means indifferent to all that was passing.

He had seated himself where he could see the faces of both, and he marked with satisfaction his daughter's skill in the art of conversation, and the wonderful con- trol her eyes seemed to possess over the grey orbs of the Senator.

Finally she leaned slightly back in the deep chair in which she was seated, and the long lashes drooped for a moment.

As the artist covers the camera when its work is fin- ished, so now, the beautiful eyes, that had read the very soul of the man before her, were hidden for an instant behind the white lids.

Then rising somewhat hastily, and as though sud- denly remembering the letter she held in her hand:

"Really, you must pardon my intrusion.   I know I must have interrupted a most interesting discussion," and with a bright smile at the Senator, "I trust you may find the time while in London, Senator Arnold, to allow us the pleasure of testifying personally that the English are a hospitable people, we of Oakdale Castle in particular," and with a smile of thanks to the American as he held aside the heavy draperies at the door, she was gone.

"And now, Senator," said the Baron, as both resumed their chairs, "I would like very much the pleasure of a long talk with you upon a subject in which I am greatly interested, and with our joint experience and wisdom," with a slight smile, "we may be of benefit to each other. I refer to the resumption of specie payments in the United States."

"I shall be quite at your service, Baron," returned the Senator, "and shall be very glad to give what facts I may have. I confess it is a subject upon which I should be most happy to hear your views, and receive the benefit of your wide experience and sound judgment."

"But," said the Baron as his visitor arose, "you are not going?"

"I think I must," answered the Senator. "I confess my first night in London was not so restful an one as I could have wished, and I fear my call may have interrupted some matters upon which you were engaged," with a wave of his hand toward the massive desk strewn with papers.

"Not at all, not at all," protested the Baron. "Merely passing an idle hour tabulating some unimportant papers. However, I have no doubt you feel the need of rest after your voyage, particularly as your first night in London should have been so unfortunate. Are you engaged to-morrow?" he went on, as they moved slowly down the room.

"Then," as the Senator replied in the negative, "do me the honor to dine here to-morrow. Quite informally, you understand; other than the members of my family you will meet no one but my friend, Sir William Cline, of whom you have doubtless heard."

"The honor will be mine," said the Senator, bowing his acceptance. "Sir William Cline's name is familiar to me as it must be to all who study finance, and I shall be most happy to meet him."

"Ah, yes," returned the Baron, "Sir William is well known in the financial world. We dine at 7," he continued as the footman appeared in answer to the bell. "My carriage will come for you at your hotel, so give yourself no concern about procuring conveyance."

"Very kind of you," murmured the American, quite overcome by this attention, and with a cordial shake of the hand took his leave.

The Baron slowly paced the length of the room, and with hands behind him halted at an open window looking out over the broad park.

His cold eyes were alight with satisfaction and the shadow of a smile played about his bearded lips. "The campaign is fairly opened," ran his thoughts, "and, if Edith has discovered what I think to be this man's nature, already as good as won."

He pressed a button at his side and as the servant responded, said without turning around:

"Say to Lady Edith I would like her to come to the library."

The young lady entered almost immediately, having been awaiting the summons since the retreating roll of the Senator's carriage had told of his departure.

'Well, Edith," said the Baron, placing a chair for her as she crossed the room, "I can see you have formed an opinion. Now let us see if your reading corresponds with mine. Give me," seating himself opposite her, "your impressions as to his character and general make up."

"Senator Arnold," began the girl, her eyes fixed on a figure of the carpet at her feet, "is a man of great pride; I mean personal pride. I believe he has an excellent knowledge of men, though not a broad knowl-

edge, as his standard of measure is self, and he is of a Puritanical narrowness, without the principle of the Puritan. He is ambitious. Fame and wealth are to him the pinnacle of success, and he cares not what wrongs make the road to it, so they be hidden ones. He is a man who uses charity as a cloak for selfishness, and to whom a philanthropic impulse is unknown. Sentiment, affection, have small place in his nature. Home and family are appreciated only as they contribute to his personal comfort and advancement. He is conservative, but it is the caution of the miser, and all his words and actions are weighed with a careful consideration of their effect upon himself. He is a lawyer of ability and wide reading, yet law and justice are as separate and distinct in his mind as the seasons of summer and winter. If he were poor, had he always been surrounded by low and evil influences, there is little villainy of which he would not have been capable, though his natural caution and cunning would lead him to avoid open transgression. I have said he is proud. There is but one influence to which he bows. Education, knowledge, fame, position; all these he has, and feels himself the peer of any; not, however, in an arrogant way, but money is the one thing to which he bends his knee."

"If opportunity should come to him," asked the Baron as the girl paused, "to obtain wealth to a large amount, through the indirect commission of crime, where there existed no possibility of punishment, or of discovery, but which nevertheless would result in great injury to his country, do you think in such an event his love of country would prevent reaching for the reward of the act?"

"No," unhesitatingly answered his daughter. "His patriotism is entirely a means to an end. Were the balance held up, country in this scale self-advancement in that, country would be found wanting."

For a moment neither spoke. The Baron's eyes were fastened upon his daughter's face, and in their depths shone a strange light. He looked at her, yet saw her not. The picture before him was not the loveliness of this dark eyed girl; it was a panorama of the years to come, when, with his purpose accomplished, his country supreme over all the earth, *he* would dictate to nations, while prince and pauper uncovered in humble submission before the power of his gold.

"That is all, Edith," he spoke at last, rising and moving toward his desk.

"Father," said the girl softly, laying her hand on the Baron's arm, "is this man to be tempted to do some wrong?"

"My dear Edith," he replied, his cold eyes striking a chill to her heart, "upon the correctness of your reading of this American depends, in part, the future history of England. As Providence with an all powerful and unseen hand guides and controls this universe, so do I and my confreres control and direct the affairs of men. Whatever I do," he continued, smiling into her troubled eyes, "you may be sure is right, and for the good of England. Be not troubled about this human puppet which England chooses to use, and know, that you have this day rendered a great service, not only to me, your father, but to the British crown."

CHAPTER IV.

The following day Senator Arnold passed quietly, for the most part in his rooms at "The Grosvenor," writing letters, reading the English papers, etc., and he was not displeased to note in the latter flattering notices of his arrival in London, one of which took the form of an editorial citing his high position in America, and his devotedness to his country and its institutions.

He had been duly "interviewed" and was agreeably surprised that for the most part he had been correctly quoted. The Senator was not given to self-indulgence in the luxuries of the appetite, and where another would have considered a bottle of wine, or a good cigar as fitting companions to an hour of rumination, he chose to forego both, and surrounded by the copies of the British Press, in love with his importance and greatness, gave himself up to thought and speculation.

Though the Senator was self-appreciative to vainness, though susceptible in the extreme to the influences of flattery from a man like Baron Rothe, it would be folly to say he did not suspect a motive in it all. Indeed it would have been strange, if in his narrow view of men he did not suspect. Just what this acquaintance with the money king might lead to, what his apparent great friendliness and interest might portend, he was at a loss to determine, but that *money* was the main-

33

spring he had not the question of a doubt. "I am of use to him," ran his thoughts. "He needs me for the furtherance of some of his plans for the increase of his already enormous store of gold. Very well," and his thin lips parted in a slight smile, "doubtless I shall obtain an inkling of what is brewing before the evening is over, and I think I can convince Baron Rothe and his friend Sir William Cline that a service which is worth seeking is worthy its equivalent."

A long time he sat there, his imagination busy with the speculations of a future built upon the foundation of a connection with the money kings of Europe, until a striking clock aroused him to the present, and reminded him that the carriage which was to bear him to the opening of a new epoch in his life was nearly due.

At exactly a quarter to seven the doors of the drawing rooms at Oakdale Castle were opened by the man in waiting, and his sonorous voice announced, "Senator John Arnold."

The Baron greeted him with great cordiality, and presented him at once to the Baroness, a statuesquely beautiful woman of middle age, who had risen as he entered and now advanced with graceful greeting for the American Senator whose name had become so well known on both sides of the Atlantic.

A cordial welcome from Lady Edith, and introductions to Sir William and Sir George Rothe, the eldest son of the house followed, and the conversation became general.

A few minutes later, indeed on the stroke of seven, for the Baron was a stickler for punctuality, dinner was announced, and obedient to the request of his host the

Senator soon found himself—the beautiful and stately Baroness at his side—entering the spacious and grandly beautiful dining hall of Oakdale Castle.

Just what influences were at work in the Senator's busy brain during that dinner never will be known.

The magnificence, the unmistakable evidences of enormous wealth were everywhere apparent, yet not unpleasantly or overpoweringly so. He ate and drank of the power of money, not because it was obtrusive, for it was not, but because he was a worshiper at its shrine and for the first time saw and recognized the extent of its empire.

The Baron had arranged with rare good taste that the dinner should be such that the American would remember it with pleasure, and with no feeling of its fatigue or heaviness.

Fatigue? Why, this politician was never so near to earthly happiness in all his long life.

This magnificently decorated hall, the sweet strains of the music just without, the splash and tinkle of the fountain, floating in through the open windows, this royally beautiful and gifted woman at his side, the wit and intellect of the conversation, the delicacy laden table with its shimmering silver and gold, all produced in his mind a species of intoxication and voluptuous delight, like the first love of a strong man. And it was for *him*, he thought; all this was in entertainment of him!

Had you but known it, Baron Rothe, you owned this poor creature from that hour, and might have spared yourself much anxiety and diplomatic fencing during the two weeks that followed. Nothing of the kind, however, was apparent in the manner or expression of the Senator. That immobile countenance wore its habitual cold reserve, mingled with the courteous pleasure of one who finds his entertainment happy and agreeable.

Whatever might stir in the inner self of this statesman was carefully guarded by that mask of austere repression.

"I hope you will not linger too long," said the Baroness to her husband, as the two ladies rose to retire. "Senator Arnold has expressed a wish to look through the art gallery and I have promised to be his guide. If you allow the Baron and Sir William to draw you into politics," to the American, "I fear I will see little more of you this evening."

"Politics shall be eschewed," declared the American with unaccustomed gallantry; I am far too eager to see the art treasures, and I trust I may prove as appreciative to my fair conductor as my heart desires."

Notwithstanding the Senator's avowal to the Baroness, the conversation drifted to a topic very like politics before the cigars were half burned, and he was cleverly led by his host and Sir William to a statement of the then existing condition of American affairs, and a brief and guarded outlining of the proposed policy of his government in resuming specie payment.

He talked well and carefully, with a full knowledge that his listeners were his peers in statecraft and finance, and were measuring his utterances as such, and with the rule peculiar to their class and station.

Yet he talked as ever, for the effect on himself. The same old sophistries, the same diplomatic cunning that marked all his public voicings were present here.

The man's real self lived so much in darkness and

behind the thick veil of policy, that he actually, in a great measure, deceived himself.

Sir William was fairly fascinated, and while astonished at the broad comprehension and wide knowledge of a man he had unconsciously regarded as somewhat superficial, his heart sunk at thought of the proposed plan to make this man a willing instrument in the undermining of his native land.

"Ah, no!" thought the nobleman with a sigh, "this broad minded, intelligent citizen of a great and powerful republic, this noble representative of a free and advancing nation, is not the tool for England to use in the forging of new chains for his countrymen."

The Baron, however, was not thus affected.

He heard the American's wisdom and rhetoric with far different feelings.

"Why," ran his delighted thoughts, "he is the very man, born and trained, for the successful working out of our end and aim. We need never fear discovery through him. He is certainly the most apparently noble hypocrite I have ever seen." And he inwardly blessed the good fortune that had cast this powerful instrument in his path.

Later, while threading the maze of sculptured marbles and wandering down the avenues flanked with beautiful paintings, the musical voice of the English woman adding to the charm of the surroundings, the Senator was thinking: "Yes, they certainly need me, and for something of international importance. I sus-pect it to have to do with our resumption, and I think I have convinced the Baron at least of my fitness to aid him. The other I do not quite understand; he seemed differently affected by my words. Possibly," and he smiled as though at the remark of his companion as she called his attention to a particularly hideous, because unfinished, painting by Rossini. "Possibly he is inclined to believe our standards of appreciation too widely at variance, to be encouraging to his plan. However, the Baron is probably the chief factor in this, and to him I shall look for the uncovering of the enterprise, whatever it may be."

The Baron and Sir William had retired to the library, the entertainment of the Senator by the Baroness being well understood by that lady, who was always aware of the enterprises of her liege, and was not infrequently called upon for counsel.

Sir William paced back and forth for a few moments in silence, while his companion, well aware what was passing in the mind of his fellow conspirator, watched him amusedly from the deep chair in which he was sitting.

"Baron," said Sir William, pausing and without raising his eyes from the carpet, "I am afraid we have made a mistake. This is not the man to lend an effort to the downfall of his country. To offer him a bribe to do our will is to accept a risk which may work incalculable harm to England, and to you and me."

The Baron laughed easily and somewhat contemptuously, at which the other looked at him in astonishment.

"Eh, what!" he exclaimed. "Am I deceived in my estimate of this man?"

"You are," replied the Baron quietly. "Very greatly deceived, and I consider it the sincerest compliment you could have paid to the astuteness and intelligence of the man who is destined to become an agent of England. My dear Sir William," he continued, rising and tapping his friend's shoulder with the point of his finger in emphasis, "I am now absolutely sure of the ground upon which we stand. You say 'bribe'? An ugly word and unnecessary. Rather say 'ally,' and therein lies success with this American. His is a singular nature. The offer of an open 'bribe' now would lose him to us forever. A proper amount of finesse and he becomes an English ally, ready and eager to advance her interests even to the cost of his country. Have not all England's victories been won through her allies? and has not the wise and discreet use of money procured for us these allies?"

"Yes," assented Sir William. "But have not these allies to whom you refer always had a mutual interest with England?"

"Very seldom," returned the Baron, shaking his head. "Was not the house of Austria directly connected with Napoleon by marriage? The Emperor's daughter, Maria Louise, was the wife of Napoleon, Empress of France, yet English money sent an army of half a million Austrians to tear from the throne this son-in-law and daughter.

"Alexander of Russia was the warm personal friend of Napoleon, yet English money poisoned his mind, and through him held together the allied powers, till they had wrenched from the people of France the imperial object of their love and esteem.

"Sir William," he went on impressively and in lowered tones, "it is *money* and not 'mutual interest,' as you are well aware, that holds in subjection the millions of Her Majesty's loyal (?) subjects in India. You will pardon me if I say you have a too exalted opinion of the American Congress and of men in gen eral, yet your experience must have taught you, as I have learned, that the power of money is paramount to any other on earth; that there is no conscience that *money* will not strangle, no nature in humanity that *money* will not warp and bend to do its will. Are you not well aware that not one, but ten 'law-makers' of the *Corps Legislatif* of France in the year 1777 were guilty of having received bribes of money? And the French are a people regarded by the world at large as superior in integrity, and those fine sentiments of patriotism and veneration for the institutions of their country. Yet, my friend," and the cold, sneering voice sank still lower, "the secret archives of my family would prove to the contrary, and while the French legislature may succeed in the future as they have done in the past, in concealing from the public their abuses of office by reason of the improper use of money, I am personally certain, that through a public matter of less financial import than this we have embarked upon, the French Chamber of Deputies could be corrupted.*

"No people," he went on, after a slight pause, "are naturally more tenacious of their liberties than the Irish, yet you will remember, through the efforts of our able though unscrupulous diplomat, Lord Castlerea, English gold, supplemented by Royalty's gifts of titles, purchased the dissolution of the Irish Parliament."

Baron Rothe might have gone further. History abounds in instances of corruption among those holding high official positions. During the period from the

*Since this statement was made four of the leading members of the national legislative body of France have been found guilty and sentenced to punishment for accepting bribes to control their votes in connection with the building of the Panama Canal. Several connected with this disgraceful occurrence confessed. Among the latter was the son of DeLesseps, one of the first citizens of France.

revolution to the end of Queen Anne's reign, bribery was openly practiced in the English Parliament. The Speaker of the House of Commons was expelled for bribery, and the great Marlborough could not clear his character from pecuniary dishonesty.

During Walpole's administration there is no doubt that members of parliament were paid in cash for their votes, and his memorable remark that "every man has his price" has been preserved as a characteristic indication of his methods of government.

A distinguished authority* says:

Bribery is the administration of a bribe or reward that it may be a motive in the performance of functions for which the proper motive ought to be a conscientious sense of duty.

The offense may be divided into two great classes—the one characteristic of despotisms—where a person invested with power is induced by payment to use it unjustly. The other, *which is an unfortunate characteristic of constitutional government*, where power is obtained by purchasing the suffrage of those who impart it.

It is a natural propensity to feel that every element of power is to be employed as much as possible for the owner's own behoof, and that its benefits should be conferred not on those who best deserve them, but on those who will pay most for the....

It is difficult to get the Oriental mind to understand how it is reasonable to expect the temptation of a bribe to be resisted, and this has been the main impediment to the employment of a native judiciary or legislature in the British eastern empire,

In no country, perhaps, is the offense visited with more dire chastisement when discovered, than in Russia, yet by the concurrent testimony of all who are acquainted with Russian society not only the official department but the courts of law are at this day influenced by systematic bribery.

It does not appear that bribery was conspicuous in England until the early part of the 18th century. Constituencies had thrown off the feudal dependence which lingered among them; and *indeed it is often said* that bribery is essentially a defect of a free people, since *it is the* sale of that which is obtained from others without payment.

*Encyclopædia Britannica.

It has been said that "the greatest danger to free government may be found in its laws;" and that "self-destruction comes through corruption." There is no doubt but that the love of money and a blunted conscience have made too many men cast their official votes and influence for measures, that pecuniary gain might accrue to themselves to the injury of their constituents.

The people of the present age are slow to believe that bribery is practiced in high places. We do not believe it, because we do not want to believe it. It requires the most convincing proof, and often confession is necessary to conviction. And yet it is one of the most common crimes extant. It is the only crime mentioned and provided against in the *Constitution* of the State of New York.

Both modern and ancient history give plenty of evidence of its frequent practice; and yet few are exposed of the thousands who are contaminated by it.

The prophet Samuel, priding himself upon his virtues, said:

"Whom have I defrauded—whom have I oppressed? Or of whose hands have I received any bribe to blind my eyes therewith?"

Amos, denouncing the condition of Israel under Jeroboam, says:

"They afflict the just—they take a bribe—and they turn aside the poor in the gate from their rights."

Nearly twenty-five centuries ago Sophocles, the Greek philosopher, said:

"No thing in use by man, for power of ill,
"Can equal money. This lays cities low,
"This drives men forth from quiet dwelling place,
"This warps and changes minds of worthiest stamp,

"To turn to deeds of baseness, teaching men
"All shifts of cunning, and to know the guilt
"Of every impious deed."

In the Illinois legislature in 1857 the City Street Railway Company of Chicago was asking for a renewal of its charter for ninety-nine years. Nearly all the citizens of Chicago were opposed to it and petitioned the legislature against it. No one expected it to pass in the form it was introduced, as it was virtually a present of millions of dollars to the company. To the surprise of every one, it went through. The Governor, who was unpurchasable, vetoed it.

An effort was at once exerted to pass it over the Governor's veto, and the people of Chicago became aroused to the danger and the methods that were being used.

Large committees of the most prominent citizens of Chicago went to Springfield to work with the members of the legislature against the bill. The experience of one of the committeemen will illustrate that of the others. The first member of the legislature he spoke to said to him: "How much money is there in it for me if I vote on your side?"

The committee representing the people of Chicago were not prepared to bribe, and the bill was passed over the Governor's veto and is the charter under which the street railway of Chicago to-day, with her nearly two million of people, is operated.

The Denver *Republican* of January 15, 1894, says editorially:

It is silly for members of the State Senate to affect suprise or indignation over the fact that many laws enacted during the regular session of the Ninth General Assembly were willfully changed in the process of enrollment. That form of knavery has been practiced for years in the Colorado Legislature, and senators and representatives have always winked at it if they have not actually prompted it.

Senators who denounced it on Saturday must have known what was going on last winter or else they must have been as blind as bats. So long as our Legislatures continue to make the committeeships at their disposal the plunder of men and women of known bad character, for personal or political reasons, they must expect that the laws they pass will be tampered with if any rogue has sufficient financial interest in the matter to pay for the dirty work.

These few instances—and they are but a few of the many that might be cited—will serve to show that the Baron, in his sweeping estimate of the power of money over the morals of men, was not without some reason and abundant support, and Sir William could but admit the force of all he had said, and the fact now disturbed, and aroused in his breast the dormant conscience, that, unfortunately for a man of his position and calling, had never been completely stifled, leading him to the expression of views that the Baron saw at once must not be allowed to ripen.

So interrupting with all the arrogance of one who allows no questioning of acts or motives, he said:

"Our right to do what we contemplate is unquestionable. All the world is at war with the man of money. In the minds of the masses a prejudice is created against the possessor of money. Juries find wealth a sufficient excuse for a verdict against it. It attracts the robber, the forger, the whole breed of human buzzards and jackals to prey upon its holder. Wealth is expected to give, not only to charity, but upon the slightest pretext, so that from morning till night it is 'stand and deliver.'

"In view of the fact," he continued, "that this is an international matter, and calculated to place England where she rightly belongs, it is our *duty* to leave no means untried, that that end may be accomplished.

This is a financial and industrial war with a nation that stands in the path to England's advancement. Since when has the use of money in war become wrong? If we have agents or allies in Africa or South America we expect to pay them. If we have an agent in the United States he must receive compensation."

Nevertheless Sir William's thoughts, as he leaned against the soft cushions of his roomy carriage while rolling swiftly homeward under the myriad twinkling stars that night, were not strictly what Baron Rothe could have wished.

Sir William sighed heavily as his mind's eye pictured the desolation to be wrought that England might gain. "And I," he murmured, with a grim smile of self-pity mingled with contempt, "I, who might have been, with the wealth at my command, an agent for all good, am become a forger of chains for the people of a noble nation; a minister, of disaster to the masses; the companion and confidante of a man to whom all possible things are right   And why? Because of my fealty to my Queen? No, the Baron is right; it is the power of money. I am a slave set to drive slaves, and *my* master is—money"

CHAPTER V.

During the two weeks more that followed, Senator Arnold gave himself up without reserve to the entertainments that so eagerly sought him.

Receptions, stately and magnificent dinners, the court ball, no festivity or important gathering in London's social world was considered complete without the presence of the distinguished American.

It was a series of fascinating pleasures and social triumphs such as had never before visited the severely regulated life of this man of policy and state. Each morning was the marble table of his dressing room heaped with fresh invitations, and each night found him the honored center of some brilliant assemblage. He was the hour's "lion," and much to the delectation of his new-found friends and his own complacent satisfaction, he roared engagingly and with proper dignity and force.

The splendid equipage of the European money magnate, with its liveried servants and armorial bearings, had borne him smoothly and swiftly, in company with the Baron, over the grand driveways of the Island capital, through the spacious and beautiful parks and along that wide show place of England's *bon ton*, Pall Mall.

He had passed hours in delightful converse and sight seeing with Baroness Rothe and Lady Edith, and at times in the added companionship of the Baron or Sir George.

The national gallery, museums, tower, all the grand and historical spots of this truly wonderful city, were duly shown the appreciative American.

And who shall say he did not thoroughly enjoy it all?

The constant, unceasing courtesy and attention from the Baron and his household; the deference, the marked respect everywhere extended; the splendor and refined influences of his daily and hourly surroundings, all presented so striking a contrast to the quiet routine of his home life, that it was quite like a visit in another world.

And so it was another world that was opened before the ambition of this servant of a free people. He saw and recognized the new empire, and while his avaricious hand longed to grasp the golden scepter of power, and his feet ached to tread the exclusive walks, he patiently waited and watched for the touch of the wand of the man he had grown to regard as his *genius* Baron Rothe.

The Senator had been in London now some weeks, when he received a note one morning written on the crested paper of the Baron, to lunch tête-à-tête the following day at the private rooms in the banking house of his titled friend.

"The hour is come," murmured the Senator, as he read the closing words of the brief invitation. "I seek your counsel and advice," they ran, "in a matter of international import, and trust you will so far honor me."

He at once dispatched an answer signifying his great pleasure and readiness to serve in any way within his power one to whom he considered himself so greatly obligated, and then he gave himself up to a mental preparation for what he felt would prove the most important as well as the most trying conference of his life.

All through the ambassadors' reception which he attended that evening his mind was busy, and if he proved a little disappointing to some of those present who had anticipated a certain amount of pyrotechnics in his utterances, it will not be greatly wondered at.

But on the next day, as he seated himself at the well appointed table, and discussed with his affable and attentive host, the Baron, the succession of the season's delicacies, the rich and fruity wines, he was never better prepared than then for the duel of intellect he felt was at hand.

Nothing, however, to hint at what was coming, was said until the cigars were brought in and the servants had withdrawn.

The conversation then insensibly drifted to matters of finance, and shortly they were engaged in an animated discussion of the experience of the United States government in procuring funds with which to carry on the civil war, and the ebb and flow of the nation's credit, as the tide of battle swept north or south during the struggle.

At the time of the opening of this narrative the debt of the United States was about $2,700,000,000, and the fact was cited and commented upon by the Baron, together with the pros and cons of the proposed specie payment resumption.

Finally the nobleman called the attention of his companion to the act of Congress passed March 18, 1869, "to strengthen the public credit," wherein the United States pledged itself to the payment of its debts in "coin," and he inquired of the Senator his interpretation or the word "coin" as here used; whether he understood it to mean either gold or silver.

In reply the Senator said: "The act itself defines the term 'coin.' It says the government is pledged to the payment of all its debts in *coin* 'except in cases where the law authorizing the issue of any such obligation has expressly provided that the same may be paid in lawful money, or other currency than *gold* and *silver.*' This exception will explain what is meant by 'coin' in the previous portion of the act. By the words gold and silver used in the exception, *coin* is thereby defined to mean *gold* and *silver*, and our debts are thus made payable."

"The most of your national securities, Senator," said the Baron, "are held in Europe,—here in England—and silver is not our standard money. It is apparent that at any time your government might unload upon us the whole of these debts in silver. This, you will agree, would injure your national credit, and be manifestly unfair to us."

"It is not probable," answered the American, "that such would occur. We have always been careful to preserve our credit intact, and will no doubt pay in gold where such is advisable. But the fact that we have the bimetallic option of liquidating both domestic and foreign obligations in either gold or silver, maintains the parity in value of those metals. Silver is now at a slight premium over gold, and it is not likely that we would pay you in the dearer of the two metals."

"It would seem to me," said the Baron, "to be impossible in the face of your present and prospective output of silver to maintain unimpaired foreign credit unless you declare your public securities payable in gold. Or, what would be better still, to adopt gold as your standard and measure of values. I was so fortunate as to be allowed to read a copy of your letter to Minister Ruggles at Paris, and was quite won by the thoroughness of the knowledge of political economy evidenced. In that I think you leaned to this view."

The Senator bowed slightly in acknowledgment, and replied: "My observation of your system of finance in England has been, that though gold had been your standard since 1816, the fact has not affected the value of silver, and the parity of the two metals has been maintained. If I could become convinced that the adoption of such a system in the United States would not result in a disturbance of the parity of the two metals, I might become an advocate of such change, as I readily recognize many of its advantages.".

"I wonder its advisability has not been advanced," remarked the Baron.

"You would not did you better understand the American people," replied the Senator. "They are wedded to silver, and among us it is known as the 'people's money.' To change our present system would require a long, arduous, and exceedingly expensive educational campaign, and even then I greatly doubt its ultimate success."

"But it would seem to me," said the Baron earnestly, "that the stability of your government depends upon the success of just such a policy. Suppose," fixing his gaze on the calm, grey eyes opposite, "I were to place at your disposal a sum which, in your judgment, would be sufficient to cultivate just such an educational movement in the United States, leaving the matter, of course, entirely to your discretion and sound judgment, do you think there is an element in the plan to recommend its trial?"

The American's sallow face had grown as white as the cloth upon which his hand rested, as the speaker drew aside the curtain which had hidden the purpose of the past three weeks; yet no tremor showed in the steady hand that raised the glass of wine to his dry lips.

Be it said to his credit that for one brief instant he hesitated.

Oh! Senator Arnold, where then was your American birthright; where your boasted patriotism and devotion to your native land?

Could the spirit of the immortal Lincoln have shed its divine dew upon that dried and rock-like conscience, in this supreme moment, this lasting infamy, this voluntary deliverance of a human soul into the keeping of the arch fiend, this black treason to a trusting and happy people, would never have been.

But no, the mighty hand of greed swept all else aside, and, with no trace, beyond his pallor, of the storm raging within his soul, the cold voice of the American statesman answered: "I think I understand you, Baron, and am quite sure with what aid you are prepared to extend to such a campaign, it could at least be thoroughly tested."

"Five thousand pounds each year," went on the Baron quietly, "placed in your hands, and supplemented by sums which you would consider necessary, I am satisfied would produce the condition in the public mind desired. No accounting, you understand, would be required, absolute reliance to be placed in your wisdom and ability."

The ice once broken, the details of the plan were not slow in appearing. No vouchers, or statement from the Honorable Senator to his employers were to be given or expected. This English money would of necessity have to be expended in a manner to preclude the possibility of the discovery of any system or plot. The method of procedure was to be left entirely to the Senator. Advice, counsel, suggestion were to be his only as he signified such a desire, and until the servants came in to light the lamps they sat there, the conspirator and the traitor, arranging the details of the nefarious scheme.

"Call here at two to-morrow, Senator, if convenient, and we will go into the matter more fully," said the Baron as the Senator rose to take his leave. "There are some parts of your coinage laws upon which I should like the benefit of your legal knowledge." And with a cordial hand pressure from the nobleman, and his avaricious nature tingling with the golden vista before him, the Senator entered his carriage and was driven rapidly to his hotel.

His sensations during the period that elapsed before he was again closeted with the money king, are better imagined than described, but it was with no intention but that of going straight forward in the path chosen that he was shown into the Baron's private office at the appointed hour on the following day. The only suggestion offered by the Baron at this interview was in saying that he had always found it advisable in matters where a nation's policy was involved that the legislation should be as quiet as possible, in a measure secret, and that education should follow and not precede the actual change.

Thus giving the Senator to understand, which he made plainer later, that the yearly payments were to continue as long as education was deemed necessary.

"I shall take a run of a couple of months on the continent," said the law-maker after all had been canvassed and arranged, "and shall return here on my way to America about the first of August."

"Very well," returned the Baron. "If you will kindly wire your arrival to me at my place in Scotland, I will come to London and will submit to you whatever new ideas I may have obtained in the interim. In this packet," he continued, handing the American a large and pleasantly thick envelope, "you will find the sinews for the opening of our campaign. The contents of that envelope," as the Senator deposited it next his heart, "will be duplicated annually, you understand, so long as in your judgment there is need." And with mutual compliment and the wish from the Baron that the statesman might find his continental tour of pleasure, and profit to his health and well being, they separated to meet again in August.

It was characteristic of the Senator that the moment he was alone in his rooms at "The Grosvenor" he should carefully examine the contents of the innocent looking envelope.

Twenty-five crisp, new, United States treasury notes of the denomination of one thousand dollars each, and his miser's soul fairly danced in exultation as he contemplated this princely addition to his already large, and rapidly growing yearly income. For right well he understood that this money was for him personally, and was not intended, nor was it received with a thought that any of it would find its way to the pockets of others.

It must be remembered that twenty-five years ago, millionaires were not so numerous as they now are, that to the average man of those times the sum of twenty-five thousand dollars was a comfortable fortune in itself, and as a yearly income was considered large. This was the amount of the salary paid the President of the United States, and comparatively few in private life enjoyed an income so great.

It had originally with Baron Rothe been the plan, to employ Senator Arnold as a lawyer to represent the English bondholders, and in that way enlist his services for the passage of the desired law; but he had substituted for this plan the other excuse, that the Senator was not receiving this money for himself, but to use in an educational campaign. This was the veneering to cover the moral conscience. Beneath this crust was the tacit understanding that this money was for the Senator, and that no educational campaign was to begin until after the law was passed.

It is presumed that Senator Arnold found his sojourn on the continent all the Baron had wished, for the latter, upon meeting him after his return, could not refrain from remarking that he was looking remarkably improved, and physically well prepared for the line of labor laid out.

The interview was not long; there was little to be said, beyond a canvass of what had already been planned, and after a glass of wine to the success of the undertaking, and a cordial "*Bon voyage*" from the Baron, the Senator mounted his carriage and drove at once to his hotel to prepare for his journey home.

He sailed from Liverpool the following Saturday, via the steamship Scotia, and it was with mingled feeling of triumph and relief that he watched the shores of Albion recede from sight.

The voyage was uneventful, and eight days later he stepped once more upon the soil of his native land, welcomed by the babel and bustle of New York's busy streets.

He drove at once to the Astor House, where he arrived in time to enjoy his lunch in company with a colleague of the Senate, and from whom he was enabled to gather a brief idea of the happenings in his country during his absence.

He had the envelope with its contents handed him by the Baron on his person.

He had returned it to the English banker to keep for him while traveling in Europe, and had received it back on the occasion of his last interview. He did not exchange it for a bank draft; it had been given to him in just the shape he most desired. He wanted no possible chance to trace this payment of money to him. The wonderful tact and knowledge of men on the part of Baron Rothe was never better shown; he had prepared himself with these United States bills, know-ing the Senator would want no record of the receipt of this large sum of money.

Now he was at home, this money must be put away; so he sallied forth and walking to the corner of Liberty Street and Broadway, entered a door beneath the sign:

"THE MUTUAL SAFE DEPOSIT CO."

Here he rented a box and in it placed, twenty of the twenty-five one thousand dollar bills. Of the other five he afterward deposited two each in banks of Washing-ton where he carried accounts, and the remaining one in the bank of which he was an officer, in his state.

About two weeks after the return of Senator Arnold to the United States, a steamer of the Anchor Line bore to England the Hon. J. W. Harrold, a New England congressman.

CHAPTER VI.

At 4 o'clock P. M. on the twenty-fifth day of November, 1872, a gentleman alighted from a train at the Pennsylvania depot in Washington, D. C. In his left hand he carried a light valise, his right swung a thick walking stick.

Refusing all importunities of the vociferous hackmen at the exit of the depot, he inquired the way to the Arlington Hotel and walked leisurely along Pennsylvania Avenue in that direction.

He was young, not to exceed thirty years of age, possibly some years younger.

Of medium height, his compact and well knit figure clothed in a neat and well fitting business suit of some dark mixture; short, well trimmed black beard and mustache covered the lower part of his face, and a pair of remarkably black and piercing eyes looked out from under the brim of the derby hat. A large but well shaped nose, and rather prominent cheek bones, and the picture is complete. Altogether rather a distinguished looking young man and bearing in face and manner that unmistakable stamp of the cosmopolitan.

The walk was long and evidently of interest and possessing some degree of novelty to the stranger.

Washington, at this period, was of the character of many of the old and sedate cities of the South. It had not assumed the metropolitan air and business rush that have later distinguished it as a Northern city.

The buildings were old and of a style of architecture prevalent through the Southern states a half century ago, and in many cases the residences had grown up within a stone's throw of the government buildings.

Arriving at the Arlington, the young man registered "*Victor Rogasner, New York City,*" and passing the checks for his baggage to the clerk, requested that functionary to send for the same at once.

That same evening, as Senator Arnold sat at his desk in the suite of bachelor apartments devoted to his use at the National Hotel, a card was brought to him upon which he read the engraved name, Victor Rogasner, and under it the written words, "bearing a letter from Baron Rothe."

"Show him up," said the Senator shortly.

As Mr. Rogasner entered the room the American rose and greeted him politely but without warmth.

"Senator Arnold?" said the caller advancing, and as the Senator bowed, continued, handing him an official looking envelope, "I am the bearer of a letter of introduction from Baron Rothe, who does me the honor to think I may be of service here."

Senator Arnold frowned slightly as the young man spoke; not at all relishing the thought that another knew of his connection with the English nobleman, and with a curt:

"Pray be seated, pardon me," he turned to the light and took up a paper-knife with which to open the message. A hasty, but searching scrutiny satisfied him that letter and seal were as they had left the hand of friend and patron.

As he drew forth the contents he partially turned his back to his caller, as though to better catch the light from his study lamp, and quickly read in the well known handwriting, that the bearer was Mr. Victor Rogasner. his nephew, in whom he had the utmost confidence and trust; that he was in the judgment of the writer, the shrewdest and most accomplished diplomat of his age in Europe, with a knowledge of men and measures far beyond his years; that in view of the delay of congress in passing upon the Senator's bill, twice already presented, he, the Baron, thought it wise to surround the measure with additional powerful influences.

He had therefore recalled Mr. Rogasner from an important mission in St. Petersburg on account of his fitness for the present occasion, and had sent him to Washington to inaugurate separately and distinctly from any operations of the Senator, an educational movement in the interests of the single standard; that Rogasner knew nothing of the existing relations between himself and the Senator, beyond the fact that they were personal friends, and that his, the Senator's views, on the propriety of adopting a single standard in finance, were the same as the writer's; and concluded by saying that the bearer of the letter knew nothing of the packet which was enclosed, but had been impressed with the importance of the whole sufficiently to insure its safe delivery.

Divining the contents of the packet referred to, he carelessly slipped it into a drawer in his desk and turned the key.

Then turning to Rogasner with some cordiality in words and manner, he said:

"I am very glad to see you, sir. Any friend of Baron Rothe is welcome here, and his relative doubly so," and the two men shook hands.

"I understand," said the Senator as they seated themselves, "from the tenor of my friend's letter, that you are here to personally assist in the education of the masses as to the proposed change in our financial system as provided in a bill which has been introduced during both of the last sessions of congress," and as the other assented, continued: "I would suggest as being wisest at this juncture, that your efforts be confined entirely, for the present, to a quiet canvass of the existing conditions in this country, and to familiarizing yourself with the laws and methods of our two houses of government. Also it would be well, if you are not already informed, to become as conversant as possible with the subjects of finance and coinage as viewed from an American standpoint. In any of these directions I can doubtless be of assistance, and trust you will command me whenever you feel such need."

Rogasner thanked him warmly, and remarked that inasmuch as his usefulness might be impaired if it were known that he was from England, he had taken the precaution to register from New York and should enter upon his Washington life as a citizen of that metropolis.

"It is not difficult to become an American," commented the elder man, smiling grimly.

It was not the purpose of the Baron's agent to make more than an introductory call, and after a short exchange of views as to the work laid out for him, and with the repeated assurance of the Senator of his readiness to be of assistance in that work, the young man bowed himself out.

The Senator resumed his seat, and a slight frown wrinkled his brow as he read again the Baron's words touching the bearer's ignorance of the foundation of the friendship which existed between him and the American politician.

He read the letter through several times, then unlocked the drawer in which he had placed the packet, and broke the seals.

Two United States treasury notes, for ten thousand dollars each, and one for five thousand, was what it contained. He sat for a moment silent, while the frown deepened and a troubled look crept slowly into his eyes. "And I am assured," he said aloud, "that this young man, this 'shrewdest diplomat of his age in Europe,' has carried this packet three thousand miles and is not aware of the nature of its contents. Either the Baron singularly underestimates the intelligence of his agent, or—he lies to me. Why should I expect he would *not* lie?" he went on contemptuously. "Perversion, deceit, hypocrisy are the arts of his class, and though I believe the Baron would make no such confidant in this matter, Mr. Victor Rogasner most assuredly knows that he has been the bearer of money from his relative to me."

He laid the bills carefully away again in the drawer, and began a restless walking to and fro over the thick carpet.

This money was not due. Thrice he had visited London since the compact was formed, and each time had received from his friend personally the sum agreed upon.

Only the previous July the last payment had been made, and no more was due for another year. Was it a hint that the approaching session of Congress must see the passage of the bill? And was it also further assurance of the generosity and good faith of his employer? Senator Arnold so decided, and while he liked not at all the thought of this young Englishman possessing knowledge that held such a power for harm, in his pride and self-confidence he felt no doubt of his ability to take the best of care of himself whatever happened.

But the feeling of annoyance and impatience that so wily and conservative a diplomat as the Baron should be so lax in what he might have considered was of grave importance to the Senator, remained to disturb and vex him. And this bill. The Senator and his co-conspirator in the house, had originally arranged their plan of action, and had frequent conferences looking to ultimate success.

The bill had once been introduced, and had passed the Senate in 1871, but an adjournment of the 41st Congress had cut its life short before it could pass the house. The same bill was again introduced as H. R. 2934 in the Second Session of the 42nd Congress. It was entitled "A Bill to Reform the Coinage and Mint Laws," and covered over fifteen pages of printed matter. It passed the house on the 27th day of May; 1872, but the two houses adjourned before it had passed the Senate. Congress, however, again met in December, which made the third session for that Congress, and if the bill could pass the Senate before March 4th, the last day for that session of Congress, it would become a law.

The bill, however, as it had passed the house, was innocent of any attempt at outlawry of one half the primary money of the government. It was the intention of the conspirators to make it the basis of their operations when it should finally be enrolled as law in the two houses. They deemed it necessary to their plans to impress on Congress the necessity of reforming the coinage laws, which were long, dry and uninteresting to nearly all the members of both houses, and at the last moment to surreptitiously substitute a new bill for the one that had been voted upon.

This when signed by the President and enrolled, would become law, and no power could repeal it, except the action of the two houses with the sanction of the President.

They counted on the fraudulent assistance of the two or three clerks who might detect the change made in the bill, and on the President signing the bill without reading. This the President often did when the bills were long and by common consent were regarded as laws regulating details only, as this bill was supposed to do.

They would insist at every step, that the old law was crude, and in view of the proposed resumption of specie payment, it was necessary to provide for many matters in the regulation of the mints; the making of new offices and the duties thereof; that the bill was only formal, and each step taken was under the advice and consent of the Secretary of the Treasury, who desired that the bill should be passed. This last statement was partially true, but that officer had no knowledge of the secret intention of the conspirators.

These were the plans, and this was the condition of affairs when the secret agent of Baron Rothe arrived in Washington. He was perfectly satisfied and well pleased with the programme, and was a powerful ally in bringing these plans to a successful termination.

The next morning after Rogasner had seen the Sen·
ator, he inquired of the clerk the address of a responsible property agent, and having been provided by that
individual with a short list, sallied forth and was soon
deep in the mysteries of rents and leases.

A few days later there appeared on the entrance
door of No. 1403 Pennsylvania Avenue a neat brass
plate bearing the modest inscription, "*V. Rogasner,
Investments.*" The house was a stone front, erected
as a residence and not unlike dozens of its fellows on
the avenue, and within easy walking distance of the
Capitol buildings; the ten rooms were tastefully though
unostentatiously furnished, housekeeper and servants
installed, and the loyal subject of the English throne
was at home.

Two rooms to the right of the entrance he had caused
to be fitted up as a business office, and as in these
two rooms were born and nourished many of the plots
that later worked such havoc among a betrayed and
bewildered people, they deserve more than passing
mention.

The front and smaller room looked out upon the
broad and well kept avenue, and from the two wide
and deep bow windows one could watch the tide of
Washington life as it swept to and from the stately
white pile gleaming through the trees.

A commodious and broad topped desk occupied the
center of the room, and the roomy, soft-cushioned
easy chairs scattered about gave one the impression
that the occupant was of the school that believes business may be transacted, though the surroundings invite ease and comfort.

A broad mahogany book-case filled the space between

the two windows, and the titles to be read on the leather backs of its contents bore out the brass legend on the outer door. Numerous pictures garnished the painted walls, of a nature to suggest a martial character, and a soft and yielding carpet of sober colors welcomed the foot of the visitor, and a couch placed across the angle to the left of the windows, invited ease and rest should "finance" become too arduous.

A heavy oak door separated the outer from the inner and larger room, and was hung with heavy curtains like those which were looped away from the broad windows. A glance at the interior of this room and it was at once evident that here the master of the house had elected to build his sanctum.

A tall and conveniently arranged escritoire was backed against the wall where best to receive the light from the one curtained window, but beyond this one article of furniture and the small but strong iron safe in one corner, there was little to indicate that this room was other than a lounging place for its owner.

The thick carpet was strewn with costly rugs, the chairs were all of that kind best described as "easy." The paintings on the walls were of the same character as those in the first room, and to the right of the door, not seen until one was well inside, stood a massive and richly carved sideboard, on which was arranged a most tempting display of cut glass decanters, crystal glasses, gold and silver trays and other accessories. Altogether this Mr. Victor Rogasner must be something of a sybarite, despite the hard character of his profession, and of the business he had chosen to represent in the capitol city.

*   *   *   *   *   *   *   *

One morning a few days later, as Victor Rogasner

descended the stairs from his dressing room, in an-swer to the summons of the breakfast-bell, the roll of departing carriage wheels, a loud summons from the heavy knocker on the door, caused him to pause a mo-ment on the lower step, and as the portal was opened by the servant and a familiar voice inquired for "Mr. Rogasner," he turned into the office with an exclama-tion of satisfaction.

A moment later a tall, spare gentleman of middle age, entered the room, and was cordially though quietly welcomed by the younger man.

We will introduce the new arrival at once as Mr. James Freeman, private secretary to Rogasner, and who had been left behind at the Russian capital to gather up and safely ship the effects of his employer when the latter had received the summons from the Baron, and who had now arrived, as the young man pleas-antly announced, "just in time to breakfast with me," and to the housekeeper as she appeared in the doorway in answer to his ring:

"This is Mr. Freeman, who will be a member of our household. Show him to the rooms prepared for him." And to his secretary as the latter turned to follow the woman: "Do not hurry yourself, Freeman, breakfast will wait."

Twenty minutes later the two men were seated at the table and Mr. Freeman was telling his employer how matters had been left in St. Petersburg.

He had called on Baron Rothe as he came through London and had been given a letter to Rogasner, which he now drew forth and handed that gentleman.

Rogasner broke the seal as the other talked, and read the contents. They were short, merely calling attention to the enclosure, which was a plain, unsealed envelope bearing the superscription, "*Hon. J. W. Harrold,*" which the young man knew to be the name of a New England Congressman, and the Baron's representative in the lower house.

"And now what next?" said the secretary as he finished his recounting, and selected a cigar from the tray handed by the attendant.

"We are here," began Rogasner when the man had withdrawn, "for an indefinite period, possibly a number of years. I am intrusted with a mission of state importance, which you will understand more of later. It is necessary that the identity of both of us remain unknown; therefore we are citizens of the United States, and of the city of New York."

To all of which his listener bowed without speaking.

"Get what luggage you have brought," he went on, "into the house and straightened out as quickly as possible, and get yourself acquainted with the city. As you noticed from the plate at the door, I am in active business and you will govern yourself accordingly." And the two men then rose and passed into the office.

"This is my place of business," continued the young man, "and this," indicating the desk, "will be your post. That room," waving his hand toward the separating door, "is my private apartment. I am now going out, and may not return before lunch.

"You are at home, Freeman; it is unnecessary to say more," and a few moments later he was walking rapidly in the direction of the home of the New England congressman.

The letter presented, and after a few moments con-

versation with the agreeable and intelligent Yankee, he
wended his way to the telegraph office and dispatched
the following message in cipher to Baron Rothe:

"Prospects good; send two immediately."

The last three words of the message had reference to
a conversation held between the nephew and the Baron, before the former's departure from London. It was
agreed that the nephew would need able assistance in
the work that lay before him, and the exceptional traits
and characteristics necessary in such assistants was
talked over and discussed.   The probable course of the
work, the methods to be adopted, both in and out of
Congress, and the many phases it might assume,
brought forth suggestions and plans from both the distinguished financiers, and it was finally agreed that the
young diplomat, whose mission was fraught with so
much importance, should first look over the situation
and then wire the Baron.

Several men were discussed as to their fitness in the
proposed work and a list of five names was made in
the order of their value, and it was agreed that Rogasner should wire for all or part of this number, and if
he named less than all, it would mean those first on
. the list.   Hence the cablegram.

He had decided to start slowly and train two men,
before using others. He also wanted to get used to the
new work himself and feel sure of his footing and his
methods, before directing others in the work they
should do.

As he sat alone that night in his office, his mind ran
on the future and its probabilities. To himself, he re-
viewed the situation, and measured his strength. "I am
here," he mused, "on the greatest mission Englishman,

military or civil, has ever been sent. In the highest sense I am a military commander. My mission is conquest, occupation, destruction; that is all a military expedition could accomplish. I am here to destroy the United States—Cornwallis could not have done more. For the wrongs and insults, for the glory of my own country, I will bury the knife deep into the heart of this nation.

"As compared with the tactics of other commanders, mine is distinctively different. To get here, they bombarded cities and lost thousands of our best Englishmen on a hundred bloody battle-fields—I arrive here without the firing of a gun, and am welcomed. They spent millions of pounds—while I will spend but a small sum compared with what they expended, or what it would cost to make war now on the United States under our army and naval leaders. I will create more havoc and destruction than they possibly could.

"In such a war as they would wage, the United States would grow wealthy and prosperous—as all nations do when there is an expansion of currency— while I will drag them down and choke the life out of their industries and commerce."

As he said this he reached forth with his right hand and clasped together the fingers and thumb as if in the act of taking some one by the throat, and a baleful light of hatred shone in his black eyes. Continuing, he muttered:

"Ay! I will do more; I will crush their manhood. I will destroy the last vestige of national prosperity among them, and humble that accursed pride with which they refer to their revolutionary ancestors, to the very dust. I will set them fighting among each other,

and see them cut each other's throats, and carry de·
vastation into each other's homes, while I look on without loss.   I am in command of the greatest campaign
the world has ever experienced—it was a great brain
that conceived it, and it is mine to execute.   Like a
chemical that passes the lips and deranges the brain,
so will I furnish the lotion that will run distracted
this nation. I only ask that I may live to see it
through."   Again his eyes flashed with a wicked and
determined light as he leaned over in his chair, staring
apparently at space.

He then arose, and threw up the window to let in
the cold air of the night, that he might restore his ex·
cited temperature to its normal condition.

An active campaign was thus about to be opened.
Under the direction of this skillful, young and dangerous leader, the movement was assuming form that
was destined slowly but surely to wrap the great American nation in the shroud of calamity and far reaching
disaster.

CHAPTER VII.

About ten days after the sending of the cable message, mentioned in the last chapter, two men of ordinary dress and appearance, and bearing somewhat the stains of prolonged travel, were shown into the private office at No. 1403 Pennsylvania Avenue.

To Rogasner, who rose from his desk as they entered, the elder handed a letter sealed with the crest of Baron Rothe.

He had been advised of the departure from England of these two men, and was therefore expecting them when Freeman had passed in their cards.

Motioning them to seats, Rogasner opened the missive and drew forth its contents, a reading of which informed him that the two strangers were Mr. Thomas Hopkins and Mr. Theodore L. Strum, both former members of the great detective agency at Scotland Yard, and for the past half dozen years in the service of the banking house of Rothe. Men of marked sagacity and ability in their line, and the two first named in the list of five as called for in his cablegram.

The letter stated that the reader might rely upon these two men implicitly, in short that the best detective intelligence obtainable in Europe was at the command of the young diplomat into whose keeping so much of the vital interests of a great nation and a powerful financial institution had been given.

Rogasner laid the letter down and fastened his black eyes upon the two men for some moments without speaking.

They were not unlike each other, and might readily have passed as brothers. Both of middle height, and compactly built, of dark complexion and prominent features, the smooth shaven faces and keen eyes gave the impress of the force and resolution of their characters, and that their intelligence and ability was of more than the ordinary man of their justly celebrated class.

"You have arrived in good season, gentlemen," said Rogasner at last, as though satisfied with his scrutiny of the two men; "while the duties you will find here are not at present heavy, you will observe the strictest caution in your words and the most careful attention to the instructions I shall from time to time give you. It is not necessary that I say more than that we are to engage in a matter of the gravest importance to the crown, which may extend over a term of years. In the meantime you will become Americans, from any city you choose, but in no event must it become known that any of us are of another nation. Mr. Freeman and myself are citizens of New York City. Find lodgings near here, look over the city and select some respectable business in which you may naturally encounter employees of the government and members of Congress, and negotiate for its purchase. Mr. Freeman will furnish all required funds. Come here seldom, and only as patrons of one who loans money. Call here to-morrow evening at nine o'clock," he continued, rising to intimate that the interview was now to close, "and I will give you instructions in detail."

The two men walked along the avenue for some distance in silence.

"That's a rum chap," commented Mr. Strum at length.

"Make no mistake about that young man, my boy," solemnly answered his companion. "That's a wise head on young shoulders, and so long as *he* directs our work, I for one shall consider our efforts to be in no danger of failure, and," squaring his shoulders and looking straight ahead, "they are likely to be properly appreciated."

Mr. Strum glanced sideways at the speaker and said admiringly:

"It's a pretty good head-piece you carry yourself, Tom. The young fellow certainly is not far behind the Baron himself, and it would not surprise me, were the truth known, that they were kin."

"Nephew," responded Mr. Hopkins briefly, to whom the fact was known and who had seen Mr. Rogasner before.

"Just so, just so," replied Strum, well pleased with his own cleverness, after which the remainder of the walk was pursued in silence.

Arriving at the hotel where they had been driven on arriving in the city, Mr. Hopkins registered for both as hailing from San Francisco, which was the only city in America where either had ever passed sufficient time to be able to talk intelligently of, as they must of need be prepared to do, of the city they selected.

The following evening at the appointed hour they entered Mr. Rogasner's private office, and after the enjoyment of a glass of what Mr. Strum afterward alluded to as "the real Irish stuff, with a burr in each drop," they settled down in the deep chairs and to the business in hand.

Rogasner was informed that his two subordinates had procured lodgings at a private and semi-fashionable boarding house within a few blocks of the former's abode, and that they had decided to establish themselves in a stock brokerage business on Pennsylvania Avenue and but a short distance from the capitol. With which intelligence the young man was well pleased.

"Now then," said Rogasner, taking a paper from a pigeon hole in his desk, "this is a list of the men in the House of Representatives of whom I desire to know more. You will ascertain their habits, tastes, and as much of their past and present as will enable you to give me an accurate account of each, that I may judge of the man's character. You will also become intimate with the clerk of the committee on Ways and Means, and the clerk of the committe on Enrolled Bills."

Mr. Hopkins took the extended paper and after a brief scrutiny placed it in his pocketbook. "This list," continued Rogasner, taking up a second paper, which Mr. Hopkins also accepted, "is that of the members of the Senate about whom I desire the same information. The last name is that of the clerk of the Committee on Enrolled Bills of that body. Your methods will be your own, but avoid delays and should you encounter a difficulty promising any such, advise me at once. As you leave here stop at Mr. Freeman's desk; I have instructed him to hand you a sufficient sum to enable you to open a bank account, either as a firm or as individuals, which will enable you to assume the position it is necessary you should occupy."

The two men had said little thus far, but had no intention of being dismissed without further information
upon what they considered important details of their
duties, and the queries, suggestions and comments
which Mr. Hopkins voiced during the next hour, satisfied Rogasner that these two men fully appreciated
what was required of them and that he need feel no
uneasiness as to their sagacity, and the intelligent rendering of their part of the programme.

He was pleased also that so little evidence of the
nationality of the two men existed in their conversation, which was quite free from those eccentricities of
speech and manner so noticeable in many Englishmen.
This was no doubt a wise forethought of the Baron,
who never left anything to chance.

"So far so good," he murmured to himself after the
two detectives had received the package from Mr. Freeman and taken their departure. "The Baron has certainly selected wisely. These two men are jewels, and
it shall go hard if I do not win success with such able
coadjutors."

And time went on.

The New Year had come and gone. Congress had
enjoyed its usual holiday; members who had sought
their homes for the season's merriments had returned
and the two deliberative bodies were again in session.

Our plotters had not been idle. Many of the members of both houses had become regular visitors at the
home of the popular young "Investment Broker," and
to be numbered among the guests at his cozy bachelor
entertainments was considered an honor to be sought
and eagerly welcomed.

This wily and unscrupulous young schemer had also

managed that several of our nation s law-makers had beome pecuniarily obligated to him, and by his generous and gentlemanly treatment was very close to the confidence of some of his intended victims.

Thanks to the spirit and dispatch with which his instructions to the two detectives had been executed, he was in possession of a volume of information about each of his guests, of the greatest value, as may be readily understood.

About this time the Credit-Mobilier scandal burst upon the startled public, and an official investigation was ordered by Congress, the result of which is well known to the readers of that day. Probably at no time in the history of the world was a national legislature so corrupt, and the integrity of its members at so low an ebb.

In a study of the records of these two years, 1872 and 1873, one is most forcibly impressed with the corrupt condition of politics and affairs in the nation at that period.

The confessions of two senators and three congressmen of complicity in the Credit-Mobilier; the disclosures of the gigantic frauds perpetrated by that company and brought to light by the investigation in the Senate; the Congressional investigation of the sale of arms to the French government by the Remington Arms Co., causing the resignation of the Secretary of War, Belknap; the Navy Department investigation; the attempted passage of the two bills yclept "The Atchison, Topeka and Sante Fé Land Grant Swindle," and "The Wisconsin Land Grab Scheme;" the defalcation at the mint in Philadelphia, and subsequent investigation; the New York whisky frauds; the impeachment of

Mayor Hall of New York; New York custom house frauds; the notorious "New York Ring" indictments; the Chicago aldermanic investigation, in which three members of the board of aldermen of that city were convicted of having received bribes.

The Chicago Fire Department investigation; the investigation of the charges of bribery and corruption in the Wisconsin legislature, and many other instances in nation, state and city might be cited, all showing the remarkable condition of the morals of men at this time. .

One of the sensational incidents that came to the surface during this most corrupt period in the history of the United States, when principles and patriotism seem to have been displaced by individual selfishness, was the frauds connected with the passage of the Internal Revenue Bill.

This bill passed the House without containing anything in it repealing the tax on borrowed capital, and went over to the Senate. Here one Clinton Colgate, as a representative of the New York Stock Exchange, with his friends, laid siege to the Finance Committee and succeeded in inducing it to insert as an amendment a few lines repealing the tax in question.

In this way the bill went back to the House, through a conference committee, and passed.

Afterward Mr. Colgate was called before the committee on Ways and Means, and after repeated denials, finally confessed to the use of money to influence legislation; testifying among other things that Judge Charles Sherman, of Ohio, a brother of Senator Sherman, had been paid $10,000.00.

He stated that Judge Sherman wrote a letter enclosing a bill for this amount which he (Sherman) alleged was for making a brief and argument before the Senate committee, and for securing the services of his brother Senator Sherman, to put the bill through the Senate, and of a member of the House to perform the same service in that body.

Colgate's report to the New York Stock Exchange contained a statement which was brought to the knowledge of the committee of investigation at a subsequent meeting, that George Basset, clerk of the committee on Ways and Means, had made a proposition to Colgate that if he would pay him $250.00 per month, and $5.000.00 when the bill became a law, he would aid Colgate in securing the repeal of the tax.

In the Chicago *Tribune* of Feb. 21, 1873, a Washington special stated that the committee had concluded the investigation of the charges against Judge Sherman, and after giving him every opportunity to explain, which he failed to do, decided to turn over all the evidence to the Judiciary committee of the House.

As Judge Sherman was then holding the position of a United States District Judge, it was expected the Judiciary Committee would take action looking to his impeachment. The report states: "The evidence shows him to have been guilty of an attempt at black mail. While it was established that he demanded money of the New York Stock Exchange, it was shown that he did not perform any service and was not in Washington when the legislation, for the success of which he demanded a fee, was enacted." In the same issue "Gath," the Washington correspondent of this administration paper, writes:

"The newest case of corruption is charged against

the Ways and Means committee, whose clerk, one Basset, demanded $250.00 per month from the bankers and brokers of New York, to assist them in repealing the tax on borrowed capital, besides $5,000.00 when the act passed. * * * * * * * At the same time one of the nepotist United States Judges of Ohio, Chas. T. Sherman, presented a claim for lobbying the bill, along with his brother, the senator." The article then proceeds to give a little inside history as to the life and actions of Judge Sherman, whom he sums up as "the belly of the Sherman family," and goes on:

"As for Geo. A. Basset, long the clerk of the Ways and Means committee, the stories of his use of his privileges are as old as my residence in this city. I heard complaints made in California that he had demanded payment for services after experiencing unusual hospitality from the corporations there. Turkish corruption under the Pashas and Beys, or Russian official rottenness, could be scarcely worse."

Impeachment proceedings against Vice-President Colfax were begun at this time, by resolution introduced by Fernando Wood, on account of alleged complicity in the Oakes Ames affair and accepting money from one Nesbit, who furnished Congress with stationery.

Then came the charges of the New York *World* against Thaddeus Stevens for having received $80,000 for services in securing the passage of the Pacific Railroad bills; the barefaced whitewash of Senator Pomeroy; the threatened expulsion of Messrs. Ames and Brooks, all conspiring to make a series of events which kept the country in a ferment of bewilderment and disgust at the continued disclosures.

Files of the leading journals of that day, covering the years 1872 and 1873, are full of these matters. Less important news was abridged or crowded out of the papers, which were given up to the reports of the investigations and their results.

Despite all, the 42nd Congress adjourned without meting out any of the acts of punishment predicted and expected. Much was proved against many men of both Houses, but by some mysterious means, all succeeded in escaping with all or a good share of their nefarious gains; and the people at large, after having been regaled with the horrifying and disgusting accounts of the prevailing condition of morals at our nation's capital, were suffered to conclude that somehow the attempt at justice had miscarried. Other disclosures, a series of disasters in different parts of the United States, claimed the public attention, and past events gradually faded and were forgotten.

It was at a time like this, and in a Congress notoriously corrupt, making one of the darkest pages in the history of the republic, that a secret foreign enemy, with all the implements of corruption at hand, was laying the foundation for the industrial ruin and overthrow of a great nation.

That enemy could not have commenced operations at a more opportune time, or under conditions more promising of success. In this hotbed of corruption, a rank and poisonous weed would grow and flourish. No great principle was before the country or animating the spirit of the two political parties, and both began an era of political drunkenness, in which the sensual tastes and individual selfishness were to be paramount to all other considerations.

CHAPTER VIII.

The time was now ripe, in the judgment of the conspirators, for the passage of the bill which should legislate into disgrace the money of the people.

The momentous day had arrived, the 17th day of January, 1873, and everything that could conduce to the success of the enterprise had been considered and arranged for. The first act in the greatest drama in the history of nations was about to be played.

The members of the Senate interested in the bill, on the calendar as H.* R. 2934, were early in their seats. Senators who had a selfish interest in it by reason of their holdings of stocks, senators who were dupes to an imaginary necessity for a reformation of the mint laws; and senators not personally interested in a bill which their colleagues saw fit to push, and who vote upon many questions as the majority vote, were all present. Senator Arnold was early in his seat.

Senator Sherman, who was chairman of the Finance Committee, was prepared to report favorably and urge its passage.

Rogasner had intended being present in the Senate chamber on this most important day, and from some post of vantage watch the course of events, but a most unfortunate and quite unforeseen obstacle had presented itself, in the form of a party of English tourists that had arrived in Washington the day previous, and, as ascertained by the astute Hopkins, some of the mem-

* House Resolution.

81

bers of which had expressed the intention of visiting this day the halls of the American Congress.

As our quondam American numbered some of these people among his acquaintances, and as it would of course be unwise to risk being seen by them, he reluctantly decided to remain at home and trust to Mr. Freeman to represent him in the Senate.

He therefore arranged with that gentleman to report the proceedings by messenger boys, that though absent he might still be advised of every move.

Rogasner was of a nature to chafe at thus being obliged to relegate himself in a measure to the background, and at this of all times; therefore it was with an anxiety and feverish impatience quite unlike his usual calm manner, that he awaited the critical moments that were to decide the fate of his elaborate plans.

The events of that fateful day are correctly reported and faithfully portrayed by the scene enacted and the communications received at the office of the English agent, to which the attention of the reader is now invited.

It was eleven o'clock, A. M., before the first uniformed boy sprang up the steps of his house and was admitted by the man in waiting at the door.

The message was brief. "Senate in session. All are present." Which Rogasner knew to mean that all the senators who were counted upon to support the bill were in their seats.

How the moments dragged to the waiting man ere the second message reached him! Twelve o'clock, one o'clock, had come and gone, and no further news. It was growing unbearable, and in spite of his remarkable self-control, he was inwardly raging like a caged lion.

The second announcement of the butler that his lunch was waiting, was met by a short, "Have it cleared away."

Though the idea of food was repugnant to him in his present frame of mind, he halted frequently in his restless pacing of the room, at the tall sideboard. Though a temperate man ordinarily, and always preferring wines to the heavier liquors, Rogasner felt the present to be an exception. He was passing through the most important epoch of his career, and the stimulant of the small potations he allowed himself, he found necessary and grateful.

He had looked at his watch the hundredth time and was very nearly at the point of throwing prudence to the winds and joining Freeman at the Senate, when the second boy came sprinting down the street.

A moment more and the message was in his hand. "Senator Sherman has just called up the bill," he read with bounding pulse. "At last," he said aloud, throwing the note on his desk. Hardly had the outer door closed after the boy when the third messenger arrived.

He read rapidly: "Senator Sherman spoke as follows:

" 'I rise for the purpose of moving that the Senate proceed to the consideration of the Mint Bill. I will state that this bill will not probably consume any more time than the time consumed in reading. It passed the Senate two years ago after full debate. It was taken up again in the House during the present Congress and passed there. It is a matter of vital interest to the government, and, I am informed by officers of the government, it is important it should pass promptly. The amendments reported by the committee on Finance, present the points of difference between

the two houses, and they can go to a committee of conference without having a controversy here in the Senate.'"

Rogasner's flushed face took on a little less anxious
expression as he read, and seating himself he slowly
read aloud the remarks of the Ohio senator.

*"I will state that this bill will not probably consume any
more time than the time consumed in reading it."*

"Good, old boy!" he exclaimed. "That's the way
to open it up! Oh! but he's a wise one," and he read
on with muttered comments of, "Good!" "That's right!"
"Once passed the Senate!" "Now passed the House!"
Nothing left to consider! "Important it should pass
promptly!"

He leaned back in the deep chair and stared up at
the ceiling, as he repeated the closing words half under
his breath, *"Can go to a committee of conference without
having a controversy here in the Senate."*

"It could not have been opened better had I drafted
each sentence," he announced to himself, chuckling
softly. "Senator Sherman, you are a great statesman."
A listener would have been at a loss to determine
whether this last was an expression of admiration or
a sarcasm. A few moments of thought, and he rose to
receive another note.

"Senator Cragin has just given notice," he read,
"that he will call up the bill providing for six war vessels as soon as the mint bill is disposed of. There
seems to be a disposition to hurry the mint bill
through."

Here was unexpected aid. Rogasner could not but
note that such an action would further impress the
listening senators with the desirability of getting a

bill well known and fully discussed, out of the way of *more important matters.* Things were certainly running very smoothly, and he felt the nervous strain relax somewhat at the prospect of speedy and favorable action.

It was with more of his habitual calm that he received and read the next message.

"They are now changing some w rds in the bill," it ran; "striking out the word *'wording,'* and inserting the word *'working'* before the word *'dies,'* also inserting the word *'office'* before the word *'assay.'* Senator Sherman is on his feet constantly, and seems to have the discussion under control."

Rogasner smiled as though indulgently thinking there was bound to be a certain amount of empty talk, but was quite well satisfied thus far.

He held the next note in his hand a moment unopened while he lighted a cigar. It was longer, and a frown settled upon his brow as he read:

"A wordy war is in progress over who shall suffer from the loss by abrasion on gold coin—the government or the people. Senators Casserly and Cole are taking the ground that the loss should be sustained by the government; Senator Sherman wants no change, wants it left to conference committee; is now speaking." He had hardly finished reading when this was handed him:

"Senator Sherman, finding he cannot shake off the two California senators, is making a masterly argument to support his position that the people should stand the loss. Some of the uninterested senators have gone out. Your London friends have just entered the gallery."

Rogasner threw the paper from him, and walking over

to the sideboard, held a moment's commune with the decanter labeled "Kentucky."

He was growing nervous again, for in prolonged debate he saw possible defeat, and he felt an unreasonable impatience with Senator Sherman for allowing himself to be drawn into a discussion so unimportant, and so fraught with peril His anxiety had returned with redoubled force, and he unmistakably snatched the next envelope from the hand of the boy, who had hardly time to cross the threshold.

"Sherman wins. People lose when abrasion is more than one half of one per cent," he read rapidly. "They are now regulating the alloy in the nickel and cent pieces. Looks like systematic delay."

A muttered curse fell from the reader's lips as he crushed the message in his hand and turned to receive the next. They were arriving faster now, and the man at the door, stationed to admit none but these blue-clad Mercurys, was kept busy opening and closing the heavy portal.

At each succeeding message the anxiety and uneasiness of the recipient waxed greater. In spite of oft repeated applications to the stimulating contents of the glass decanter, the nervous tension was growing with each moment. The Senate was not taking everything for granted, notwithstanding the persuasive opening of Senator Sherman. The very thing most dreaded, full discussion, was threatened, and as note after note told of the growing debate, and failed to announce progress, the mental condition and actions of this waiting leader, forced thus to play a passive part in the drama, may better be imagined than described.

A lull of a quarter of an hour in the arrival of the

messengers only increased the feverish impatience with which he received and read the following:

"They are now discussing whether or not the eagle shall remain on the silver dollar, halves and quarters. The bill as reported takes the eagle off and stamps in its place the weight and fineness of the coin. Senator Casserly is fighting for the eagle. Says it's American sentiment; that silver is the money of the people, and that the people want the eagle on the coin, emblematic of liberty. If Sherman could shake off Casserly all would be well. Half the seats are empty and few senators present seem to be listening to what is going on."

"Great Heavens!" ejaculated Rogasner, now thoroughly alarmed, "if that man, Casserly, keeps this up, there is no knowing where it will end."

It had been his hope that a discussion on silver would be avoided, as it held possible defeat if carried to any length, and rendered complete concealment of design impossible. When the bill which he had arranged should be surreptitiously substituted for the one now under discussion, should become a law, it would possibly annul the months of patient labor if it were to be discovered that there was contradiction between it and the debate now going on, and at any rate make the succeeding years to be spent in educating the American people, wearisome, dangerous and expensive.

And now this meddlesome California senator must threaten the whole structure with his idiotic sentiment over the eagle. Rogasner fully recognized that though a small matter in itself, it was liable to draw the attention of more than one of the waiting senators, and he stamped in impotent rage and vexation as he contemplated the possible result. That so few senators were in their seats was the only consolation.

His hands shook and his bloodshot eyes gradually lost their strained and angry blaze as he mastered the contents of the next communication from his secretary.

"Senator Sherman has just spoken as follows," it read:

" 'If the senator (Casserly) will allow me, he will see that the preceding section provides for coin which is exactly interchangeable with the English shilling and the five franc piece of France; that is, a five franc piece of France will be the exact equivalent of a dollar of the United States in our silver coinage; and in order to show this wherever our silver coin shall float—and we are providing that it shall float all over the world—we propose to stamp upon it, instead of our eagle, which foreigners may not understand, and which they may not distinguish from a buzzard or some other bird, the intrinsic fineness and weight of the coin. In this practical, utilitarian age, the officers of the mint seem to think it would be better to do that than to put the eagle on our silver coins. I must confess I do not think it very important, but I think the senator ought to be willing to defer in these matters to the practical knowledge of the officers who have charge of this branch of the government service. I will say that Mr. Linderman, whom the Senate must know, has suggested this as being a convenient mode of promoting international coinage. The trade dollar has been adopted mainly for the benefit of the people of California and others engaged in the trade with China. The intrinsic value of each is to be stamped upon the coin.' "

Rogasner was filled with astonishment as he read, at the boldness of these statements. Senator Sherman had here affirmed that silver was to be enobled; that United States silver coins were to be good all over the world; used as an international money. He laid the message on his desk and resumed his walk up and down the room.

"That man would have been chancellor of the Exchequer had he lived in the time of Richard III.," he thought; "what masterly nerve in thus uttering words that might some day be used to his undoing! What a fall there will be from international money to no money at all; subsidiary coin!"

He repeated the sentence aloud as he read again the words looking up at him from the desk:

"*We are providing that it shall float all over the world,*" and he laughed at the irony of it, as he stepped into the outer room to greet the boy he heard entering.

This was brief and somewhat better in tone, as it disposed of the eagle question.

"The eagle wins," it ran, "retained by a vote of 26 to 24. Casserly rallied enough senators from the cloak rooms to win by a scratch. Had it not been for the Californian the American eagle would have flapped its wings no more on the *'people's'* money."

Rogasner felt a little relief, and inclined to think the worst was over. He lighted another cigar and was standing at the window when the bearer of the next message came running up the steps. It read:

"Senator Sherman is forcing consideration of bill. Seems confident."

"That's better," muttered the young man; "now comes the run in. If he isn't headed again, he'll win in the next half hour."

But the dread that the senator *would* be "headed" and the dangerous discussion break out again was so great as to be almost intolerable, and pending the arrival of the next note he walked nervously and erratically about the two rooms, muttering to himself his hopes and fears.

As he heard the step of the messenger in the hall he sprang eagerly to meet him, flinging the door open before the boy could reach it. With mad haste he tore open the note, and the retreating youth was startled by the fierce imprecation that burst from Rogasner's lips as his eye raced over the few words on the paper:

"Sherman again tackled by Casserly, who is bringing up another objection. Sherman has grown pale and seems anxious."

"Good God! How long will this last?" raged Rogasner as he violently flung the door shut, and mechanically ran his fingers through his disheveled locks.

"This infernal Casserly will be our ruin. Oh, that I could be on the floor of that Senate for five short minutes! *I* would find a way to silence his meddlesome tongue. Sherman is an old woman, to wheedle and coax in this way." And he went on pouring vituperation and unreasoning condemnation on the defenseless head of the unconscious and gallant Casserly, and heaping bitter blame and reproaches upon the name of Sherman.

Rogasner years afterward acknowledged to Baron Rothe that on this day for the first time in his life he utterly lost his head, which the reader will not find difficult to understand when the decanter is remembered.

In the midst of his raving another message arrived, and so great was his agitation and haste to get at the contents that he dropped the missive twice ere it was opened and spread before him.

As he read the hurriedly penciled words the pallor of fear that overspread his face when the note was handed him gave place to the flush of hope and expectation.

The message was long and he read slowly and carefully, commenting as he read: "Sherman spoke as follows:*

" 'I must express my regret that the senator from California should raise this disputed question at this stage of the bill, just as it was about on its passage. ("The fool is *showing* his disappointment.") The people of California are very largely interested in the revision of the mint laws. Indeed, I have received more letters from that state about this coinage bill, desiring it to pass, than from any other portion of the country. ("Which bill?" with a grim smile at the sophistry.) I can see the great importance of it to them, and I believe it to be one of great importance to the whole people of the United States. Therefore I do not wish to enter into a discussion in regard to this coinage change, that may possibly weary the Senate and delay the passage of the bill. I promised that the bill would not take more than an hour and when I made that promise I supposed these amendments which have been acted upon, would be acted upon *sub silentio*, and that other questions which had been settled would not be revived.'

"Casserly seems to have good-naturedly given in. Looks as though a vote would now be taken."

Rogasner jumped from the seat he had taken on the desk, and hurriedly poured himself ' full glass of the fiery juice of the corn, and tossed i. off at a gulp. His glowing eyes, undimmed by the fumes of the liquor he had drank; his disheveled hair and person; the disordered rooms, with the litter of torn and crumpled paper on the floor, all gave evidence of the awful strain of mental disturbance and enforced physical inactivity the

*The speeches of Senator Sherman, reported by Freeman, have been compared with the congressional record and found to agree verbatim. PUBLISHERS.

man had experienced since the first message was handed him that morning.

The end was now drawing near, and the next note from Freeman must tell the result. Was the labor of the past months, the worry, the strain of the continual fear of discovery, the carefully and as cautiously executed plans leading up to this day, the vast sums of money expended; was it all to go for nothing? Was he to fail?

He, the trusted agent and confidant of the most powerful man in Europe, to suffer defeat, and seek his relative and master as the conquered and not the conqueror?

For a brief space Rogasner suffered as only a man of his indomitable will and inordinate pride can suffer when confronting defeat. He buried his face in his hands and groaned aloud as these bitter reflections swept in a wave over his mind.

Suddenly the hoof-beats of a rapidly driven horse sounded without. The roll of the wheels ceased at his curb, the door was flung violently open, and as Rogasner sprang across the floor to meet him, Freeman entered crying:

"It has passed!"

The record of the events on that fateful day, as to the words uttered in the Senate chamber, may be found on the last pages of part one, and the beginning pages of part two of the Congressional Globe, third sesssion of the 42nd Congress. It begins on page 668 and closes on page 674 of the proceedings of Januray 17, 1873. It closes by saying, "And the bill passed," without giving the vote. In fact, it passed without a dissenting vote.

The object of the bill was supposed to be a measure to revise the mint laws so the Secretary of the Treasury in his preparation might more readily facilitate the resumption of specie payments on January 1, 1879, the day subsequently fixed.

That it was intended to conceal within its folds a deadly sting, blighting and withering to the hopes and prosperity of the American people, was only known to the few conspirators whose characters are so faithfully portrayed in our story.

Senator Casserly's eloquent words in defending the emblem of American liberty—the eagle—on the silver coins, would have rung out like a trumpet and rallied to his support the sleeping and benumbed integrity of even that rotten and speculating Congress, had he known the impending danger to the primary money of the nation.

When told that the silver coins of the United States were to be given a higher function than they had yet enjoyed, by being made to circulate throughout the world—that Americans wherever they might travel in foreign lands would meet a friendly face, and recognize in their coin the power of their great republic—it appealed to Senator Casserly's patriotism and gave assurance of the patriotic intention of his fellow senators, who were supporting the bill. Greater duplicity was never before practiced in a national legislature.

When Senator Sherman proposed to take the eagle off the silver coins and in its place put the weight and fineness, Senator Casserly in reply uttered the following beautiful sentiment:

"The eagle, it is said, suffers little birds to sing, and the eagle will not object to having his value in the countries of the world put under his wing on the coin."

The bill as it had passed the Senate was different in detail from the one that had passed the House; so it now had to go to the conference committee.

It was considered in that committee on January 27, and again on February 6, and was agreed on and reported back to both houses, where it passed as reported and was enrolled on February 12.

In the meantime the real work of the conspiracy was being consummated. As soon as the bill passed the Senate, Rogasner became the inflexible and determined leader that he was. His English friends had left the city and he was no longer hampered by their presence.

Strum and Hopkins were now reporting daily, and about this time a veiled woman mysteriously came and went, calling each night about 10 o'clock, and seldom leaving before midnight.

On the night of the 11th she was late, and Rogasner sat at the front window, where he commanded a view of the entrance, and waited impatiently. The last card was being played. Checks and balances had been provided, so if one plan failed another would succeed.

But now the worst was over, he was not prepared to admit failure as possible. Backed by unlimited wealth, and aided by skillful and intelligent subordinates, he felt himself fully equal to the future demand and entered upon his arrangements with greatest confidence.

It was nearly midnight, and Rogasner was standing in one of the deep windows idly drumming on the pane, when a carriage drew up at the curb without. A quiet, fine rain was falling, and at this late hour the avenue was quite deserted. He had closed the door to his inner office, excluding the light from the outer and dark room, and as the figure which stepped from the carriage and ascended the steps to his door, glanced at the two broad windows, no sign of light or life was visible.

"She has come at last," murmured the waiting man at the window, and he stepped to the door of the inner room and threw it open, admitting a glow of light as his midnight visitor entered from the hall.

Rogasner advanced to meet her and with low voiced greeting led her to the lighted room and closed the door.

"It will be done just as planned," the woman announced as she threw off the enveloping cloak and sunk into one of the deep chairs.

"Are you sure?" said Rogasner, seating himself opposite her, and fixing his eyes upon the veiled face.

"Remove your hat and veil," he continued. "I wish to talk with you at length."

"Yes, I am sure," she replied, uncovering her face, and laying the veil aside with her hat. "There is no room for doubt. I have just left him. He is intoxicated with anticipation, and the $10,000.00 I gave him, with a promise of $20,000.00 more, has purchased his innermost soul. He is mine; therefore yours."

Rogasner expressed his satisfaction, and then they settled down to a conversation carried on in low tones that would only mystify and perhaps not add to the reader's interest were it given here.

That this woman was another of Rogasner's numerous aids has doubtless been surmised, and as she sat in the soft light of the glowing study lamp she presented the appearance of one that would prove not the least powerful and effective. Dressed in some material of sable hue, plain and unrelieved by flounce or ruffle, the only visible articles of jewelry a plain ring on the fore finger of her left hand and the plain gold brooch at her throat, it would have required a face of unusual

beauty to have attracted attention from a casual observer. But the face was of unusual beauty. Young,
not yet out of the teens, the dark, almost dusky skin
glowing with the rich blood of youth and health, the
full red lips disclosed teeth white and regular as nature's
best. The raven eyes, and tresses black as Rogasner's
own, the rather prominent, though well moulded nose,
spoke her to be of his own race, that race which has
shown to the world some of the most beautiful of that
type of female beauty called brunette.

It was nearly two o'clock when she rose from the
chair, resumed her hat and veil, and wrapped the water-
proof about her small but exquisitely rounded figure.

Rogasner sat with his head thrown back, and eyes half
closed, listening to the musical voice of his companion,
when she leaned over him and lifting her thick veil
pressed her fragrant lips to his.

As he sprang to his feet she eluded his grasp with
a soft laugh and held up a finger warningly with the
word: "Remember!"

"Ah! Temptress," he exclaimed, "the time will come
when I shall be suffered to 'remember,' without the
chains."

She had reached the door while he was speaking and
turned with her hand on the knob.

"*Is* it hard for you? And do you think I too do not
find it so? As you have said, the day will come when
to remember will bring no fetters, and then—and then
—Ah! Victor, there is no hour in the day or night I
do not long and pray for the coming of that day. It
is my whole life; how small a part of yours!"

With which passionate and somewhat bitter words
the door closed after her and he was alone.

He stood a moment where she had left him, as though listening to the departing sound of the carriage wheels, then, as the rumble died away in the distance and the hush of the night enveloped him, he shook himself impatiently and passed his hand slowly across his eyes as though awakening from a dream.

A half hour later one looking down at his sleeping face, calm and peaceful as that of a child, could never guess that behind the quiet mask lived a spirit controlling the destinies of a great nation; th t held by the long white fingers resting so lightly on the coverlet, was a power greater than that of kings; that that lurking spirit, that mighty power, had set in motion the ponderous wheels of time that should grind beneath their merciless weight the beating hearts of countless thous nds of the human race.

Sleep well, Victor Rogasner, imperial servant of a royal master; sleep while you may. Your life is young, your feet well over the threshold of ambition's glittering hall, and no shadow of the years to come, when the misery nd anguish in which you are now wrapping a free and gallant people, falls this night upon your slumbering eyelids.

*   *   *   *

All transpired just as had been designed. The bill enrolled in both houses was as Rogasner desired, and as one may read it in the statutes to-day; and a report of the conference committee that should be consistent with the bill as enrolled, was substituted for the original. The dollar of the size of a "five franc piece of France," and "the size of an English shilling" is not mentioned. Gold was made the unit, and the old law by which the silver dollar of 371¼ grains was the unit, was abolished. Silver was demonetized. When the time should come to resume specie payments, gold alone wo il l constitute the money of redemption, and be the basis of our currency system.   Silver would be subsidiary coin redeemable in gold.

CHAPTER IX.

And now the progress of our story must be hastened.
Congress adjourned on the 3rd of March. No one had
discovered what had been done. Most of the instru-
ments used in its accomplishment knew nothing of the
real facts, and those who were in a situation to know
that something unusual and fraudulent had occurred,
were too ignorant of matters of such import, to comprehend their true meaning.

The few who did know what *might* be the result,
were conscience deadened, and their selfishness gorged
with money It 'is probable, however, that even these
had no conception of its far reaching effect.

Not a whisper was to be heard—not a word in print
was to be seen, about the demonetization of silver.
The greatest crime ever committed in the world—one
that was to cause more suffering than all other crimes
committed in a century, had been quietly accomplished,
and all traces removed as effectually as would be the
case when the ocean closes over its victim and the
billowy waters roll on as before.

An era of falling prices would now set in, and more
and more property would be required to pay debts.
Gold would increase in value, as it would now be required to do the work of both gold and silver, in supplying the needs of a redemption money, and all money
redeemable in *it* would necessarily be of the same value.
The rise in the value of gold would be marked by the

decline in the value of silver, as the latter was measured in this new standard of values, and all other property would decline with silver.   Debts would be harder and harder to pay, as property would bring less and less when converted into money.

The conjecture with the English conspirators was: "How long would it take this crumbling process to strangle the industries of the United States?"

Any reader having a doubt as to the secret and silent stealth used in the demonetization of silver, can satisfy himself by going to any city library where the files of papers are kept that were published in January and February, 1873, and he will discover that no mention was made of the passing of such a law.

The only account of what was enacted will be found in the telegraphic news from Washington sent out by the Associated Press that:

"The mint and coinage bill that passed the Senate this afternoon is a codification of all existing statutes on the subject."

It was not regarded as of sufficient importance to be noticed editorially by the papers.

That which has since 1876, the time of its discovery, convulsed half the world and consumed millions of words in the news and editorial columns of the papers and journals of the country, went by at the time of its enactment without being noticed.   It has since been intrenched and defended by all the power that capital could wield, and the people have been powerless to reverse the great wrong.

General Grant, who was at that time President of the United States is on record as saying that he had not read the bill, and signed it on the representation and understanding that it was a codification of the then existing statutes, with detail changes only.

The history of the world has been a struggle between the few and the many. The few have used money as the instrument to enslave the many. It is said that nothing occurs that has not had its precedent in history. But the events transpiring in this and other countries, culminating in the demonetization of one half the money that had theretofore measured the values of the property on the earth, is without a parallel in the known history of the world.

The power of money is so great in controlling the avenues that influence the minds of the people it is a serious question whether they will ever again succeed in bringing it under subjection.

Napoleon struggled with the old world for twenty years to free the masses from the domination of a selfish few, that had held them in subjection for fifteen hundred years. At one bound France threw off the galling chains of debt and class rulers, and as if by magic, prosperity sprang up on every hand, and gave support to its young and brilliant leader to battle with the combined wealth of Europe.

What he fought against was the old story of despotism. Abbott says of that period:

"The millions were ground down into hopeless degradation and poverty, to pamper to the luxury and vice of a few haughty masters. Voluptuousness and luxury reigned in the palaces of the kings, beggary and wretchedness deformed the mud hovels of the defrauded and degraded people."

After successes unprecedented, and victories in battle that astonished and amazed the world, English gold broke his power and drove the people of Europe back into a dependency on the mercy of the few.

The people of the world have never been sufficiently on their guard against the unjust and improper use of money. They are too slow to believe that others would do that which they feel they would not do themselves. The commonly accepted idea of crime is the infraction of an existing law. It does not occur to the ordinary citizen that it is possible to successfully covet and possess your neighbor's property by and with the use of statute law.

Rogasner remained in Washington, with all of his agents at his command, till after the adjournment of Congress on the third day of March, 1873. He then made arrangements for an early departure and for a suspension of hostilities till the new law was discovered.

He gave to Strum and Hopkins each a present of $10,000 and a leave of absence from duty for one year, unless they should be earlier recalled. And other aids he rewarded in proportion as their services had been of value.

It must be remembered that none of these agents knew the ultimate object of Rogasner's plans. They believed that the secret of his designs was to secure the payment of United States bonds held in England, in gold, or at least in better money than the war greenbacks that had been issued by the United States and which were then, with national bank notes, exclusively the currency of this country.

The United States had suspended specie payments —silver and gold—during the war of the rebellion, and had since maintained a purely paper money system,

and there were grave fears that it might not return to
specie payments at all, and would perpetuate its paper
currency.   It afforded Rogasner ample opportunity to
mislead his secret agents as to his purposes.   As they
believed that a return to specie payments substantially
the same as had previously existed, was just and right
and as good faith required, they did not feel as if they
were parties to a crime. So that they felt amply paid
when they received what they regarded as munificent
presents from an employer they had been pleased to
serve.

The secret intentions, and the ultimate effect on the
United States to be expected, were known only to three
men, Baron Rothe, Sir William Cline, and Victor
Rogasner.   Two others had a somewhat similar knowl
edge.   One was working for the same end in France,.
and the other in Germany.

Senator Arnold and the New England congressman
knew that gold was to be the standard and silver
demonetized, and that in the judgment of the world's
leading financier an advantage from this was to accrue
to capital, but the· thought that it would be of such
serious consequence as to bankrupt the nation, neither
entered their minds, nor was considered in their money
grasping natures.   Rogasner rewarded his secretary
liberally, and arranged that he should be left in Washington to watch.

His instructions were, to keep the house open, read
the daily papers, and watch with a hawk's eye for the
first sign of discovery, and to cable Rogasner of that
fact.   On the 8th of March Rogasner left for Europe.
A year rolled around, and no sign of discovery was yet
apparent. Freeman continued at his post.   Strum and

Hopkins returned to England. The years 1874 and 1875 both passed, and not a line had yet appeared in print that would indicate that the bill had been examined or that its effect on silver was known. The danger of detection increased as the time for resumption approached (January 1, 1879), and would be certain to be fully known and understood at that date.

In July, 1873, Germany passed a similar law to that enacted in the United States, and the same object was accomplished in France in January, 1874. The work was prosecuted very much in the same way as it was done in this country, and Rogasner, after leaving Washington, had spent much of his time with the trusted agents in charge of the measure in those countries.

It was on the 16th day of August, 1876, that Rogasner received from Freeman a cablegram bearing the single word:

"Discovered."

The next Cunard liner sailing from Liverpool bore Rogasner to the shores of the United States. Five assistants followed on the next steamer, among whom were Messrs. Strum and Hopkins.

Later Edward Rogasner, the younger brother of the English diplomat, established himself in the banking business in New York City, where he would be of assistance in the adroit plans of the elder brother.

CHAPTER X.

The discqvery produced consternation and indigna·
tion among the people who at once recognized the
effect such a law would have.   Members of the 42nd
Congress nearly all denied responsibility for the law.
A few were noncommittal; many did not like to admit negligence of duty in not having watched the
proceedings under their control, and deferred any
statement on the subject till they had examined the law.

A bill was at once introduced at the next session to
wipe out the objectionable law and to restore the old.
But with far swifter efforts, and a more perfect organi-
zation, the agents and proponents of the new law were
coming to its rescue.   Rogasner bore letters from the
banking houses of London to the prominent bankers
of New York, and placed in their hands English editions of books favoring the single gold standard.

In lesss than three weeks from the time he had left
London, his office in Washington was in active operation, and books and other literature were going through
the mail to all the bankers in the United States, to
the editors of the metropolitan newspapers, to politicians and others in high places.   He immediately sub-
scribed for all the leading daily papers in the United
States, and put clerks in charge of them to clip and
lay before him all their utterances on the subject.

A newspaper directory was on his desk, giving the

list of all the newspapers, magazines and journals in the United States.

Works on the "single standard" were mailed to all the professors of Political Economy in all the colleges in the country, and these were followed later by letters from a publisher in New York City to the professors of political economy in the leading coll ges stating that this publisher had a demand for a book on the side of monometallism that would advocate th desirability of a single gold standard for the United States, and that he could afford to pay the sum of $5,000 for such a book from the pen of the professor to whom the letter was addressed.

This tempting bait had the desired effect, and in less than a year exhaustive and able books from American authors were in the hands of leaders of public thought, and confus'on and pandemonium reigned until the public wav arried from its moorings of nearly a hundred years, an serious doubts began to creep into the minds of s me of the most patriotic as to what was best for the United States to do.

The bankers and money lenders in the United States, as had been foreseen by Baron Rothe, as narrated in our second chapter, now began to rapidly allign themselves on the side of the new law, and their influence was a powerful factor in molding public opinion.

The most outlandish exaggerations were circulated as to the present and prospective production, of silver in the Rocky Mountains, and the miners, prospectors, and promoters of mining schemes and their daily and weekly organs unwittingly aided in this general misrepresentation. If a miner opened up a vein of silver ore a *foot* wide and assaying *twenty* ounces to the ton, before the report left the mining camp it was *three* feet wide and *fifty* ounce ore; by the time it had traveled to Denver the pay streak was *five* feet wide and the ore would "mill run" *100* ounces; and by the time the account of the "new strike" reached the East it was *ten* feet wide and *1,000* ounce ore, and shipping in *car load lots.*

At the next session of Congress Mr. Bland, a member of Congress from Missouri, introduced a bill to wipe the obnoxious law from the statute books. A strong and powerful lobby was at once encountered, to delay and prevent the passage of the repeal. Everything possible was done to manufacture sentiment against any change in the new law. But the underground swell of indignation that came up from the people was too strong for the combined money influence of the world, and the bill passed both houses of Congress.

In the meantime the most powerful influence that could be brought to bear was being thrown around the President to veto the bill. Senator Sherman was now Secretary of the Treasury, and he laid siege to President Hayes, with specious arguments; with dire forebodings as to the success of a resumption of specie payments if the repeal was allowed to become a law. The protest of bankers, and through their influence the protests of Chambers of Commerce and other mercantile bodies, crowded the mails of the President and were piled upon his desk. The New York bankers assured the success of resumption if the President would veto the bill. but predicted its utter failure if the free coinage of silver was restored. Threats from Wall Street of impending panic and the numerous protests had it, effect upon the President.   The people as usual were quiet in trying to influence the Chief Executive, and were not aware of the pressure being brought to bear upon him.

The President wavered.   Senator Sherman renewed his efforts.   Finally the President yielded, and like a clap of thunder in mid air to the astonished people the veto was announced.

The struggle was renewed in Congress. A compromise followed, influenced by the known attitude of the administration—in the Bland-Allison law of 1878, which was a signal triumph for the single standard forces. By it silver was to be purchased as a commodity. The silver dollar in limited quantities was restored.   Gold remained the standard measure of values. Notes. bonds, and contracts, payable directly in gold to the exclusion of all other forms of currency, was legalized by the bill.

The conflict was renewed again in the next Congress, and continued to agitate each session, with a strong aggressive and unrelenting lobby, ever ready to meet the onset of the silver forces.   Party platforms of the two national parties both declared each four years in favor of the free coinage of silver, and the people each time trusted to this promise inscribed on the party standard they loved and that had so often led them in their political struggles.

Disconcerted by bad faith, weakened by treachery, and discouraged by defeat, the representatives of the people again rallied in Congress in 1890, and after a long and fierce political battle were vanquished by what is known as the Sherman purchase act.

This was substantially the enactment of the Bland-

Allison bill of 1878, with a change only as to the limited quantity of silver to be coined. Gold was still retained as the *unit* and measure of values, and all bonds, notes and mortgages were still authorized to be taken payable in *gold*.

In the meantime Rogasner was guiding the forces of monometallism. He had been conducting the most powerful educational bureau that had ever exerted its influence in the world. With the use of unlimited wealth at his command, vast possibilities unveiled before him, and his sagacious intellect took advantage of every opportunity.

He imagined himself a great general, engaged in a gigantic campaign, that had for its object the conquest of a nation—in a struggle with the greatest government in the world. He would at times compare himself to Wellington, and would fight over in his mind the battle of Waterloo. Again he would drink his inspiration from Lord Nelson, and had once taken down a history from its shelf in his office and read the account of the battle between the English and French navies in the Bay of Aboukir.

The history of that great naval conflict was already familiar to him, but now a new feeling took possession of him, when he read of the victories of these renowned English commanders. Lord Nelson shattering the French fleet, the greatest naval production of the great Napoleon—a cannon ball strewing in fragments upon the quarter deck the body of the French admiral—the brave words of Lord Nelson as he fell wounded—the ships drenched in blood, and the storm of shot and shell, that ended with the French fleet at the bottom of the bay, and England again the mistress of the seas

K

—all this had now a charm that had never before taken possession of him.

He had at one time doubted the financial sagacity of Baron Rothe, in the latter's prediction that the change in the financial system would utterly bankrupt and ruin the United States, and once when expressing this doubt to the Baron, his uncle had told him to watch the effect on the prices of products and manufactured articles. Since then, when reading the newspapers, he would turn the pages to the market reports. It was now a daily custom with him to notice the price of wheat and cotton, and he no longer had any doubt as to the ultimate outcome.

He knew perfectly well what effect the enormous and rapidly increasing debts, municipal, corporate and otherwise, would have as it required more and more of these products to pay them, and could see in the near future the victory for which he was waiting.

Twce he had been in doubt as to his success in the conflict he was waging; once when the bill was passing the Senate, and again when he had been defeated in both houses and was saved by the intervention of the presidential veto. During the period last referred to, when everything hung in suspense on the action of the President, he remembered what his uncle had told him when first sending him to the United States: that if the act of demonetization once became a law, he would have three chances of maintaining his position; one chance to defeat a repeal in the house; another in the Senate, and a third with the President. But while the suspense lasted waiting on the action of the President, Rogasner had suffered intense mental anguish.

He had, however, never relaxed his efforts, but had

redoubled them with added energy. At this critical period he compared his situation to that of Wellington at Waterloo, when driven from his first position; with the roads in his rear encumbered by wagons, artillery and baggage deserted by the drivers; with retreating fugitives spreading confusion and consternation throughout Bussels; with the Irish and Highlanders making a last desperate effort to hold the then victorious French in check, and his last hope the coming of Blucher. To Wellington it was Blucher or ruin. To Rogasner it was veto or disaster.

This young commander, as he was pleased to term himself, was never cooler or more determined than at this time. He cabled in cipher to Baron Rothe to make heavy purchases of gold in New York, and to set the tide of yellow metal flowing in streams from this country. He had such a connection with one bank in Wall Street as to be able to exaggerate the size of these shipments. He saw to it, that telegrams were sent to the President from the New York banks advising him of these heavy shipments of gold, and stating that it would all leave the United States if the silver bill was allowed to become a law.

This and many other things he did. Among them was to send agents south and west to travel in hot haste and mail letters to the President protesting against the bill becoming a law; these would be from the dear people. Thus a shower of letters poured in on the President. Rogasner knew that these letters would not be closely examined, and that the President in fact would never see them, but that his secretary would tell him that many letters were coming from the West and South against the bill. It was a small mat-

ter, but in the absence of letters asking him to sign
the bill, it would have its influence; and when the
veto finally came, he felt that it was his work that had
been most instrumental in wrenching victory from defeat.

Since that trying ordeal everything had gone smoothly
with him; the long struggle in 1890 he regarded as
won before it began, and the result confirmed his judgment.   It was now mostly a matter of routine to keep
his educational bureau, and his other plans for molding public sentiment in operation.   He believed that
industrial disintegration would soon set in, and he
waited impatiently to see the republic rock upon its
foundation.

Then came the struggle in 1893 to give the last finishing blow to silver, to stop its coinage even as subsidiary money.   It succeeded.   But the battle waged
fierce and long.

In the house, the power of the President, who advocated the complete destruction of silver as primary
money, was invincible. Public patronage was used with
unstinted liberality as bribes to influence the votes of
members of both houses of Congress.   A long and desperate defense was made in the Senate, where the
friends of silver stood like the Greeks in the pass at
Thermopylæ.   But the power of money, and the influence of the President, as he dispensed the thousands
of offices at his command, bore down these defenders
of the people.

Senator Palmer of Illinois is an illustration of many
others whose loyalty to the people was destroyed by
public patronage. He was elected upon the pledge that
he would vote for free coinage of silver 16 to 1.

without any condition or equivocation. He basely vio-
lated this pledge, and became a common suppliant at
the White House for the control of the Illinois patronage.

The reports as published from Washington in the
Chicago papers represented him in the most disgusting attitude, as beseeching the President for the appointment of his friends. Like a child crying for toys,
Senator Palmer begged for offices.

Not since the day the blood-stains of national dis-
honor were bespattered upon the escutcheon of England
by the use of titles of nobility and official salaries, to
abolish the Irish parliament, and destroy the constitutional liberties of a free and noble people, has such a
disgraceful act been chronicled in the history of nations, as the open, flagrant and intended use of public
patronage by the President of the United States, to
procure votes to repeal the last vestige of law that
authorized the coinage of the money of the people at
the mints of the country.

Bribery! Bribery! In so high a place! By what
other name would you call it? It is not money alone
that constitutes a bribe. The giving of an office may
be a bribe. The office may have a salary attached to
it, and this salary is money.

It is sufficient to say that history records a similar
act of an English king, in destroying the constitutional
liberty of Ireland, as "*bribery*," and impartial history,
when the fawning friends and partisan advocates of the
present administration in the United States shall have
passed away, will use no less harsh a word in speaking
of this act in American legislation.

He has done more than any other one man, except-

ing the actual conspirators, to tie the hands of the people of this country and place them as helpless victims
in the power of a soulless gold oligarchy.

CHAPTER XI.

Has the reader ever chanced to be at our nation's capital during the period immediately following the holidays and the reassembling of Congress?

If so the gay scenes, the days filled with streams of sight-seeing visitors, the nights of gorgeous entertainment, given over to a pleasure-loving populace, are well known and probably happily remembered. To such, Washington will ever be the Mecca of a pilgrimage toward which our pleasure-loving, happiness-seeking natures of clay will always turn.

To him who comes to this city of sybarites, as a stranger, I extend an invitation to accompany me this bright January morning of the year A. D. 1894, to the halls where wisdom sits, and the power of knowledge sets up its lamp that the light of its rays may extend to the farthest corner of our land of free thought and free speech.

Stand with me in the gallery of the United States Senate, and watch the unreeling of the tape that is fashioned into law, to protect and nourish your welfare and mine. Listen to the eloquent words of the wise men selected by an admiring people to serve Columbia and fashion new jewels for her crown.

If you weary of proceedings which you may possibly not understand, here at your elbow is variety to claim and hold the wandering interest for hours.

It is a day of visitors, for Senator Jones is to speak

upon the tariff, and you find that during your brief attention to the floor below, the gallery has filled with those on pleasure bent, and drawn here like yourself to see and hear all that may be seen and heard of one feature of Washington life.

The gentleman to your right is evidently of some foreign legation, and his companions of his nation. This is Count De Lonne just beyond, and the beautiful woman at his side is an American girl soon to become a countess. Over here is a party of our English cousins, apparently not strangers to their surroundings, and judging from the interest evinced by those near, of some importance in the social world. This charming young girl at your left, with the saucy eyes and prattling voice, is the daughter of the wealthy Senator Pembrook, and if you will look closely as she waves her fan to and fro, you will notice her engagement finger wears a ring.

Young? Oh! yes, not more than seventeen, but years count little; she is older than her years. Yes, that vapid, monocled, slender young Britisher at her side is her fiancé.

Not much to look at, certainly, but then he is "Sir Varian." Waste no pity upon this fresh young bud; it is considered a fair exchange; title, social position, a generous bank account, and she knows exactly what she is doing.

Do you notice the modest looking young woman just behind our young beauty? Pretty, isn't she? and quite respectable looking, yet she can not be respectable, for beauty has just cast a glance of withering contempt and insulted pride at her for sitting so near.

Beauty is right—the offending one is not respectable.

She is a member of the *demi monde* of Washington; yet do you know she has more claim upon my respect than has our dainty beauty?

The vapid escort suddenly seems to feel a thrill of life; he has dropped his monocle in his agitation, and as he hastily readjusts it we hear him exclaim: "By Jove! what a lovely girl! Who is she?"

If you are a man your eye will instantly seek the object of this youth's involuntary compliment, and found, will dwell upon it as a vision which even Washington, with its kaleidoscopic pageant of grace and beauty, may seldom duplicate.

Lovely? The word would be weak had it not been used by the brainless fop, whose exclamation discovered her to us. What of all the words which our poverty, stricken language gives to beauty, shall apply? Select your own, while your eyes feast, and if one be not enough take them all; you will not do injustice.

Tall, above the average height of her sex; a figure of the most graceful and lovely proportion, and in whose carriage there was no trace of the awkwardness of many tall women. Skin like the velvety blush of the ripe peach; eyes blue as Heaven's deepest hue, and beaming with that sweet womanliness that mark them truth itself; hair, and such rich, thick tresses, of a sunny golden brown, with lights and shimmers that envious lips called a gleam of "red;" a mouth—here I own I hesitate.

Only once before in his lifetime has the writer seen a mouth like this, and never one of sweeter or more alluring curves. Cupid's bow never cut its form more perfectly to upper lip, and the full red freshness of its fellow, smiling over the even white teeth, was—was—

well, looking was longing, and if the arrow has not reached its mark, it can only be because you are led captive elsewhere.

You echo the question of the young Englishman:

"Who is she?"

And turn to catch the reply:

"That is Grace Vivian, Senator Arnold's ward."

Grace Vivian. Truly a fitting name for this radiant type of the American maiden; and since interest in the proceedings on the floor has waned, let us move nearer where she has seated herself surrounded by the members of her party, and see if the evidence of our ears will belie that of our eyes.

Have no scruples; it is quite usual in the Senate gallery, and we shall not be noticed. She is speaking now, and the mellow, sweet tones are such as we have expected from so lovely a creature.

"I did not go," she is saying in reply to the question of a gentleman near. "Our guests arrived yesterday, you know, and hardly felt equal to it. I am told it was one of the successes of the season."

"In point of numbers, yes," said a young lady at her side. "A regular crush, and after an hour of struggling and pushing about the overheated rooms I was thankful to escape. I wish I had had anything like the presence of guests as an excuse to remain at home," she added plaintively, as if the punishment had indeed been severe.

At which the rest laughed merrily, for it was well known, best of all to the young lady herself, that an excuse that should serve to keep her at home when a reception like that of the night before was in progress, must be more than ordinarily powerful.

"But your guests will not claim your attention *this* evening, Miss Vivian?" inquired a gentleman of the party, bending over her as he spoke. "Surely you will grace the Atweld ball by your presence to-night?"

"I have accepted the invitation," she answered lightly, without meeting the persuasive black eyes above her. "It is now too late to send regrets, so doubtless I shall be present for a brief space."

"And will you not dance?" questioned he of the black eyes.

"Probably not," she returned, meeting his ardent gaze for a moment, then dropping her eyes, while a slight flush crept into her cheeks.

"I am sorry," he returned; "I had hoped to receive the favor of a waltz. Do you know, Miss Vivian, that I am most unfortunate?" And continued as she looked up questioningly, "Although I have often sought the pleasure, do you know we have never enjoyed a dance together?"

"Why, Mr. Rogasner," said the girl, a little annoyed at his bad taste and his too evident admiration. "I am not conscious of having behaved illy to you. I will make amends, and promise you now a dance from my card at the first ball at which we are both present."

He had taken the seat vacated a moment before by the young lady who desired an excuse to remain at home from a social triumph, and now leaned toward her with low voiced thanks.

"Let us listen," she said presently, hushing the whisper on his lips as the session was opened on the floor below.

Obedient to her wish, he relapsed into silence, and his heart in his eyes, sat gazing at the beautiful face of his companion, while she, forgetting his very presence, leaned forward in rapt attention to the eloquent words of the Senator from the Rocky Mountains, Jones who had commenced to speak.

Rogasner cared nothing for that eloquence, indeed when in the presence of this lovely girl took note of little else. He is older than when last we saw him, but time with its changes has dealt kindly with him. The black hair is slightly tinged with grey, and his figure is fuller than that of the young leader we knew twenty years ago. He does not look to be over forty-five, and is probably not so old. The black eyes have lost none of their brilliancy and power, and if we may believe their unspoken language now, his heart is still young.

The impulsive, handsome young broker of then has given place to the fine looking, dignified banker of to-day. He has prospered; that is evidenced by his face and appearance, and until this proud young beauty flashed the light of her blue eyes into his heart, had deemed all things worth winning were at his call.

Not that he doubted yet, but he had learned that the heart of a true and womanly woman is not to be plucked like overripe fruit, and may not be won by the glitter of dross, and its surroundings. He had spoken no word of love to the girl as yet, nor did he purpose to until he was much more sure of success than at present.

In the whole of his busy and eventful life he had never set himself to attain an object that did not sooner or later become his. In all his years of power, comfort and plenty, he had never felt a need as he craved now the love of this beautiful American girl, and it is small wonder if he refused to believe, what he sometimes feared, that it was far beyond him.

The slight ripple of applause that swept over the floor told that the senator had taken his seat, and many rose to go. Miss Vivian, with her party, had risen and were standing adjusting wraps and discussing the speech just ended, when a gentleman entered the gallery and pushing his way through the crowd, gained Miss Vivian's side just as Rogasner was turning from the assistance he had been rendering an elderly lady who had dropped her lorgnette under the seats.

His eyes flashed and a scowl swept over his forehead as the new comer greeted the girl with a directness that failed to see any one else for the moment, and his keen glance noted the light in the blue eyes and the heightened color of her cheek.

In a moment he had accepted the proffered hand of his rival, and the three were making their way down the wide stairs. As they reached the floor and joined the guests of whom Grace had spoken, she introduced the young man on her right as "Mr. Melwyn, member of the House from Nebraska."

There was, among the people visiting at Senator Arnold's house, a young lady from the far west, whose father was a railroad magnate and one of the Senator's closest friends. He, with his wife and daughter, had come to Washington to spend a few weeks of gaiety and recreation as the guests of the Senator. This young person was of the true breezy western type, and as her description of John Melwyn is truthful and somewhat interesting, we will, with her permission, copy here a part of a letter written that night to her friend and intimate in the western city.

After a page or two devoted to the trip hither and the people among whom they are sojourning, she writes: "We visited the Senate to-day, and heard Senator Jones speak on the tariff. I suppose it was a very grand speech, for the senators applauded when he had finished, and you know that is not usual, but I confess I was more interested in watching the queer actions of the men and the constant coming and going in the gallery. There was a Mr. Rogasner there, a banker with piles of money, and he is just dead in love with Grace, Miss Vivian, you know, but she doesn't care two straws for him. Just as we were leaving we were joined by Congressman Melwyn, and you would have laughed to see him march up to Grace without looking to the right or the left. The rest of us might have been so many wooden images, for all the notice he gave us. We left the three talking, and when they joined us at the bottom of the stairs, Grace introduced him. Oh! Maud, there is a *man* for you. He is very tall, over six feet, I should think, and a splendidly proportioned figure; a long, heavy brown mustache, and lovely dark eyes with dark eyebrows and lashes, the kind of eyes that look friendly, and make you like him immediately. His voice is deep and very pleasant, and Senator Arnold says he is one of the finest speakers in the House. He was dressed faultlessly, and I think him one of the handsomest men I ever met. He too is in love with Grace, and I think she likes him a little bit, but he is poor, awfully poor, only has his salary, and the other has so much money he can not count it. But then he is young, not over thirty, and papa says has a brilliant career before him.

"His manners are so nice, too. Not a bit of the 'great
I am' of the banker, and when he says a thing you feel
that he means it.   I hope Grace will marry him; they
are so well suited to each other, and they are quite the
finest looking couple I ever saw."

By which we may infer that the writer, true to her
sex, had scented a match and desired its consummation.

She may have considered significant the circumstance, that as the two men escorted the ladies to their
carriage that morning it was Melwyn's hand Grace
touched as she stepped into the waiting vehicle, while
the gloved fingers of the banker were unheeded.

The two men stood for a moment chatting pleasantly
of social matters, then separated, Rogasner to be
whirled in the waiting coupé to his bank, Melwyn hurrying back to the House.

Doubtless there would be a diversity of opinion in
the minds of those seeing them together, as to which
of these two men was the superior.

Rogasner with his immaculate apparel, distinguished
manner, and general air of prosperity and ease, speaking the aristocrat and man of substance, and Melwyn
with his strong figure and intelligent face, no less well
clothed, presented a type of young American manhood
which, though common in our land, is not the less
worthy admiration and is a credit to our institutions
and systems.

No two men could be more dissimilar and more on
the same plane, not only in physique, but in character,
tastes, habits and manner.

The banker, his stout and well groomed person, soft
skin and disinclination for bodily exertion, certainly
presented a marked contrast to the broad shouldered,

bronzed young giant striding toward the capitol building.   No, there could be no doubt about the result of
a personal encounter between them, but if they ever
became antagonists, it would not be physical powers
that would decide the contest; it would be a duel of
the mental faculties, and there, it must be confessed,
Rgasner held an advantage.

The honest heart and frank directness of the younger
man; his simple rearing, uneventful, in a sense, furnished few weapons with which to meet the wily diplomacy and cunning, the broad knowledge and teachings
of a life of intrigue, possessed by the polished,nephew
of Baron Rothé.   And money! It would not be strange
if, in the light of what Victor Rogasner had accomplished with the aid of money, he looked upon it now
as the most powerful ally in his determination to make
the beautiful ward of Senator Arnold his wife, and mistress of his home.

As for Melwyn, he never felt the sting of poverty to
be so bitter as since this radiant girl had come into
his life.   He believed he judged her rightly when he
considered that such a nature as hers could never allow the thought of his circumstances to influence her
attitude toward him, or her decision, should he win
her heart.

But what an undertaking he had set himself! To
win for his wife the ward, and rumor said the heiress,
of the wealthy, proud and honored Senator Arnold; a
girl at whose feet had been laid titles and wealth, and
whose hand was now sought by a man, handsome, accomplished, whose wealth was great, and whose position and power were second to that of no man in the capital city, and above all, who was the warm personal friend

of the man who stood in the position of protector and father to his divinity.

Possibly the young man overestimated the obstacles in his path, and vanity was not a part of his nature. Great love is timid, ."vaunteth not itself," and it was with anything but a light heart that he resumed his seat among his brothers of the House and forced his attention to the matter under discussion.

Meanwhile Grace and her guests had arrived at the palatial residence Senator Arnold had but recently erected, and after a dainty and toothsome lunch had separated to their several ways of supplying the interval to dinner; . the railroad magnate, Mr. Willets, to make some business calls, his wife and daughter to do a little needed shopping, and Grace, after writing a few short notes, to "lie down" in the darkened sanctuary of her own apartments.

Which means that upon her arrival home she had found a note from Mrs. Atweld, containing a most cordial and pressing invitation to Grace's guests to attend the ball she was to give that evening. A consultation at lunch resulted in acceptance, which accounted for the shopping and also for Grace's retirement, for when one intends to turn night into day, it behooves one, and the fair sex fully appreciate the fact, to reverse the rule. So it has been discovered that beauty's star shines the more brightly for the indulgence of a nap before the fray.

While the girl who is the heroine of our tale and who has so large a part in the subsequent lives of Rogasner and Melwyn, is peacefully sleeping behind the silk curtains of her couch, the reader shall be told how she comes to be of the household of the austere and selfish Senator Arnold.

CHAPTER XII.

As will be remembered, when Lady Edith Rothe had portrayed to her father the character of the man with whom the Baron was to deal, she had stated that "sentiment, affection, have small place in his nature," which was perhaps true at the time, but Senator Arnold had lived his romance and buried it, and for many years its memory had small influence upon his daily life or actions.

In his early youth he had met and loved a beautiful and high born girl; met her while spending his college vacation with his friend and her brother, at their home in the South. And in the short weeks of that happy vacation he learned to love her as he had never thought it possible to love, and with all the force of a strong and selfish nature. He wooed and lost, and some months afterward read with a strange clutch at his heart the account of her marriage to his rival, an old friend and neighbor of her family with whom she had grown up from childhood. Then came the war, with its four years of strife, and its sacrifice of human hearts, offered up at the altars of the two flags.

His friend, her brother, fell at Bull Run among the ranks of the gray. His successful rival sheathed his sword at the surrender of his commander and soon after took his wife and went abroad. Since then he had heard nothing of them, and gradually in the press of his busy public life the old sting died from his heart, and the beautiful image of the one love of his life from out his mind.

He had married, purely as a means of advancing himself, a woman as cold and selfish as himself, and she had died after three years of wedded calm, leaving him childless but with added wealth and influence.

Little of the past lived in his memory, and it was with a new and unaccustomed stirring at his heart that he one morning received and read the following, brought to his desk at the Senate among his other mail:

"SENATOR JOHN ARNOLD,
            "United States Senate,
                    "Washington, D. C.

"DEAR SIR:—In pursuance of the request of our late client, Mrs. Grace Vivian, I send you the enclosed from her pen, with the request that you communicate with us at your earliest convenience as to your decision relative to the request therein made, and allow us to express the hope that you may be able to comply with said request.   It was   much   desired   by Mrs. Vivian.
            "Yours very truly,
                    BARD & STOLL

Senator Arnold laid the curt, business communication from this law firm upon his desk and took up the enclosure.   It was sealed with wax and addressed in the fine hand he so well remembered to

JOHN ARNOLD,
        Personal.

The room resounded with the hum of the assembling Senate, and the pattering feet of the busy pages.   He was in the midst of noise and disorder and yet was far away. Again he stood by the moss-grown spring in the sunny south-land, listening to the sweet voice that stilled his hopes, crushed his love, and ended the one romance of his practical life. How beautiful she was that bright afternoon, and with what gentleness and womanly sympathy she had told him what he wished could never be! He had blessed her then for her pity of his sorrow, and had told her he was the better man for having loved her, and that though she was not for him, he would be her sincere friend so long as he should live.

And now she was dead. A mist rose to his eyes, and a sigh swelled from the heart that had so long lain dormant. It was over now; what request had the dead to make of him? He slowly ran his paper knife along the edge of the envelope and drew forth its contents. Then becoming aware where he was, he rose and made his way to a retired corner of the lobby and read the message from his old love.

"My friend," it commenced, "I know not if I am forgotten, or if remembered, as one to whom you may extend such a kindness as I am about to ask. I must of necessity be brief, for the sands of life are fast running out and I grow weaker with each hour. I am alone now; you have heard of my husband's death, and like many of the people of my land who suffered the shock of the cruel war, I have survived my nearest of kin. I shall leave behind me a daughter who has been my one blessing and comfort in the dark hours of the past year, and it is her future, a desire to feel that her welfare and happiness is assured, that induces me now to turn to one upon whose kind heart I once inflicted pain, but in whose goodness and truth I have every faith. In the memory of the friendship you once expressed for me, I venture to ask you now to protect and guide my little daughter through the years of her girlhood, and until she shall arrive at that period where her life and future become her own. I am able to leave her amply provided for, and do not mean that she shall become a burden upon you in any way, nor do I mean that she should become an inmate of your home, for others' rights must be considered. But I ask that you give her your care, your counsel and advice and to protect her by your guardianship from the pitfalls that yawn at the feet of the orphan. I have left full and complete details with my lawyers here, Messrs. Bard & Stoll, as I am not equal to the task of writing all. Have no hesitancy, my friend, in expressing to them any inability to comply with what to you must seem my strange request, though I feel that it will be granted. I have taught my little Grace (for she has her mother's name), to trust and honor you as her mother's friend, and such is her nature and sweetness of character that, should you assume her charge, you will not find the care extended burdensome or unappreciated.

"I have marked your course in public life, your noble utterances and acts in our nation's affairs with greatest interest, and no one can be more truly glad of the well earned distinctions and honors that have come to you than I. I wish for you their continuance through the years to come. I can write no more. I have left all with the gentlemen who will forward this to you. Forgive me if I ask too much.

'GRACE VIVIAN.'"

Who can fathom the feelings of that silent man as

he sat there, alone and busy with the past and what it contained? His colleagues wondered at the empty seat and remarked at the absence of one who had become as regular as the great clock behind the speaker's chair.

That night he left for Montgomery, and in a week, after repeated interviews with Messrs. Bard & Stoll, returned with his "ward," then a young girl of twelve.

He resumed the house rented at the death of his wife, and aside from the two years Grace had passed at a finishing school, had kept her with him constantly.

She had grown to be more like her mother with each succeeding year, and Senator Arnold, who once thought the fount of his affections dried and broken, now lived for little beside the happiness and well-being of this lovely young woman.

For her he had laid aside his aversion to society and its exactions; for her he had later built the palace she looked upon as home; to gratify her slightest wish was become a greater happiness than the winning of a victory for his party; to hear her happy laugh was keener gratification than the receipt of a handsome check.

By which we may know that our Senator was somewhat changed. Changed truly to his friends and political associates, who knew him as we have known him, and from whose presence he would hurry when matters of grave moment were under discussion, if it so chanced he had promised Grace to attend her at a certain hour, and that hour had arrived.

Never fond father doted on only child, as this reserved man of affairs doted on the bright haired maiden who had so entwined herself about his heart. It was matter for comment among their circle of friends, and the struggles which took place in his heart, sometimes apparent to the world, between his natural avarice and selfishness and his love for his beautiful ward, were really pitiful, though the world said "silly."

He might nave been, nay, he must have been a different man, had such an influence as this girl exerted over him, come in his earlier years.

CHAPTER XIII.

It was the evening of the Atweld ball.

The magnificent mansion of these recognized leaders of Washington social life was ablaze with light, and the spacious and brilliantly decorated rooms were thronged with beauty and its ever attendant train.

Arriving carriages deposited their freight of pleasure-seeking humanity at the carpeted and canopy-covered walk, and departing, swelled the turbulent stream of the broad avenue.

Strains of sweet music floated through the open windows, to regale the ever present crowd of curious ones filling the sidewalk to the curb.

The resplendent ball room was a sea of bright color and fairy-like beauty, on whose undulating crest gleamed the bright faces and white shoulders of lovely women, and sparkled with the flash of happy eyes, outrivaling the brilliancy of the gems where enmeshed in heavy tresses, and nestling against soft throats.

The sober-hued dress of the conventionally clad men added the finishing shade to a living picture, never complete that shows not the union of strength and beauty.

Never completed, for beauty were less beautified without the protecting presence of strength; and the latter—how wofully weak without the added grace of beauty at its elbow!

It has been said that "all men look alike in a dress suit."

If a woman were the author of such an opinion the fashion would have been changed long ago, for the majority of them prefer an individual to the sex.

Look at this individual over by the window, cooling his flushed and heated face, while he pompously entertains the slight girl at his side. His short, rotund figure, his fat and shaking shoulders, that seem about to burst the seams of the tight-fitting coat; and what an expanse of white bosom, and swelling vest unrelieved by a single thing, and rather emphasized by the two tiny shining studs beneath the double chin! How much better dressed is the gentleman just beyond! A long, lean and lanky person, all angles of elbows and knees, the whole surmounted by a huge head, the bald surface of which is now affording the merry and mischievous girl behind him an opportunity to air her knowledge of phrenology to her amused companion.

Now notice the young man standing by the doors opening from the drawing room. He is engaged in conversation with the minister from Italy, but his eyes seem ever to scan the faces of the entering guests. Yes, we've seen the gentleman before; it's Jack Melwyn; but look at him well and then say "all men look alike in a dress suit." That sober costume, which differs in no way from that of the others, reveals the noble proportions and sturdy length of limb of the perfect man. He is dressed becomingly; what shall we say of the others?

Well, it is not given to all to be Jack Melwyns, and until the decree goes forth that man's taste and good sense shall clothe him for the ball, all men must dress alike.

It is not hard to understand why Jack watches the entering ones so closely. He has not come early, but that he has come at all is simply that he may see and be near the girl who is now so constantly in his thoughts.

He is not at all a devotee at the shrine set up so high in Washington, and the occasions when he had lent his presence to its gatherings since his election to Congress had been few, until he met Grace Vivian. Since that meeting it was safe to assume that where she held her court he would be found among the courtiers.

The musicians were just playing the opening strains of one of Strauss' delicious waltzes when she entered, and upon the arm of Rogasner.

They stood a moment to catch the beat of the music, then glided away down the long room. As she swung lightly about, facing Jack, she caught a glimpse of his face, and its expression positively startled her.

Although but a glimpse, she read it as one reads written words, and she years afterward acknowledged that waltz to be the most uncomfortable she had ever danced.

Now, Jack was perhaps somewhat old fashioned, possibly owing to his Puritanical blood, and in the brief instant the girl had stood, her companion's arm resting lightly against her waist, he felt so keenly the profanation of such contact from a man like Victor Rogasner, and so fiercely did the unreasoning jealousy of the lover sweep over his heart that it was reflected for an instant in his face, and Grace saw and understood it.

She had never danced with Rogasner before. The

few times they had met that season at such entertainments he had sought her card for a waltz and she had
avoided the giving instinctively, why, she could not
have told. She knew now. When she had been met
by him in the drawing-room, just after her greeting
by Mrs. Atweld, he had claimed his dance in fulfillment
of her promise in the Senate gallery that morning, and
had selected a waltz, not only one, but had scribbled
his initials against four different numbers of the same
character of dance.

Such cool effrontery could not fail to be unpleasant,
and then to see such unmistakable—well, disapproval,
in the face of Melwyn, did not tend to soften her feelings toward Rogasner.

Jack watched them till they were lost to view among
the whirling couples at the other end of the room, then
with very scanty courtesy to the Italian minister, excused himself and made his way to the smoking-room,
to try the soothing effects of a cigar.

The waltz over, Rogasner handed his fair partner to
a seat and stood over her murmuring the pretty noth-
ings he knew so well and so eloquently how to say,
until she was claimed by the gentleman whose name
appeared next on her card. He noted her stately bearing
and noble form as she moved away and took her place
in the set, and thought to himself with an exultant
smile, "You are cool now, my lady, but you are to be
won and you shall yet be mine."

It was some time after, and Rogasner was seated
with Grace waiting for the band to signal the beginning of his second waltz, when Melwyn approached and
after greeting both, somewhat constrainedly to be sure,
asked to see Grace's card.

"I am afraid you will find it quite full," she said laughingly; "although I intended to be so very temperate this evening, I find it difficult."

"It could not be otherwise, Miss Vivian, once your card is surrendered," he returned gallantly. "It is indeed full, and I am doubly unfortunate in that I was unavoidably cornered in the smoking-room by a very prosy and merciless member of the House, and was thus prevented from seeking it earlier. Surely," he continued, smiling at Rogasner, "you will be generous in my misfortune and allow me at least one of your three remaining favors," and he coolly drew his pencil through the banker's name and substituted his own. This was assuredly a somewhat high-handed proceeding and can be excused in Jack only on the plea that he felt recklessly determined not to be robbed of all his evening's happiness, and after being obliged to listen to a tiresome harangue when his mind was anywhere but on the speaker's subject, and after finally breaking loose, to hurry to Grace, only to find his chances of a dance with her gone, and the initials V. R. showing in four different places on her card. No wonder he felt himself unfortunate and was guilty of a grave breach.

This headstrong young congressman cared little for that however, so long as it did not bring upon his head the displeasure of his love, and he did not read that in the blushing face.

Rogasner however, was not the one to voluntarily relinquish such an advantage, and at the same time forego a pleasure secured to him.

He laughed lightly as he replied:

"My dear fellow, you clothe me with a virtue undeserved. I assure you I am prone to be extremely selfish in such matters. I could not think of giving away a pleasure granted by Miss Vivian."

"I am quite at your mercy, Mr. Rogasner," began Jack, "and must—"

"Pardon me, Mr. Rogasner," interrupted Grace with quiet dignity. "You forget that I granted you *one* dance. I think you must allow me to dispose of one of those you claim."

Rogasner's dark face flushed at the reminder that he had appropriated more than had been granted, but nothing remained but to relinquish the waltz to Melwyn, which he did as gracefully as possible under the circumstances, and Jack went off with a lighter heart and the feeling that the banker's victory had not been altogether complete after all.

"How cruel of you!" murmured Rogasner as the young man turned away.

"Not at all," said Grace, her face still burning slightly at the dispute; "it was only just, since Mr. Melwyn had not the advantage of asking my card earlier, and seemed to so regret the circumstance."

Rogasner was about to reply deprecatingly and in excuse of his refusal, when the musicians struck into the waltz they had been waiting for, and Grace, not relishing a prolonged tête-à-tête over a subject at which she felt some vexation, rose to her feet as though to join the dance and in a moment they were in the maze.

Meanwhile Jack took his way back to the smoking room, to beguile the time that must elapse before he could again seek the presence of his lode star, carefully avoiding, however, the corner where the merciless one was still holding forth.

He joined a group near the window from which came a burst of laughter as he entered the room, and was immediately assailed by the center figure with:

"Here's Melwyn; I'll prove it by him."

"What's to be proven by me?" said Jack, laughing at the excited face of the speaker, whom he recognized as a Western member, dubbed in the House "The Red-Headed Rooster of the Rockies."

"Who's the peacemaker of the House?" demanded the red-headed one.

"The peacemaker of the House," repeated Jack, catching at once at the fact that 'the boys' were having a little fun with the congressman reputed to be the most pugnacious man in the House. "Why, I think you must be, McNaught."

"Exactly!" pronounced McNaught, sweeping a glance of triumph around at the grinning faces. "This feller, Wilfer, says I'm the chap that always makes a row," and went on in support of his claim. "Didn't I spile a scrap between Waugh and Moses the other day? Didn't I, this very mornin', spill ile on the water when Funk jess the same as told Meredeth he was a liar?"

Which was met by a roar of laughter from his audi tors, as McNaught's method of "splling ile" on the occasion in question had been to forcibly pull the offended Meredeth back into his seat and hold him there while he whispered stentoriously: "Don't take no notice of him now, wait till you get him outside, I'll back yer up," which proceeding had so astonished that gentleman that he had suffered the discussion to pass on without him.

"An' I'll be durned," he continued in a tone of dis-gust as the merriment subsided, "if them two fellers want talkin' and laughin' together like brothers fifteen minutes afterwards."

Jack laughingly agreed that Meredeth's conduct was past comprehension, and thus reinforced the "peace-maker" launched forth in a variety of citations as to how differences were settled between "gentlemen" in his beloved West.

This McNaught was a character, and afforded his fellows in the House a fund of amusement that was practically inexhaustible. An immensely wealthy, and in his own country, very popular, mine and ranch owner, he had literally bought the honor of a seat in Congress, and whatever his faults might have been it could never be said he was not loyal to the people that sent him there, or failed to represent them to the best of his knowledge and ability.

In appearance he was striking enough to draw attention anywhere, and the appropriateness of the title bestowed by some wag in the House was unquestionable

Very tall, with a massive, bony frame, a well shaped head covered with a shock of fiery red hair, blue eyes, a long, heavy, drooping mustache of the same hue as his hair, a bronzed and weather-beaten face, his whole person suggested the life of hardship and activity meted out to those who cast their fortune on the frontiers.

Honest as the sun, with absolutely no knowledge of fear in his composition, an uncompromising, hit or miss kind of directness in all his speech and manners, with a good deal of native shrewdness and ability, he was a thorn in the side of some of his fellow representatives, and had inspired a wholesome respect for his rough, but honest tongue, and his rugged and incorruptible nature.

With all his pugnacious talk and despite his fierce aspect, those who knew him best, knew his heart to be as tender as a woman's, that the blue eyes that had so often flashed terror into the heart of an antagonist on the frontier, and that lighted up at what he called a "circus" in the House, could melt with sympathy at sorrow, and shine with merry jest and story in the presence of childhood.

Children adored him and he fully returned their worship, and it was a sight refreshing and to be remembered to see this red haired giant surrounded by a happy crowd of youngsters, himself as young as they.

A warm friendship had sprung up between this man and Jack at the session when both had first assumed their seats, and subsequent events during the fight for the rehabilitation of silver, when each had found his views and opinions reflected in the other, had cemented the relation. McNaught had the highest opinion of Jack's ability and his knowledge of law, and it had grown quite the common and natural thing for him to consult the young man on matters connected with his affairs at home as well as upon the business of the House.

Melwyn liked the sturdy honesty in the man's nature, and his natural intelligence and broad comprehension of a subject so near his own heart made him a companion and friend of double value where so many were arrayed on the other side.

"I say, McNaught," spoke up Wilfer, returning to the charge as that gentleman wound up one of his narratives with an explosive, "That's the way we treat such a critter in my country,"

"You said in the lobby this morning that gold will

soon have grown so in purchasing power that it will take double the amount of property to be equivalent to a dollar that it did before the repeal bill passed. If that's the case, why is it not perfectly fair to all, since all are paid with that dollar, and all get the benefit of its increased value?

"Why, you doggone gold bug," replied Mr. Mc-Naught, eying the questioner suspiciously, "do you ask that because ye don't know, or 'jess because you wanter see what I'll say?"

"I ask for information," returned Mr. Wilfer, joining in the laugh that followed the reply of McNaught.

"Well then," said the latter, "I'll tell ye a little story by way of answer," and he began as the circle grew closer:

"We used ter have a feller out on my ranch, that made a business of ridin' bronchos. A regular '*buck-aro*,' as the Greasers call 'em. He used ter brag about the hosses he'd rode, and tell how there never was a critter that wore hair that he couldn't ride to a finish. He was a good rider, that's a fact, best anywhere in those parts, but his everlasting braggin' made the boys mad, and they was always on the lookout ter put up a job on him, an' hed scoured the country fer spiled hosses. But this feller he jess rode 'em all as fast as they'd trot 'em out and then laugh at 'em.

"Well, one day a family of immigrants come along, and camped that night near us. Of course the boys went over ter yarn a little and it want long afore they found that the fellers had a mule that nobody had ever rode, and he swore the man didn't live that could. This was jess what the boys was looking for, and they told the man to bring his mule over in the mornin' and get him rode, an' he promised.

"Next mornin'," continued McNaught as he pulled at his vest, which seemed to fit him uncomfortably, "over he came, leadin' the mule, an' our feller started in. The critter was a big, raw-boned, long-legged animal, quiet and innocent lookin' enough, but the oneryist white eyes you ever see. 'Twant no trouble to put the saddle and bridle on, but the way he braced himself on them long legs, and laid back his ears, tickled us half to death, for we knew by the signs he wasn't no rockin' hoss.

"Well, the feller got on quicker 'n a cat an' without waitin' to give the mule a chance ter plan what he was goin' ter do, he socked the spurs into him."

McNaught paused impressively and sighed, as though words were not equal to the description of what followed.

"Gentlemen, I'd ruther have tackled a full-grown comet with a tail ten miles long, than that 'ere mule, an' I'll bet that feller would a give anything he owned to 've been on 'terriferma.' He got there finally, but not jess the way he calculated. Of all the buckers that mule certainly beat anything I ever see in my life, an' I wouldn't of believed it possible for a four-legged critter to tie itself up in so many knots as that one, an' chain lightnin' was like molasses to her. In a mighty few seconds she had him loose in the saddle an' his head snappin' like a whip lash, then she give him a final boost an' away he went, an' I'm a Dutchman if she didn't kick him twice 'fore he hit the ground. We worked over that chap for over an hour gettin' the breath back into him, an' the first thing he said when he came to, was, 'Say, boys, the only way to ride that beast is to take a sap-wood club and kill him first.'"

The peal of laughter that followed, as much at the inimitable manner of the narrator as at the tale itself, penetrated even the music-filled ball room, and brought the idlers at the door to join the circle of which Mc-Naught was the center.

"Your story is a good one, McNaught," said Wilfer when he could be heard, "but I hardly see the application. What is the untamed, unridden mule supposed to typify."

"*Debts!*" roared the westerner at the top of his powerful lungs, "debts! the one mule that all yer gold bug, single standard doctrines from hell ter breakfast can't. ride."

"Here, Jack," he commanded, waving his hand to Melwyn, "give Wilfer the English of my yarn, n' then perhaps he'll understand it."

Jack would have preferred not to have taken part in the discussion, but others pressed him for a reply, and Wilfer himself turned toward him as though expectant of an evasive answer, so he quietly but earnestly gave his views as follows:

"My friend McNaught's story, gentlemen, said Melwyn, "means that debts do not decrease with all other values, and they thus become doubly burthensome. It takes more and more property to pay them.

"We read in history," he continued, "of a bedstead constructed for the purpose of smothering the innocent victim while asleep. This bed had a top to it that noiselessly came down to where its deadly work of suffocation was accomplished. Debts, that do not shrink in value, while all other property does, will have that effect upon our people."

As he finished speaking, a movement of the group

near the doors apprised Jack that he was strangely remiss in his social duties, and as the discussion was taken up by a well known senator who had been a listener to the closing words, he departed in search of a companion to take in to supper.

Grace was already bespoken, that he knew well, and like many another man who finds himself denied the object of his thoughts, determined to seek out one who was near to her, in this case Miss Kitty.

He espied her just entering the ball room, from the conservatory, on the arm of a young secretary of one of the foreign ministers, and watched them as they crossed the floor, and the young lady was safely deposited under the maternal wing. Melwyn noticed with satisfaction that the girl was evidently unsought as yet, by a cavalier on supper bent, and made his way quickly to her side.

Miss Kitty was very glad to see him, and being a young lady of truth and veracity and accustomed to speak her thoughts, said so, whereat Jack looked duly gratified and hoped he might be allowed to escort her to the supper room.

The permission granted, they were soon seated at the long table, and Jack with a leaping pulse beheld the face of his charmer almost opposite. Rogasner was not at her side, and our lover suddenly found himself not nearly as miserable as he had imagined. He noted the bright smile and little nod with which she noticed their arrival, and if Miss Kitty had half formed the impression that her companion was inclined to be "dull," from the fact that she had not seen him dancing, she recanted mentally, and pronounced him afterward to Grace, "one of the nicest men I ever saw."

He quite gave himself up to the entertainment of the charming and refreshing young girl at his side, which was not difficult, as that same person was enjoying herself as only a girl can that leaps at a bound from the confines of a boarding school to her first "real ball."

"Mr. Melwyn," she said suddenly, with a sigh of content, "do you know, I believe this is quite the happiest moment of my life."

"Indeed!" said Jack, smiling, "and may I ask why you find the present so superlatively happy?"

"You mustn't laugh at me," she replied impressively, "but this is my first ball, my very first, and it's *so much* more than I *ever* pictured it, I am having *such* a good time. I've dreamed of my first ball many a time, but my dreams fall far short of this. I am *so* happy I feel like hugging somebody," and she gave a little shiver of very ecstasy.

Jack looked down into the pretty, eager face as he answered with twinkling eyes:

"If you will restrain such a desire, Miss Kitty, until we return to the other rooms, I shall be happy to offer myself as the 'somebody.'"

"Poufe!" she exclaimed at his literal acceptance of her expression. "That's so like a man. You always take to yourselves everything a girl says. I did think *you* were above that, Mr. Melwyn."

"Above it?" questioned Jack mischievously. "There is a difference in our statures truly, but then, that is easily overcome. You might stand on a chair, you know."

"Now, that's unfair of you," said the girl, laughing in spite of herself at the absurdity of the suggestion. "To tease me about a thoughtless speech like that. I'll take it back.   I *don't* feel like hugging anybody.   But if *you* do,'' demurely, "you should select somebody that wouldn't need the chair; Grace, for instance."

Which was turning the tables with a vengeance, and Jack felt himself blushing like a boy at the mere thought.

"You needn't blush so,"went on this refreshing young person,"I shouldn't blame you; she's just the sweetest, dearest girl that ever lived, and *isn't* she just too lovely to-night?" looking over at the beautiful face across the table.

Indeed she was, thought Jack, too lovely for his peace of mind, but his heart's theme had been sounded, and finding his companion as enthusiastic and willing to pursue the subject as fondest lover could wish, they talked of Grace.

If that young lady's ears did not burn during the remainder of the supper there can be no truth in the old saying.

But it was unfair of the roguish Kitty, in view of Jack's efforts for her entertainment that evening, that she should say to Grace the next morning at breakfast that "Mr. Melwyn wanted to talk of nothing else but you all through supper."

And Grace? What was she thinking about through the long, and it must be confessed, to her, not very enjoyable hour at the supper table? The man at her side was undesirably heavy, and though he no doubt brought forward all his powers of entertainment, she found her eyes often straying to the merry pair opposite.

How handsome the young congressman looked, how good and noble his face, and how strong! Well, she remembered her first meeting with him. She had heard him speak once in the House, and knew him to be considered one of the ablest men in that body, and she had gone one morning to the Senate to hear her guardian, Senator Arnold, speak upon the repeal bill. And immediately following him had heard the loyal Teller give utterance to the heartfelt prophecies that later events were to prove so true. Had listened with swimming eyes and beating heart to the mournful and eloquent words with which the Colorado senator pictured the peril of his beloved country. She had heard behind her, as silence followed, a deep voice say softly, "God help my native land." It was almost like an "amen," and under the influence of the moment the impression produced upon her was vivid and profound. They were introduced a moment later by her escort, and Grace returned home that day with a new and strange feeling in her heart of the seriousness of the duties of one selected to draft laws for a nation of people.

They had met a number of times since then, and she frankly confessed to herself that she liked him better than any other man she knew. It was of course impossible that she should not be aware of the feeling she had excited in his breast, and it was with little dismay that she now felt the stir in her own as his speaking glance sought her face. And she was glad, nor bothered to ask herself why. When he rose when the signal was given for the ladies to retire, what more natural than that he should lead the seemingly unconscious Kitty to seats near her, so that they might form a trio by themselves?

It was undoubted bliss for Jack, and he had to laugh outright when the elfish Kitty, as the attention of

Grace was drawn away a moment, leaned over and said *sotto voce*, "If you were to voice your feelings, you would echo what I said at the supper table."

The long waited for waltz was the second number after supper, and Jack afterward thought it the shortest bit of dancing he ever indulged in. Like all great happiness it seemed ages in coming, and went like a passing ray of light.

She had been unaccountably shy with him, as she sat with the chattering Kitty waiting for the resumption of the dancing, and no intuitive sense told Jack it was but the maidenly diffidence of an awakening heart.

And that blissful waltz.

Never was scene so fair, never music so entrancing, never did polished floor respond to lighter footfall, as they floated away on the strains of the dreamy "Immortelen."

All things must have an end, and the Atweld ball could be no exception, and as our hero waited in the broad hall to conduct his fair one to her carriage he pronounced it to the genial host, quite the most enjoyable affair of the kind he ever attended. And Grace, was it possible, did you so far unbend from maidenly modesty and pride, as to, not squeeze perhaps, but actually *press* Jack Melwyn's hand at parting?

CHAPTER XIV.

"How do you feel this evening, father?" asked Melwyn as he entered his father's room one evening a few weeks after the Atweld ball.

"A little better to-day, Jack," he answered, and then continued querulously, "If Congress would stop this infernal tariff agitation and let the law stand as it is, I would very soon be on my legs again, and go at business with some hope."

"An argument would only weary you," said Melwyn, "but I wish you would get this tariff business out of your head. Think of something else, and let us talk of something else."

"I can't think of anything else," returned the old man with some excitement. "I am ruined, and the work of a lifetime destroyed, if this attack on the tariff system is persisted in."

"I don't want to argue the matter, father," said the young man, "but if you must dwell upon these matters, I will say this, and when you are alone you can give it a little thought. The present panic began in 1890; the country was ripe for it and the failure of the Barings started the land slide. The Republican party was then in power, and you as a manufacturer had all the protection a tariff bill could give you. Mr. Harrison was in a dilemma as to what should be the proper course to sustain the gold reserve. His secretary of the treasury had bonds printed and was about to make a loan,

when the President stopped him.   His term was ex
piring and the load that was becoming too heavy for
him was gladly thrown off onto Mr. Cleveland's shoulders.   Let us talk no more about it now, father.   I
want to tell you about my efforts to locate Sam."

"Any news?" interrupted the old man eagerly.

Jack shook his head.   "No, I received a letter this
morning from the man I had written to, to look into
Sam's disappearance, and he tells me he can find no
trace of him after they left Los Angeles, where it seems
Sam worked for some time in a store.   He says there
is not the faintest clew by which to trace him."

"My poor Sam," murmured the father, while a tear
stole out from under his closed eyelids and rolled
slowly down the wrinkled cheek, "he too is a victim
to the times, and maybe, Jack," and he looked at his
son as though the thought were new to him, "maybe
he is suffering, perhaps finds it hard to get enough to
eat."

"Oh! father, I hardly think it as bad as that.   Sam is
proud, and after losing his place he may have found it
difficult to get work, and would not let us know about
his condition, but Sam is too bright a boy to go hungry
in a land like America," and Melwyn smiled reassur-
ingly at the distress in the father's face.

To himself, however, he thought differently.   He
knew that the best directed energy could be exerted in
vain and that tens of thousands were searching for employment they could not find.

The old man's fears were aroused, however, and Jack
passed the next half hour trying to satisfy him that
though the son and brother was lost so far as they were
concerned, he was well and getting along somewhere,

but probably too proud to let his family **know of his**
poverty.

They talked for some time of the absent one, **and his**
probable whereabouts, and of the father's **financial**
affairs, Jack offering what advice and consolation he
could.   It was growing late when, after bidding his
father to "cheer up" and not to "dwell upon these
tariff complications," he took his leave, promising to
call in again in the morning.

On his way down stairs he encountered the landlady
of the house, and after exchanging a pleasant word he
slipped a five dollar bill in her hand, with the request
that she spare no pains in making the old gentleman
comfortable.

Mr. Melwyn, senior, had begun life as a factory boy,
and had by dint of hard labor and the gains accruing
from several labor-saving devices evolved from his
practical brain, risen in time to a partnership, then to
sole ownership of the mills he had entered as a poor
boy.   Prosperity had attended him, and he had been
accounted in the New Jersey manufacturing town as a
wealthy man, up to 1873, when he felt his business war-
ranted an increase in his plant; and in order to do so
had made a loan of $100,000.00, which he secured by
mortgage on the whole plant.

Everything had indicated at the time that it would
not be difficult to pay this loan within the term of its
life; but when the time for payment arrived he felt
the need of the ready money in his business and considered it wiser to renew the loan for another five
years.

Like many another man who once gives a mortgage,
he found it easier at the time to pay interest and put

off the paying of the principal, than to take from his business so large a sum at one time. "It is well invested," he argued, "and is earning me much more than the amount of the interest I am paying."

When it became due in 1883, the mortgagee was again willing to renew it, as he had regularly received his interest, but when it was again due in 1888, the owner of the mortgage desired to make a safer investment and had insisted on payment. Mr. Melwyn, after much trouble, finally succeeded in making a new loan with which to pay off the old debt, and this loan was now due, and his new creditor was anxiously seeking payment.

The manufacturer in late years had had much trouble in raising the money to pay the interest on his loan, and to do so, and meet certain losses in his business, had sacrificed all his other property, except his home, on which he had also made a loan to meet the demand upon him for more money in his business. His business had not been profitable, as of old, now for many years.

His family consisted of two sons and one daughter. His children were now all of age. One was our young congressman, who had moved west after finishing his college course, and had settled in Lincoln, Nebraska. He had graduated in the law school at Yale, and having a natural love for his profession and being a man of unusual ability, had risen rapidly, and had finally been elected to Congress from his district.

The other son, Samuel, two years younger than Jack, had not prepared himself for any profession, and when he left college went west to visit his brother at Lincoln, and then drifted to California. He had there purchased himself a ranch and had industriously gone to work to improve it, and set out a fruit orchard. The news had first come back that he was happy and doing well in that far-off land of fruits and flowers. His letters depicted him full of hope and energy. Then came the tidings that he was married. His written accounts of his happy home had made glad the hearts of his father and mother, and increased their longing to see him. For a time "Sam's wife," as she was familiarly alluded to, wrote frequently to Mrs. Melwyn; then came news that the younger son was meeting with reverses, and finally that he had been obliged to give up his home to his creditors; then letters came seldom and finally ceased.

The son too had ceased to write, and it was now two years since they had heard from him. After waiting some time and suffering much anxiety, when their letters were returned to them through the mails not delivered, they had written to the postmaster and others and learned that he had been sold out of his fruit farm by the man from whom he had purchased it, and to whom he owed about one half the original purchase money; that real estate had declined so in value the property had only brought the debt and cost, that the son had lived for a time in the village and had then moved away, taking his little family with him.

One of the letters they received was from a lady, who knew him and his wife. She said that as he became poor his pride rose proportionately, and that he would not allow his wife to write his folks; that he seemed to think it was a disgrace to not be able to make a good living, and have a respectable home for his family; that he had become very melancholy, and that he could not be traced as to his whereabouts through his

wife, as she was an orphan, her father and mother having died there, leaving this only child, and they knew
of no relative of hers to whom to apply.

Thus had Sam Melwyn dropped out of sight, and
the thoughts of him and conjectures as to his circumstances and troubles were a gloomy reflection at
nearly all times in the minds of his parents, brother and
sister. But what added more to the troubles of Mr.
Melwyn, senior, than his debts or his lost and wandering son, was the death of his wife in 1893.   This had
been the severest blow of all. He had married late in
life, but thirty odd years of companionship with such
a woman as his devoted wife had been, had left a void
that could not be filled. Now his mind ran almost
constantly on his debts, and he attributed all or most
of his trouble to the threatened change in the tariff
laws. He had a loud and harsh voice, and when discussing with any one the condition of business he
would soon be engaged in an animated argument in
which the tariff was his principle theme. If he chanced
to be standing near others who were discussing the
times or condition of the country, he would take part in
the conversation and would soon drown out all desire
in any of the others to continue the controversy, by
reason of the vehement manner in which he advocated
his views.

He had closed down his factory the fall before, and
was now in Washington on his own responsibility,
lobbying against the tariff revision. His creditor was
pushing him for payment of the mortgage, but had not
yet brought foreclosure proceedings. That gentleman
held the same views as to tariff that Mr. Melwyn, senior did, and believed that the defeat of the Wilson

bill would enable his debtor to soon make a new loan and pay him off, which he could not now do.

The father was much worried at his son for refusing to agree with him in his views, and the two had held many long arguments upon the subject.

The son did not hold to the opinion of the father that tariff pro or con was the cause of industrial distress. He believed that the secret was to be found in our monetary system, and that trusts and combines, strikes, riots and the general distress were all to be traced to an erroneous monetary system; but he did not wish an argument with his father, by reason of the latter's excitable nature and poor health, so when it began he usually led the conversation to some other subject.

"Poor father," thought Jack Melwyn, as he walked with rapid strides down Connecticut Avenue, "he will never save a cent from his property, no matter how the tariff bill goes. They said we would have good times when the silver purchase bill was repealed; now these men that are throttling the government will claim that prosperity will return as soon as this tariff question is settled; when they find it does not, I wonder what they will lay it on next."

Just as he was passing Seventeenth Street his attention was attracted by a noise in the shadow of a building where there was a vacant lot. He looked in that direction and made out what he took to be two people struggling together. He broke into a run as the sound of a blow, followed by a woman's scream, fell upon his ear.

Assisting the woman to her feet and finding she was not much injured, Melwyn discovered her to be

a comely, nice looking girl of the servant class, who
had been enticed out by some new acquaintance
and refusing to enter a building, the man had first
attempted force and then in temper at seeing Melwyn
approach, and that he was discovered, had struck
her. Melwyn treated her with greatest respect and kindness, escorting her to her home. When told by her
that they were approaching the place, Melwyn asked
whom she was living with, and her reply, "Mr. Rogasner," a little astonished him.

Our Western congressman had no idea when he said
"Good night" politely to this girl, that she was to return his kindness a thousand fold before many months.

He now walked on down Pennsylvania Avenue to his
room.   Melwyn had forebodings as to the future, not
as to himself, but as to his country; this visit to-night
to his father had set him thinking anew of the causes
of his country's distress; and when he reached his
room he lit a cigar and rolled a chair into the bow
window, and seating himself, gazed out on the quiet
avenue, his mind busy with the vexing questions of
the day.

This young congressman had traveled much in his
own country; he had visited and talked with the people
of all sections of the Union, and had acquired both by
observation and study a very fair knowledge of the
different interests of different people engaged in different pursuits.

He was now trying to picture in his own mind the
probable political and industrial future of his country
for the next year. In his judgment he thought it would
drift from bad to worse, and he wondered in what way
the distress would manifest itself so as to claim the

attention of the nation. He considered the total wiping out of silver legislation as the last straw necessary to break the camel's back, and no argument could have changed his mind in this respect.

The fact that Mr. Cleveland, the unrelenting enemy to silver, was to be the President for the next three years, was the great and overshadowing fact that depressed his spirits. It assured the perpetuation of the gold standard for the term of his office. He could see the further breaking down of prices of all property belonging to the people, as it adjusted itself to the new measure of values, and that this meant sweeping disaster all over the land.

He had lately been investigating the extent to which the people were in debt, and he was amazed at the figures which had been furnished him by the census bureau. He had figured out that the people of the United States were paying a daily average interest of five millions of dollars. The census bureau admitted to debts of $20,000,000,000. This amount was greater than the assessed value of all the real estate, or the assessed value of all the personal property in the government as shown by the census returns, and it was many times larger than the total value of the cotton crop, or wheat crop, and while all these property interests were constantly shrinking in value this enormous debt would call for payment in full—more and more property as prices declined would have to be given in exchange for dollars with which this debt and the interest on it would have to be paid.

He saw in the future nothing but confiscation of property to satisfy the demands of debts and the transfer of the property of the many to the possession of the few—and he saw no remedy but rising prices, to enable the people to satisfy their creditors and save the remnants of their property—and this he regarded as impossible so long as gold was the measure of values.

He looked for new evidence of this distress to manifest itself among the people. He knew they would struggle against it—against what they did not understand—and through a sense of pride would redouble their energies, and seek to maintain their credit, but with a force against which resistance would be vain, the economic conditions would destroy their business and be continuously adding to the army of the unemployed.

These were somber thoughts, and he arose to shake them off. He bethought himself of a remedy to cure the effect these evil forebodings were having upon him, and throwing them off, he disrobed and was soon asleep, dreaming of Grace Vivian.

When Melwyn opened his mail the next morning he was greeted by a new trouble in the shape of a letter from a broker in Chicago, who wrote to inform him that he, the broker, had purchased the mortgage which Jack had been obliged to place on a small block he had some three years previously built in Lincoln. The obligation was overdue and its present holder demanded immediate payment.

CHAPTER XV.

A few days after the Atweld ball Melwyn had called upon Grace and was cordially received and pleasantly entertained by the young lady.

Upon inquiry for the other ladies of the household, he learned that the charming Kitty and her mother had departed for a few days' visit to other friends in Washington, and the conversation naturally drifted to the ball, and its pleasures.

A remark of Grace's touching her girlhood led Jack to ask of her Southern home, which she described at length and in the tones and manner of one speaking of very dear memories.

Her birthplace and childhood's home in Alabama had passed into other hands, and she had not visited the old familiar scenes for some years, but it was all still very dear to her.

The formal hour of the call passed as time never passed before to the infatuated Melwyn, and he took his departure thrilling with the hope expressed by the sweet lips that he "would soon call again."

He wondered, as he walked away down the avenue, if this his first call had left with her an impression favorable to him. He was conscious during the short hour of a curious constraint, and thought with impatience that he must have seemed dull and heavy to the girl. His confidence and ease of manner, ever present in his addresses in the House; the eloquence and ready

flow of language that had charmed and held spell-bound
vast audiences, and won the rapt attention of court
and jury; all seemed stricken dumb and as though they
had never been, in the intoxicating presence of this
lovely young woman.

Holding the sex in the abstract in the chivalrous
regard and veneration accorded woman by your true
man, he looked upon this divinely beautiful girl as the
embodiment of all graces and virtues, and the perfec-
tion of noble womanhood, and was filled accordingly
with an adoration that touched the innermost recesses
of his being, and made him silent and constrained from
the very excess of his emotions.

This feeling of reverential awe in the man, did not
prevent in the mind of the lover the wildest dreams
and speculations during the next few days, as to whether
this divinely perfect woman had come into his life to
sadden and destroy his future, or to render that future
bright beyond compare with a fulfillment of his
fondest hopes.

He saw her once or twice in the few days that in-
tervened before he called again, but only for a moment
and to pass the ordinary salutations of such meetings;
but it served to keep fiercely burning the fire in his
breast, and it was with the determination to better
acquit himself in this second interview that he approached the palatial home Senator Arnold had erected
for his ward.

Arriving, he found the Arnold carriage at the curb,
and the Senator with Grace, and accompanied by Rogasner, coming down the walk to the gate.

Poor Jack, in his embarrassment at the disappointment, and thus seeing his rival in possession, greeted

them in some confusion, and with regrets that he should have called so inopportunely, though he knew of course this was not Miss Vivian's day "at home."

Grace had been very kind, softening his disappointment, and restoring him somewhat his self-possession by sweetly regretting the circumstance and a happy allusion to the "next time."

As the carriage rolled away and Melwyn was left standing at the gate, the thought presented itself more forcibly than ever how mad he was to aspire to the love of this beautiful patrician. A girl of her education and surroundings to give herself to a poor man like him, while men like the polished courtier and wealthy banker, Victor Rogasner, sued for her favor!

He was more fortunate after that, though he never but once found her alone. Sometimes he met Rogasner there and with his direct and honest nature, and feeling so keenly the advantages possessed by the banker, made his calls on such occasions short, and found it difficult to appear natural and unconstrained with his rival's black eyes continually regarding him.

With the spring came additional duties and cares for Melwyn, and a series of unfortunate and discouraging financial troubles served to occupy his time and mind to such a degree that he found little opportunity to seek the society of the girl he loved at her home, on any but occasions when society was also present, and her duties as hostess, and always attendant train of admirers, made it impossible to see her as he longed to see her, and enjoy converse with her, without the disturbing element of a half dozen or more poor moths like himself, striving to bask in the flame.

It was late in May, and our nation's capital was

fresh with the bloom of flowers and redolent of the sweet breath of spring, when our hero, seizing the opportunity offered by a postponed committee meeting, wended his way to the home of the girl who now more than ever dominated his every thought.

It was a fair, warm afternoon, when all nature seemed to be in song and attune with his desires, and when told by the butler that "Miss Vivian was in the garden," he begged that functionary not to call her, that he would go in search of her himself, and entered the fragrant walks with bounding pulse and eager delight, that now surely she would be alone.

As he rounded a curve in the broad pathway, and espied a vine-clad arbor close at hand, he came upon the bent and frost-crowned figure of an old negro slowly advancing, leaning heavily upon a stout cane.

Melwyn halted, and looking with kindly interest at the wrinkled and intelligent face before him, inquired pleasantly of the old man if he had seen Miss Vivian. That he had been told she was in the garden and was in search of her.

The negro bowed profoundly and not without grace, as he replied:

"Miss Grace sho yere Mas'r, she be erlong terreckly, I reckon. Ah done see 'er comin' dis yer way jess now."

Melwyn had always taken a great interest in the colored race, and recognizing in the white haired old fellow before him a type of the Southern darky of the old plantation days, felt a curiosity to draw him out a little, while he awaited the appearance of the one, from the negro's words, he judged must soon come in sight.

"Do you live here, Uncle?" went on Jack, smiling at

the searching scrutiny with which the black man was favoring him.

"Yes, Mas'r," he replied, as though satisfied with his examination, and displaying his white teeth in an answering smile. "Yes, Mas'r, I live yere, live yere eber sense my missus come yere."

"Miss Vivian is your mistress?" said Melwyn inquiringly.

The old man nodded and Jack went on: "And what is your name, Uncle?"

"My las' nam' same as Miss Grace's mudder, but folks allus call me 'Abe;' been call 'Abe' more yeers 'n I c'n reckon. I's poful ole man, Mas'r," he concluded with gravity.

"Yes," replied Jack, "but you are a well preserved man; and have you lived in Miss Vivian's family all your life?"

"All my life, Mas'r," answered the negro. "Wuz borned on de ole place down in Alabama, an' I ain' never bin 'way frum de family sense. Miss Grace she couldn't git 'long 'out ole Abe noway." And he chuckled with pleasure at thought of his importance to his mistress.

As the old man squatted down on the turf at his feet with the apology, 'Scuse me, Mas'r, dese er ole laigs 'gin to git kine er rickety," Jack began plying him with questions about the childhood home of his young mistress, and listened with pleased interest as this old slave rambled on, in his musical though quivering tones, about the land he loved.

Melwyn adroitly led him to talk of his young mistress, which he found the old fellow nothing loath to do, all the while keeping a bright lookout for her coming.

That young lady, however, was at the present moment snugly ensconced in the arbor referred to, and
enjoying the dialogue quite as much as Jack, though
from entirely different emotions.

She had entered the arbor from the opposite side,
and hearing the voices but a short distance away, and es-
pying Melwyn through the tangle of leaves, mischievously refrained from making her presence known.

She was somewhat surprised at the friendliness of
her old servant's manner toward this stranger, as Abe
usually required to know a person before unbending as
he now was doing, and afterward when she expressed
as much to him, she was struck by his reply:

"Dat Mas'r Melwyn's er good man, honey," he had
said. "*He* am no nor'vin trash. Dis ole man no loss
his eye ef he *be* mos' a hundred. Ye kin *truss* dat man,
honey, an' I kant say dat for mos' people what I see
round dis yer town."

Grace did not intend to listen to a conversation not
meant for her ear, and after a moment, and blushing
slightly at hearing herself the topic which seemed to
so interest the young congressman, she left the arbor
as she entered it and walked round to where she was
visible to the two men as she approached.

Jack advanced, hat in hand, to meet her, expressing
his pleasure, and as she asked if he had been waiting
long, declaring with a smile at the now standing negro
that he had been most pleasantly entertained during
the few minutes since he entered the walk.

Then they walked slowly along the flower-bordered
paths and under the spreading branches, while she
pointed out the rare plants and named for him the pro-
fusion of buds and blossoms surrounding them.

He discovered that the garden was one of the girl's chief delights, over which she exercised a personal supervision, and in whose shady nooks and quiet, fragrant walks she passed the greater part of her leisure time.

They seated themselves by the musically splashing fountain, and Jack discovered with delight and ever increasing love that there were many planes on which their two minds met, and he was surprised at the familiarity and understanding with which she discussed subjects not popularly supposed to be of interest to a belle of society.

No word of love was spoken, nor did they descend to the small chatter of society conversation, yet when Melwyn took his leave he felt that they were better acquainted, and that he had learned more of her real self than he could in many meetings such as had gone before.

It was with double impatience, therefore, and a feeling that fate was indeed unkind to him, that the next morning he received a telegram from home saying that he had been sued on the mortgage alluded to in our last chapter. He left on the night train for Lincoln. On his arrival he found that the investment broker in Chicago who had purchased his note, had ordered suit of foreclosure. He found it difficult to make a new loan, as money men were very conservative, and one of them had even laughingly suggested that he could hardly expect it, as he himself was responsible in part for the hard times. He finally instructed attorneys who would appear for him, to secure all the delay possible, and then returned to Washington, after securing the promise of a friend in Omaha to try and procure him the money with which to pay off the loan.

This trip had kept him away three weeks, and when he returned, his fondest hopes received a crushing blow when he learned through rumor that Miss Vivian and Mr. Rogasner were engaged to be married.

In the meantime, since that night at the winter ball when Rogasner had sworn to win this fair girl, he had improved his every opportunity. Frequent calls, all the diplomacy and arts possible to be used by the accomplished man of society, were brought into play to make a favorable impression on this accomplished and lovable ward of his friend the Senator.

Drives had been followed by invitations to join him in horseback rides in the beautiful parks and suburbs. Grace was an expert rider and delighted in the exercise, and had gone with him for the pleasure of the ride more than for his society. She had learned to think him agreeable and a pleasant companion and did not hold that dislike she had felt for him when they first met.

He had been materially aided by the influence of Senator Arnold. The latter was not blind to the fact that two men were suitors for the hand of his ward. He openly disliked Melwyn, who had constantly scored him for his connection with the demonetization of silver, and had used other uncomplimentary language about the Senator in his speeches, as well as in conversation. Melwyn held that having started through corrupt means, but in what way he did not know, on the side of the gold standard, Senator Arnold's prejudice toward those whom he termed his traducers, made him the more bitter toward all opposing his financial policy. The American suitor was right in his estimate of the Senator, and was now to feel the weight of that prejudice.

The Senator was too wily a diplomat to give his real reason of such dislike to his ward—so he waited for convenient opportunities to express himself, and then little by little he made an impression on her mind. He spoke of Melwyn as having impractical ideas; as supporting doctrines that were visionary; of being in favor of dishonest money, and inferentially that he was a dishonest man.

He read aloud to her, while masking his object, of wind storms on the Nebraska prairies, when only storm cellars furnished a safe place. Again at one time he read in her presence of a hot air that had swept over Nebraska and Kansas and killed all the corn, and almost suffocated the people. It was an exaggerated account, that slandered the rolling plains and invigorating air of that billowy state and western empire, but it answered his purpose to try to prejudice the girl against the man as well as the section in which he lived.

He also impressed upon her mind the threatening danger to the peace of the country, as he claimed, from men like our hero, who were creating a discontent among the poorer classes, and thereby making anarchists.

There was coming to his house at the time a certain daily paper from a Western city, in which Rogasner owned a majority of the stock; this paper was very bitter toward silver men, and in violent editorials stigmatized them as "blatant orators," "thieves, swindlers and repudiators," "dishonest tricksters," "brazen charlatans," and containing other articles well calculated to mislead and convey the desired impression on a pure and innocent mind, taught to think her guardian one of, if not the wisest statesman of the government. These articles in this paper were shown to her in a way that did not excite her suspicion as to the reason for having her attention attracted to them.

He pursued exactly the opposite course with regard to Rogasner.

The banker was in his opinion a model man, who could cope successfully with any of the emergencies of life, and he had frequently found him, as had others, to be the soul of honor and generous and large-hearted to a fault.

The fact was that the Senator was at heart one of those American worshipers of title and wealth. Had he been a girl whose hand was sued for by one of the English nobility, he would have accepted, and the shape or size, or character of the suitor would have cut but little figure. True, she did not know that Rogasner was one of the English nobility, or one of a family commanding unlimited wealth, but she would in time learn that, if necessary to influence her mind.

In the contest for this girl—fair and beautiful enough to typify Columbia—between the Englishman and the American, the Senator preferred the Englishman.

He did not want to see any one win his ward from him, but he knew in all probability some one would, and he meant, if he could help it, that it should not be Melwyn, whom he had learned to dislike.

There was another side to the character of the Senator, and of late it was growing more pronounced. He seemed to devote most of his thoughts to his ward; he would leave the Senate early to spend the afternoon with her; he would have her read to him, and appeared to be happy only when in her presence. It was the doting love and devotion a fond father would hold for an only child, and recently it had become a mania with him.

If she came to the Senate gallery, he would go to her. If he were going out driving he would send for her, and if not otherwise engaged would have her go with him. As the summer came and waned, this had grown on him until it was almost childishness. This caused him to become selfish in regard to her disposal in marriage, and he would sometimes look with disfavor on any suitor.

After his return Melwyn, having heard of the reported engagement of Grace and Rogasner, and determining to ascertain if it were true, called at the Arnold mansion, intending to so shape the conversation that he would discover the truth, but learned that she was out riding with Mr. Rogasner. He left a note that he had called and asking when he could come again, and received an answer that she could not fix a time, as she would leave the next day on an excursion with a party down the bay, but would let him know when to call after her return.

Later the now discouraged Melwyn learned that it was as Rogasner's guest on his yacht that she had joined the excursionists. Two weeks later he saw them on horses cantering up Pennsylvania Avenue, and they seemed happy. Why had she not let him know that she had returned? Certainly, he argued, under the circumstances his note and her answer would have required it, if she had wanted to see him. This was proof positive that she did not, and he would act accordingly, crush her memory from his mind, and her image from his heart.

The fact was the note had been sent, telling him that she had returned and would be glad to have him call, and setting a time. She had given the note to her guardian to mail, and had asked him that same evening if he had done so, to which he had replied that he had. In truth he had not done so, but had deliberately torn it into small pieces and thrown it into his senatorial waste basket.

Melwyn did not come. She wondered and felt the slight. Her Southern spirit was aroused and she sought no explanation. Thus they grew apart and Rogasner improved the opportunity. Jack now believed the report to be true that they were engaged and soon to be married.

It was not true, however, although late in June Rogasner had declared his intentions to Senator Arnold, and had asked his permission to pay his addresses. The Senator was a trifle testy about it, but was as gracious on the whole as could be expected, and the banker was now waiting for a favorable opportunity to declare his love.

The man of cool and determined nerve, whose ravaging work was creating havoc in the country he had come to wreck and destroy, was now preparing to carry off the "Helen of Troy"—the most lovely product of American beauty. When the earth should tremble with revolution under his feet, he would sail from the shores of the dying republic with this girl in his arms and an apostrophe on his lips to a vanishing nation, a victim to the wants and wiles of the kings of money.

CHAPTER XVI.

It was on the evening of April 30 of the same year (1894) that Jack wended his way to the National Hotel, in search of his friend McNaught, and arriving found the red-headed gentleman in the lobby and in heated argument with Melwyn, Sr., and a surrounding crowd of politicians and lobbyists as to the cause and effect of the great industrial upheaval then making itself manifest in the marching armies of unemployed men toward the capital.

It was a subject engrossing the attention of all Washington, and the name of "Coxey" was on every lip.

This rumbling from the west like the approaching roar of a storm was the sole topic where men gathered.

What did it portend? was the burning question. Men who left all political matters to others, men who deemed they had no personal interest in economic questions, were now seeking light and reading literature on the subject.

Like a deluge, this inundation of the people now threatened to engulf Washington. From far-off Los Angeles an army of one thousand had started for Washington; regiment after regiment was leaving San Francisco; Northern Pacific trains were being stolen and headed east by these roving armies; the bowels of "socialistic" Chicago were beginning to rumble; an "army" was forming on Boston Common and great crowds were besieging the capitol of that city and demanding of Governor Greenhalge work or bread; from every quarter of the country north of the Ohio river, and from the Atlantic to the Pacific, moving bodies of men, disciplined to obey the orders of their commanders, were swayed by the one impulse, "on to Washington."

They claimed to be going to Washington as "a living petition;" as a petition "with boots on;" they said Congress had paid no attention to their written petitions, and now they were going there with a live one that could not be pigeon-holed.

At one time it was predicted and believed in Washington that this movement would grow with the excitement and that over a hundred thousand half starved and poorly clothed people would assemble at the national capital before the end of May. The government was alarmed. Drastic measures to suppress and scatter this host of idle men might arouse the countless thousands of their friends that had staid at home.

It was a critical moment for the government. Mr. Cleveland at once brought into operation all the powerful influence of the administration. Letters and telegrams were sent to governors of Western states and to mayors of cities to throw every possible obstacle in the way of these advancing "hordes." Detectives were sent to mix with these industrial armies and note their character and designs; railway managers were appealed to, to refuse to carry them, and to call on the governors for militia to protect their property; the United States troops in the Northwest were put in the field to arrest armies from Montana, Oregon and Washington, that were racing toward St. Paul on stolen trains as fast as steam could carry them, and the influence of the press was set in motion to discourage the movement.

But still that awful detonation of popular unrest came with every vibration of the wires. Kelly's army was coming through Iowa like the roar of a lion; Frey had reached St. Louis; Saunders' six hundred miners were "running wild" on a train through Kansas; the Chicago army had started; Coxey was in the suburbs of Washington; army officers were coming and going from the White House and consternation existed at the national capital.

McNaught had just closed a horrible recital of the awful butchery that might be expected to result from a hundred thousand or more indignant people infesting the city, that was bringing a pallor to the face of a Washington dude, when Rogasner entered the office from the opposite direction to which Melwyn had arrived.

"Here comes a banker; let's see what he thinks," said a well known merchant of Washington, as he turned to the new arrival and asked him what he thought of the Coxey invasion.

"It all depends on the Railroads," replied Rogasner. "If they stubbornly refuse to run their trains when captured, the government will owe them a debt of gratitude, and it will prolong and finally check the movement. Everything now depends on the action of the railroad managers."

"To me," said another gentleman near, "a more important question is the cause of this great upheaval."

"What say you, Rogasner, to that?" asked the merchant.

"The failure of Congress to settle the tariff schedule," replied the latter, with a smile which might have been ironical.

"Melwyn," said McNaught, appealing to the young congressman as he was about to turn away, "tell these tenderfeet the cause of the Coxey business. Why are they hungry, out of work, and tramping through Uncle Sam's vineyard?"

"We might differ—probably would," said Jack, annoyed at being brought into the discussion in this way, "as to the cause of the general industrial distress, and I would rather leave you in the hands of my friend here," motioning toward McNaught.

"Mr. Rogasner says it is the tariff," said the merchant, "but for my part I think it is over-production."

"Do you know what I think?" said the dude, rising and pushing his way toward the center of the company, with his legs straddled out and adjusting his eyeglass. "I think there is too much silver money; the haw'ed thing is too heavy to carry; I detest it."

"I want to say," said Melwyn, senior, in a high voice, bringing his right fist down into his left hand, "that if we had a tariff wall around this country that would keep out the manufactured articles of all the other nations, there would be no Coxeys—this country never prospered so much as it did as a result of the high tariff during and after the war—that is what we want and nothing less will satisfy us."

More to check the rising excitement of his father than to engage in the discussion, young Melwyn began, and his rich voice and commanding presence won him the attention of all his auditors.

"Gentlemen," said Melwyn, "blind indeed is the man who has not observed the continued fall in prices for these many years through changing administrations. All classes of industries have been conducted upon falling prices. If it were not for this awful and real fact on which tariff legislation has had little or no effect in checking now for twenty-one years, that subject would receive its just attention. As to over-production; there is no over-production except in tramps and idle men."

"To what do you attribute it, sir?" asked Rogasner, with a keen desire to test his power of false logic and dissimulation with this champion of the people. He knew what the cause was—and knew with what powerful force it was driving the ship of state upon rocks prepared for its destruction—but he would draw out this legislator and rival, and confuse and irritate him if he could.

"I attribute it, sir, to our financial legislation that has gradually but persistently pulled down the prosperity of the greatest nation on earth," replied Melwyn.

"But the people do not agree with you, and it is said the people solve all questions wisely," said the secret English agent.

"The *people* do agree with me," replied our young American statesman. "They may not understand the subtle effect of a change of standards, but they do know that silver was the money of the people, and that it has been grossly discriminated against, and if they had the opportunity to vote upon its full restoration the result would be an overwhelming majority in favor of the proposition."

"How do you account for the fact, then," asked the banker, "that they haven't sufficient strength in the present congress to even get a *free coinage* bill reported from a committee?"

"It is true," replied Melwyn, "that the committee on *Coinage, Weights and Measures* is a tie on this subject, and this prevents Mr. Bland from reporting a bill, but when you measure the sentiment of the people at home by this, you are in error. Never was a people more basely betrayed than by this administration. The Roman senate, implements and tools of money changers, never more grossly deceived the peasantry, than has our President and congress the people of this distressed and suffering nation. Human nature among our office-loving congressmen is not made of the material that followed Marion through the swamps of South Carolina, or led at Bunker Hill and Lexington.

"The appointment of some friend to a petty office in their districts presents a substance more remunerative than the promise in a law antagonized by the President. This power of patronage has been used as base bribes to thwart the will of the people. No democratic congressman avowedly in favor of the free coinage of silver can get any party favors shown him at the White House. Enmity to silver is the test of official favors. Only he whose neck bends to the will of Wall Street, and whose feet tread the golden path of the money trust, can bask in the sunshine of the administration influence. The average farmer has more love of country, and clearer comprehension of this financial subject, than has our average congressman. The human wreckage strewn over this land, is evidence of the corruption and mismanagement of succeeding administrations that have breathed their inspiration from the money changers."

The office of the hotel was now filling up and something like three hundred people were in the rotunda. Half a hundred were packed together in the crowd of which our characters were the center. Reports were being circulated of labor meetings then in progress in the city, and of a possible uprising of the unemployed.

The police force had been doubled, and this fact was, now noticeable from the increased number seen on the streets. The dashing of a cavalry officer down the avenue, and the report of large shipments of arms by the government to Washington, all tended to increase the nervousness and general excitement in the capital city. Every one in this crowded hotel office at the 'National" partook of the general feeling, and there was much difference of opinion upon any branch of the subject that might have been discussed.

What prompted the man to do it, or what started it, no one knows, but of a sudden the attention of every one was attracted to a large man standing on the office counter of the hotel. He had begun to speak and every one stopped talking to listen to what he had to say. He wore a low-cut vest exposing the full front of his white shirt bosom, and in the center was a large diamond stud.

He began speaking of the danger to Washington from the Coxey armies, and continuing said:

"These men should not be allowed to enter the city. They should be shot down. Shot down like dogs. They are no better than dogs. They are idle, meddlesome men, too lazy to work, and every honest citizen in this city should stand by the authorities in repelling this rabble and driving them from our midst. If necessary we should assist the police and army by organizing volunteer companies. They are anarchists, and should be so dealt with. "

Some one shouted from the crowd, "Will you volunteer?"

A chorus of "no's" from the crowd greeted this question.

The exceptional often happens. No one can tell how or why. Thus this speech-making from the marble office counter began. Mr. A. H. Lewis, the Washington correspondent of the Chicago *Times*, a boarder at the hotel, was standing back of the counter in full dress suit preparatory to attending a reception at one of the foreign legations that night, and had listened to the speech just quoted.

The clerk would have put a stop to the whole proceedings, and reprimanded the belligerent speaker, had it not been for the *Times* correspondent, who said to the clerk, "I will answer him," and first stepping on a chair and then on the counter, addressed the people. By this time the numbers had increased. The rotunda of the National Hotel is very large, and there were now four or five hundred men packed together and all facing the new speaker.

He was known to many, and hand-clapping from the crowd greeted his appearance. Mr. Lewis is probably the brightest and brainiest newspaper correspondent in the world. He is not a man to obtrude himself or air his opinions on an occasion like the one now presented, but he was incensed at the sentiments that had just been uttered.

"It would be inhuman," he began, "to let such remarks as you have heard, go without a protest. When a rattlesnake sticks up its head it ought to be killed. That was the hiss of a rattlesnake."

This was cheered by some, but from the murmurs the crowd was evidently divided.

"The men," continued the *Times* correspondent, "who act like this man talks, are fools. To lapse into the vernacular, they overplay their game. They pile up money as a young one does blocks, and then scream for guns and sabers and government aid when it starts to tumble. They should go to night school and study humanity, and particularly should they study and try to solve the Anglo-Saxon. They should learn that if they want to rob men, and ruin them, and play the autocrat and be the moneycrat, they must have heed to a brace of matters. They must not let the men get hungry, and they must not permit them to become cold and wet. An Anglo-Saxon kept warm and dry and with a full belly may grumble and roar, but he will stand an obstinate deal of bullying and plundering before he'll attack you outright. Not because he's lacking in either courage or ferocity, for, mark you, your Anglo-Saxon is the bravest, cruelest, most ferocious animal the Lord ever breathed life into. But when he is full-fed and warm his motives for exertion are much suspended, and he won't take the trouble to tear your head off, although he may deem it a proper, virtuous exercise enough. When your Anglo-Saxon has been made hungry, and his house and his rags no longer keep him warm; when your plunderings and your robbings and your strippings have set him cold, comfortless, and famine bitten, don't go in his cage. He'll eat you up. And remember, no government and no millions of dollars will ever be swift enough to get there in time to save you. Every millionaire's library should contain Goldsmith's "Deserted Village" and Carlyle's "French Revolution." If one failed to reform, the second might scare the rich student to happier and better paths."

These were burning words Every one was now listening. There was no noise or confusion. No one moved for fear he would lose a word, and many had their hands to the back of their ears to assist those organs.

"What have our congressmen been doing here for many

years, but making millionaires and tramps?" continued
the speaker. "There has not been a principle involved
in politics since 1866. Your average congressman is
here for boodle—for patronage. And who runs them?
The money sharks, the stock gamblers, the 10 per cent
gang of New York, Boston, Philadelphia and Balti-
more. There isn't in all of these aggregations for
sucking blood—these Eastern boards of trade and chambers of commerce—a man who isn't an idler, a para-
site, a leech, a wolf. There isn't one but feeds by the
labor of others. They produce nothing. Their whole
membership—every kite or condor, buzzard or vulture
of them all—doesn't compare in national use or value
with any farmer, or mechanic, or laborer one ever heard
named. Their religion is rapacity; their vocation comes
merely to be piracy within the pale of law. They never
feed, nor clothe, nor slake one's thirst. They neither
elevate, instruct, nor entertain. Their mission is the
mission of a cancer; their hope is corruption, their
gift is death. They are the panthers of commerce, of
business, of labor; they live by tearing honest throats.

"They are the shark's brood, to prey, and guzzle, and
drink at the expense of others. The Savior in his day
made a scourge of cords and drove them from the temple. In this, the hour of Cleveland, they occupy the
temple to the exclusion of others, and are even nego-
tiating a mortgage on it. The politician's god is gold.
He makes sacrifices to money like an old Greek to his
gods. He builds his temple in New York; he makes
Wall Street and the national banks its high priests;
Mugwumpery is its altar boy, and attends in charge of
the sacred knives, while the powers that rule sacrifice
the West and South to the end that their blood may be
incense in the nostrils of gold. Coxey has only touched
a match to a powder magazine that these false gods
have made.

"The trouble with you moneycrats," and he looked
down at the diamond-studded individual, whose face
was as red as a beet, "is that you don't leave the
rest of mankind destinies worth working out. Hap-

piness is, after all, a matter of comparison. You set your embossed, cushioned, diamond-studded comfort alongside of the pain and weariness, the hunger and nakedness, the darkness and no hope of your neighbor. Do you wonder he feels the unequal injustice of a system which breeds you both? He beholds the splendid and sunlit lives of your wife and children. He sees his own wife galley slave to a tub; his boys heirs to his own half-fed fate; his daughters, perhaps, the playthings of a vice-paved street. Do you wonder the contrast excites him to rebellion? And do you marvel that in July and August, the fight months, when rattlesnakes double their poisons and men are more cruel and blood-eager, he tears you to pieces? Why, bless your dollar-blinded intelligence, this sort of thing has been done millions of times, in ages we've forgot, on this bullhead world of ours, and unless we solve this problem, the future will fill the pages the same way. Have no fear of Coxey; the most patriotic and law-abiding people we have are the poor people If this government is saved, they will be the ones that will save it. The most criminal and dangerous men we have are these rich men infesting the capital, and who are ready to trample on all laws that may oppose their selfish purposes."

He had finished, and after uttering this terrible philippic had stepped down from the counter. His words were prophetic when he spoke of what might be expected in the coming summer months. Cinders from another great industrial volcano were soon to fall over the land. Chicago was the crater, and nearly the whole United States army was soon to bivouac in that city to smother the new fires of passion and discontent.

For a moment after Lewis quit speaking and had disappeared the crowd stood still as if paralyzed, or as if waiting to see if any one would take his place. The murmur of conversation and the confusion of moving about began. Then some one exclaimed that "every word he spoke was a lie."

A large, sinewy iron moulder, with muscles like bands of steel, was standing near the man who spoke the words above quoted, and the epithet intended to apply to Lewis had not more than left his lips, when the mechanic struck him a terrible blow.

In a moment all was confusion, and a half dozen fights seemed to be in progress at the same time in different parts of the rotunda. A minute later a squad of police charged through the office, and in another moment it was empty.

Ten minutes later a telephone message went to the White House, conveying the intelligence of the riot at the National Hotel, and the reply came back:

"The President advises drastic measures and the further increase of the police force."

CHAPTER XVII.

When the row began in the office of the hotel Jack linked his arm in that of his father and walked rapidly into the wash-room, and remained there discussing with some others who had sought refuge in the same place the sensational features of the disturbance, till the office was cleared.

He and his father then started to leave the hotel and were approaching the entrance, when suddenly Mr. Melwyn, Sr., halted and the ruddy glow dying from his face, gazed at three men just entering.

They were poorly dressed, in fact ragged, and the stubble of beard on their faces gave them an added appearance of roughness, and with their battered hats and gaping shoes they looked strangely out of place in that spacious corridor, accustomed to being filled with the flowing stream of well-dressed and prosperous looking men.

Jack Melwyn paused and looked inquiringly around for the cause of his father's abrupt action. In a moment he was at the side of the advancing men and had grasped the youngest by the hand with a glad cry of:

"Sam, my dear fellow!" and then released him as the white-haired old man hurried up trembling.

"My boy, my boy!"

As the curious ones following closed about them, Jack led the way to one of the reception rooms at the side, and there, seated in one of the deep plush-cov-

ered   chairs, surrounded   by all the elegance and
comfort of the modern hotel, and holding his father's
hand while he talked, Sam Melwyn spoke in a general
way of his trials and hardships in the land where he
had hoped to build his home.

"And what is this?" asked Jack, as his brother
paused in his recital, touching a badge of white
ribbon on the coat lapel of the other.

"That's a Coxey badge, Jack," he replied, smiling
and flushing a little.   .

"A Coxey badge!" repeated Jack, "do you mean to
say you are a member of the Coxey army?"

"That's just what I mean to say," said the other
a little defiantly. "I have come to Washington with
them, and am one of them. They are my friends and
companions in misfortune, and I stand or fall with
them."

"Don't misunderstand me, Sam," said Jack gravely.
"They have no better friend than I, and you should
know that. While I am sorry to see you in such
straits, there is no disgrace in it, and I honor you and
your companions for your courage and fortitude in up-
holding a principle and for seeking a betterment of
national affairs in so earnest a manner," and he grasped
his brother's hand and pressed it warmly, while the
old man on the other side patted his shoulder in affec-
tionate approval.   .

"I might have known, Jack, that *you* were on the
right side," returned Sam. "I have read enough about
Congressman Melwyn's championship of the cause of
the people. Tell me, father," turning to the old man,
"how comes it you are in Washington, and how are home
matters?"

"Tell us first, my boy, about yourself," replied his father. "How you came to join this industrial army, and your experience in gettng here."

"Well," said young Melwyn, "it is something of a story, and perhaps we had better go where I would feel more at ease than here in this parlor," glancing down at his shabby apparel.

"Come to my rooms; they are nearest," said his father, rising to his feet.

Outside the door they came upon the two men Sam had entered the hotel with, and the young man halted to explain to them the state of affairs, and introduce his father and brother. One he introduced as Jack Carroll, from Iron ton, Colorado, the other as Colonel George Frame, of Los Angeles, California.

"Sam," said Jack, "it is late, and father should retire. Come with me and bring your two friends," and he turned and went back into the hotel, followed by the others.

Arriving at the clerk's office, he had the three register, introduced his brother and friends to the clerk, and paid for their lodging and breakfast, and then with, "Will see you in the morning, Sam," bade them goodnight, and after seeing his father home, returned to his own room.

The next morning Jack Melwyn was at the National Hotel early and breakfasted with his brother and companions. This fragment of the Coxey army had slept the last night in a bed for the first time in more than a month, and the refreshing rest obtained, a bath, breakfast, and later a shave was making them feel greatly improved.

As Sam's two friends are characters of no mean

reputation in the West, they will be introduced to the reader.

If any one has ever visited Ironton or the Red Mountain mining camp in Colorado and not become acquainted with Jack Carroll, it was because Jack was on one of his periodical trips to Ouray, or the visitor was too much of a tenderfoot to remain long enough in the camp to get acquainted with its celebrities.

Jack could pick a tenderfoot out on the arrival of the "buckboard" (a mountain stage) quicker than any man in the camp, and there were many there with a broad knowledge of men.

He had an opinion, and a very lucid one, on all subjects that could be discussed, and he bore the same relation to all conversations that a pepper castor does to the cuisine. "Grub stakes" was his strong hold, but he never worked on anything but the "stake."

There was one notable exception, however, in his history as to his industry. It was on the occasion when a man from Jackson, Michigan, let a contract for a hundred foot tunnel to be run on his mining property in Red Mountain. This man from Jackson had advertised for bids, and Jack having managed to "side track" most of the bidders, got the job at eighteen dollars per foot for running the tunnel.

It was in early winter when the contract was let, and the man from Michigan went home, to return later in the winter when informed by letter from Carroll that the contract was completed. On his arrival the owner inspected the tunnel, and found it the required width, height and length, as called for in the contract. It was nicely timbered and the space between the posts on the sides and overhead was covered solid with "lagging," thus making a number one job. The "breast" was in rock, but showed no mineral. This was the only disappointment to the mining investor, as the work appeared to be excellently done.

He settled with Jack, paying him the $1,800 called for by the contract, and left for home, to return again in the spring. When he did return he could not find the tunnel. The snow had melted, and the tunnel had gone with it.

Jack had run the tunnel in a snow bank, carefully calculating to have the last ten feet hit the solid earth.

Carroll had a broad knowledge of affairs generally, and loved to discuss matters of state, national or international. He was the central figure in every argument in the saloons, and the hotel in Ironton that secured him as a guest was sure to do the larger business, as every one knew that where Jack stopped there must be the best "grub," to say nothing of the added pleasure of his society. He therefore got his board free, and liquor was thrown in.

Sam's other companion, Colonel George Frame, was originally a Missourian. He was by profession a newspaper reporter, and was also something of a politician, and could poll more votes in the thickly settled wards of a city, and cause more men to vote "early and often" than probably any other man living.

He was thin, tall, spiral, always wore a plug hat, and was as courteous as a "Virginia gentleman." Carroll was short, and Frame was long, both were fluent talkers, and the two in animated conversation made a picture as novel and striking as the famous "Judge and Major" of the stage, though, to the credit of both Carroll and Frame be it said, they were the possessors

of no mean brains.   Frame was the greater traveler of
the two, and owned more experience with politics and
active social relations on an extensive scale.   Time
was when in St. Louis, his advice and aid were sought
by the shrewdest of state politicians, and when, as
chief clerk of the Missouri House of representatives,
his sonorous voice had resounded from the capitol
throughout a good part of Jefferson City and well across
the Missouri river to the Callaway county · shore.   He
could deliver a toast, he could tell a story and he could
determine instantaneously, either by eye, nose or pal-
ate, whether the amber mocker in a glass · was born in
a cornfield of the Kentucky lowlands when the summer
sun was high or amid the billowy green sea of some
northern rye fields.   He had drifted eventually toward
the setting sun and enlarged both his vocabulary and
his acquaintance with the quality of such humanity as
the United States affords.   There was scarcely a town
of any importance between the Missouri river and the
California coast that he had not lived in.   He won his
title at a carnival in Pueblo, Colorado, during the real
estate boom in that city, by performing the difficult
feat of running a printing office on a float in the procession and commanding a regiment of cowboys at
the same time.   From the printing press he turned
out copies of the *Evening Press*, and amidst flying
rockets, Roman candles, the glare of red fire and the
cheers of the multitude, he received from the king of
the carnival, the commission that dubbed him a colonel
in the army of His Majesty, Rex.
   He rejoiced in the past, and his mind frequently
wandered back to those early days of his political triumphs, when the most effective electioneering argu-

ment in his native state was a jug, and a good anecdote. He could appreciate the humor in either, and could use the former to polish the latter.

No man had a kinder heart, and if all the world belonged to him he would not hesitate to slice it up without charge and give every one a piece, reserving only enough to insure his living the balance of his days like a prince of the royal blood. There is no man living who has buffeted with the billows of fortune and misfortune, in their alternating changes in the far west, for whom the writer has a more kindly feeling than for Colonel George Frame.

When Melwyn returned with Sam from a clothing store about ten o'clock that morning, the latter now looking more his natural self in a new suit of clothes, they found Carroll and Frame in the bar-room, drinking "cocktails." The latter was standing in a chair, and was just closing a speech to a crowd with whom he and Carroll had gotten acquainted and were making themselves at home. This was not hard for these two men to do in any country. If they had both by some process been suddenly landed in China, in twenty-four hours Frame would have been running a newspaper and using wooden blocks for type, and Carroll would have been assisting the American consul or minister to receive and entertain the guests of the legation, and it would have been difficult to tell which of the two, the American official or Carroll, was the one more in authority.

The brothers arrived just in time to listen to the peroration of Colonel Frame's defense of the Coxey movement, which he concluded with a toast:

"Here's to the tear of friendship: may it crystallize

as it falls and ever be cherished in the memory of those we love."

There had joined the group by this time quite a number of people, among the faces of whom were recognizable more than one well known in Washington. There was the shrewd face of John Chamberlain, greatest of restaurateurs, and standing beside him was his inseparable companion, Hallett Kilbourn, his grimly quizzical face and natty, well-groomed figure making him a man to look at twice. Interested in all possible new parties were these two veteran men of the town, for had they not a party of their own, a fantastic creation which was a jest! Yet, jesters though they were, there were few shrewder politicians in all Washington than these two men, as had been demonstrated an hundred times when some grant was to be secured or the district commissioners made complaisant.

After the conclusion of Frame's address, some one ordered more cocktails, and then came a discussion of what Congress ought to do for the benefit of the country.

"What is your idea of what ought to be done?" asked Kilbourn, addressing Carroll, with a keen desire to hear the latter talk.

"My opinion is," said Carroll, putting his hat on the back of his head and expressing· himself with all the confidence of an insurance agent, "that instead of us marching over the country, Congress and Mr. Cleveland ought to go on the tramp and learn something.

"They don't know anything about the condition of this country, and it's mighty little they'll find out traveling through the country in parlor cars.

"Why," continued Carroll, "I met a man up here in

Maryland the other day, who said he was going out *West.* I asked him how far. He said to Buffalo, New York." And then the Red Mountain miner laughed.

"Why, do you know," he went on, addressing Kilbourn, "that that damn fool didn't know how big a country this is? Buffalo," and he laughed again, "is an eastern town. It ain't west at all. When you've got to Chicago, you are only one third the way to Frisco. And when you get to Omaha, you are only one half the distance, with two thirds of Uncle Sam's possessions still lying west of that town."

"Now let me ask you a question," concluded Carroll, facing the Washington jester, "and if you fail to answer correctly it's your treat."

"The question may be a hard one," said Chamberlain.

"No," replied the Coxeyite, "it is a simple, easy question in geography, and I'll bet you, nor old Cleveland, nor any of his cabinet can answer it."

"Well, let's have it," said Kilbourn, "and if he doesn't answer correctly we'll make him treat." And Frame looked down with great pride at what he regarded as the shrewdness and superiority of his companion.

"Tell me within 200 miles," began Carroll, putting the question, "where the half way point is between the east and west lines of the United States."

"Omaha," answered Chamberlain. "You admitted that yourself a moment ago."

"No, I didn't," was the reply. "I said Omaha was half way to Frisco You are darn near as ignorant as an average congressman. *Frisco is half way.* The

most westward island of Alaska is as far west of Frisco
as the most eastern island of the United States is east
of that city—here, barkeeper, cocktails," and Carroll
turned to that individual, who had been an interested
listener to the conversation.

"Do you know," continued the Westerner after they
had all drank at Chamberlain's expense, "that Mr. Cleveland has never been west of Buffalo or south of Washington, except in one of Prince George's private cars,
and then only for a short distance, and under circumstances surrounding him with corporation agents and
office seekers?"

"Well, I guess that's so," interposed Chamberlain.

"Now," continued Carroll, "how do you expect a man
to know how to run this government, that knows no
more about it than Cleveland?

"He wouldn't admit it," he went on, "and thinks
he's broad-minded; so was I, I thought, before I left
my native state, but I have since learned what a 'jay'
I was. Now I am going to prove to you what the effect
is on a man like the president, who thinks there is
little or no country outside of what he has seen," and
the speaker turned to the bartender, who had shoved a
cocktail toward him with his personal compliments.
Bowing his thanks, he picked up the glass, and while
holding it in his hand, continued:

"A straight line drawn north and south through the
center of population of the United States, throws it a
little west of Evansville, Indiana. Mr. Cleveland selected six of his seven cabinet officers from the east
of that line,—Gresham's town is a little east of the
line—" he added parenthetically, "and only one from
west of it. Thirty-five million of people west of that

line are virtually without representation in the cabinet,
for, mind you he only gave that half the secretary of
agriculture, an office that was only intended to save
congressmen the trouble of sending garden seed to their
constituents.   And what a man!" continued Carroll, as
he rolled his eyes up and whistled.   "We don't count
Morton as anybody out in our country.   He's a gold-
bug."   And the Westerner looked the contempt he felt
as a silver miner for the new botanical insect he had
mentioned, and then he added: "If that man ever has
time to study his own country he'll not do it; he'll go
to Europe."

. "A man can't learn the West on one visit either,"
broke in Frame.

"Say, Colonel," said Carroll, addressing his partner,
"tell 'em about that fellow from Chicago that was going to swim the ditch."

And with a little persuasion and another cocktail
Frame told what proved to be a good story.

"A fellow," began the Colonel, "from Chicago, by the
name of Scudder, came out to Colorado to write up the
cost of mining silver.   He didn't seem to understand
that there were no two silver mines in the world alike
on cost of production, or any *one* mine that would be
the same for three days in succession.   He either
thought they were all alike, or was sent out by some
one who wanted to 'black-eye' his own country, and
was paying this fellow to do it.

"Well," continued Frame, as he leaned up against the
counter and took off his plug hat, "this fellow stopped
at a ranch where I was to stay all night, and the next
morning he was up early, some time before breakfast,
and so was I. He said he wanted some exercise and

was going to take a walk to give him an appetite for breakfast, and as he started off across the flat he asked me how far it was to the base of the mountain.

"Well, the distance was about twenty miles, and so I told him.

"To a tenderfoot it looked about two miles, and he was about the rankest tenderfoot I ever saw. Well, he turned around and grinned, and said he was going to walk over there and back before breakfast, and off he went.

"After breakfast two of us that were going in the direction he had gone, got on our horses, and about two miles out we came up with him by a little *arroya.*"

"What's that?" interposed Chamberlain.

"That's a natural ditch, where the rains wash out a furrow in the ground," Frame replied, and then went on:

"The arroya was about three feet wide. He was standing there half undressed, and was taking off the balance of his clothes.

"We asked him what he was doing. In fact we felt a little uneasy about him," said Frame, as he pointed with his forefinger toward his head.

"He told us that when he started on that walk he did not believe the base of the mountain was more than two miles away, and he had been fooled once that morning, and he wasn't going to be fooled again.

"We couldn't still understand what he meant," added the Colonel, as he selected a cigar from a number in his pocket that had been given to him that morning, and lighted it, "and we told him so.

"'Why,' he said, 'I have been fooled once this morning, and I'll be damned if I am going to be fooled again. *I'm going to swim that ditch.*'"

Everybody laughed heartily, including Frame, and Chamberlain ordered the drinks, and said that he had learned more geography and politics in the last sixty minutes than he had before in six years.

And they laughed and talked for several minutes longer, for your genuine American will laugh and chaff even in his most desperate straits—a happy national disposition, else, under existing conditions, there would be more suicides here than in France or Germany. Sam Melwyn alone did not enter into the reckless spirit of the moment. His face was grave. The other men had perhaps only their own burdens to bear. Upon him depended the existence of others.

Even into the shrewd faces of such men of the world as Kilbourn and Chamberlain came an expression at least of sympathy for and approval of the courage of the men who could laugh in misfortune's face, as were doing some of those before them. "This beats our new party, John," said Kilbourn, half laughing, half earnestly, and the two left the place together.

There was a clamor upon the streets.

A policeman, red-faced and ex ited, looked into the lobby of the hotel, then disappeared. Something was happening upon the Avenue, and all went outside. The sidewalks were lined with people. Down the street, across the way, above the rather shabby foreground of the great Avenue's south side—the boundary of "the Division"—loomed up pleasantly the elevated greenery of the mall, and the stately structures of the Smithsonian Institution, the buildings of the department of Agriculture, and of the Bureau of Engraving and Printing, while to the southwest the Washington monument pointed its great finger toward the seat of final adjudication of all these matters.

Meanwhile close at hand was presented another picture. Down the Avenue marching toward the capitol came, wearily but confidently, an army in uniforms such as army never wore before since Falstaff marshaled his regiment. No two men were dressed just alike and no man was dressed as he would have been in prosperity. But the faces were rarely those of tramps and "hoboes," and there was perceptible even in the countenances of these jeered-at trampers something of that enthusiasm which once made thousands of the English yeomanry face blindly forth toward London, and which, before that, had impelled its myriads of all degrees to march to Palestine. All crusades must lack a certain dignity, but all earnest crusades must have a dignity of their own.

And, as the motley procession moved by the hotel, three men, as if by instinct, saying no word to each other, stepped from the sidewalk and fell calmly into line. They were Sam Melwyn and Frame and Carroll. Their garb now assorted but illy with that of their companions, but it did not matter. Carroll and Frame walked side by side cheerfully and almost jauntily, while Sam Melwyn joined a creature whom he did not know; a brother in trouble, that was all, a being ragged and unkempt, pinched and white of face, tottering as he walked and seemingly almost at the gates of death.

The Coxey army was marching on the capitol

CHAPTER XVIII.

Of what happened when the army reached the capitol all the world knows. The father of Jack and Sam had arrived to join them just before the latter took his place in the ranks, where he felt he in honor belonged until the end was reached, and he with his elder son were on the hill in time to witness the closing scene. They saw the possibly fantastic but certainly honest attempt of the humble yet earnest citizen of Ohio to carry out the programme planned. They saw the foolish roughness and brutality of a needlessly alarmed District force in dispersing what they called a dangerous mob, but which was only a few of the more greatly suffering or hopeless representatives of a vast, restless force in the nation, seeking to exercise the right of "petitioning for a redress of grievances," upon ground in every foot of which the humblest of them had as great a proprietary interest as has the President of the United States. They were witnesses of the whole miserable scene, one lacking the elements of a physical tragedy, because no man was killed, but one which indicated that, under existing conditions, there were lacking in the national government all tact and perception, all broad sympathy and sense of national brotherhood, all genius in recognizing the difference between an ebullition of the discontented few and a movement which, though it may be blunderingly and vaguely done, represented the suffering and unrest of millions.

Sam had no difficulty in keeping out of the immediate fray, and recognized his father and brother, who had made themselves purposely conspicuous, and he joined them before the affair, so small and preposterous in one way, so significant and far-reaching in another, was fairly ended. The three left the capitol grounds together and went to the young congressman's room, where Sam told his story, and he told it with all the earnestness and vigor, and sometimes the bitterness of a man who has done his best and has yet suffered because of the conditions surrounding him. It was a story calculated to affect strongly the two men who were listening to him.

He first referred to his wife and child, whom he had left in a little village near Oakland, California. As we suffer always most through those nearest and dearest to us, so it was evident that he suffered more because of them than on his own account. Tears came into his eyes when he mentioned them.

He had improved the farm he had bought in Southern California; planted fruit trees; cultivated a few acres in raisins; had built him a little cottage, intending to build on to it later, and had cleared and otherwise improved their home. To do this he had been compelled to borrow money and mortgage his place.

Then followed the old story.

When the mortgage fell due he was unable to pay it. The market for his fruit was in San Francisco, and the railroad charges for freight were so great there was not sufficient left to more than meet actual living expenses, and, after considerable indulgence on the part of the mortgagee, the foreclosure came about and he was left without a home.

"Could you not sell it, thus improved, for more than the mortgage?" asked the father.

"No, father, there is scarcely a price to be set on anything in that country, where it is to be paid for in money," was Sam's answer. "We tried hard enough," he said, "to find some one who would loan the money, or who would buy it in, and let us work to redeem it, but it was useless; no one seemed to have as much as $3,000, the amount we owed, except the bankers, and they said they only loaned to their customers, and were not able to accommodate those. So our place that had cost us $6,000 when it was unimproved, was sold, and we moved out when a tenant came to take possession.

"Jack," continued Sam, rising to his feet, and turning to his brother, who was sitting with his elbow on a table and his head resting in his hand, "what is the matter when energy such as mine, such as animates these arms, cannot make a living?" and as he said this he held out his arms, showing those muscular and well developed limbs of the perfect man.

"Go on, Sam, and tell us what you did next," was Jack's only reply.

"We then rented," said Sam, "a little place in the village near the ranch where we had built our home, and I secured work on a fruit farm for a time, but Chinamen came who were willing to work for so little that I had to quit. What little I was getting would not support us. You two may never feel it," he continued, with emphasis on each word, as he sat down in a chair and looked dejectedly at the floor, "but to feel—to know, that one's own wife and offspring are suffering for the common necessities of life, and liable at any moment to be turned out of doors, and to feel in the face of such a situation the helplessness of despair!" And Sam looked as if he were living over again the experience he was narrating.

Both the father and Jack sat quietly and said nothing while Sam paused in his recital.

"Piece by piece we sold off our furniture," began Sam again, "and then went with a friend in his wagon to Oakland. There we rented rooms, risking to chance for employment to pay for them. I secured a little work, but it was only enough to buy food, and at the end of a week we had to give up our rooms. But why tell what we did? I tried everywhere to get work, but failed. I went over to San Francisco and from morning to night tried to get a situation. I told the firms I applied to that I was well educated. It was of no use. One man asked me in what I had had experience. That settled it."

He paused for a few moments, then continued, with an effort: "The six months that followed seem like a nightmare, even now. No matter what may come to me and mine, the memory of those months will be a blackness and a horror all my life. From bad came worse. I struggled in San Francisco to get just food for my wife and little ones, to carry to them even a few cents nightly that body and soul might be kept together, until I became a tramp in appearance and a thing forlorn and weak at heart, with moods which at times almost changed me into a desperado. I understand now what the conditions are which make some, at least, of our ciminals. My feet protruded from my ragged shoes and left blood-stains upon the cobble-stones of the street, but my own sufferings were noth-ing. The horror of it was with the helpless ones; the woman so eager to assist, so brave and patient, yet so helpless, and the little ones growing pale and thin from want of proper nourishment. I tell you that time and again they went to bed hungry—yes, hungry!" and the tears rolled down the poor fellow's cheeks as he gulped forth the concluding word.

He resumed with resolution "There came one little pitiful gleam of hope at last, though of brief contin-uance. There came an opportunity to get back to Los Angeles by work on a boat, and a grocer whom I knew there and whom I met in San Francisco, said that he would give me a place in his store if I would come. I borrowed one dollar from another man who had been almost as unfortunate as I, but who had found work at low wages, and leaving this with my wife to be her sole support for ten days—think of that!—I went to Los Angeles. I received the place at $8.00 a week, and it seemed a fortune to me! I lived on almost nothing and sent nearly all my salary to my wife. She bought food; she bought a few cheap things for the poor little half naked bodies, and a new world seemed opened to us. It was not much of a world; it was a world with a day's life, but it was too good to last. The grocer failed, and at the end of four weeks I lost my position. The little money I used in getting back to San Francisco was bread taken from my children's mouths.

"How shall I tell of what followed? It was the former ghastly experience repeated, but with one happening which can never be remedied!" and his voice trembled as he spoke. "We starved. My blessed wife, brave and resolute as she was, grew weak, and the babe at her breast could not get the nourishment required for the sustenance of life in its small body. It died, died of its mother's starvation, and we could not even pay for the little pine coffin in which it was buried. My God! I can hardly realize it, even now—much as I have seen since of the misery existing in this boasted country!" And the man's voice grew hoarser.

After a few moments Sam resumed: "I could get no work save an occasional trifling job, and we still went often hungry, but my wife gradually regained a degree of strength. One day I went home weary and hopeless a little earlier than usual after a day of tramping, and found the remaining child alone in our single, shabby basement room. My wife had left word that she would be home at six o'clock. She come in then, that blessed woman, and there was a new light in her eyes. She held in her hand what was to us the great sum of forty cents. She had found work in a pattern store, where, with a gift she possessed for pattern cutting, she could earn at least that pittance daily. And upon that sum so earned by that noble wife we existed until I left San Francisco, for work for myself I could not find.

"It could not last! Had I been alone the case might have been different; but with the responsibility I had assumed for the welfare of others, to have cherished further pride would have been wickedness. I resolved to come East again, to come alone, to get work if I could and if not, then, father, to come to you, to tell you all simply, to confess myself the miserable failure I have been, and ask you in the name of all ties of blood, of all humanity, to help me if you can. And, father, here I am!"

The old man had risen; tears were streaming down his cheeks and his arms were outstretched toward his son. He fairly roared out:

"Failure! You're no failure at all! You are an honest, unfortunate man, God bless you, whose only fault has been that you waited too long before coming to your own. Thank God it is possible to send money by telegraph. Your wife will be happier to-night. Why, my boy, I"—but here the old man broke down. He could not command his words.

As for Jack, he was hardly less affected, though more self-controlled. His eyes were dewy as he grasped his brother's hand and wrung it warmly "You're all right now, Sam," he said, "but," he added as he became more thoroughly himself again, "you must tell us the story of your journey. How did you get here? Were you with the industrial army all the way?"

"Practically so," said Sam. "I could not afford to ride, and so I had to walk. The hungry, restless force was already organizing on the coast. I saw an opportunity for making my way eastward without being entirely alone in my misery; I joined the army."

"Tell us all about it," said Jack.

CHAPTER XIX.

"At the time of which I speak," said Sam, "not far from the first of April, the army on the coast had passed under the command of Gen. Kelley, and was encamped at Oakland, about six hundred strong. You have, of course, become familiar through the newspapers with the story of the earlier part of the journey. The Southern Pacific Railroad Company provided us with a train of box cars, and we were not interfered with until Ogden was reached. There the bumptious Governor West of Utah made a demonstration as arrogant and presuming as it was ineffectual, and which resulted but in a temporary delay. He called out the militia, he had a gatling gun planted in the public square of Ogden, and he informed the Southern Pacific authorities that the industrial army must not be brought into the territory. His bluster was of no avail. The Southern Pacific train ran into Ogden, unloaded its carloads of human freight, now over 1,200 men in all—and the army went into camp on the property of the railroad company. The army began its march across the territory, a freight train evidently put purposely in the way by the politic Union Pacific company, was taken without formal consent and, though living hardly, we did well enough after a fashion until we reached the borders of Iowa. Then ensued what was a disgrace to a state and to humanity.

"The train reached Omaha April 15, and was met

by a platoon of police officers and 3,000 citizens. Under the inspiration of Omaha's broad-minded and resolute mayor, Geo. P. Bemis, there had been provided thousands of pounds of bread and cooked beef, and the train passed on over the bridge into Council Bluffs, where nearly 10,000 citizens met and welcomed it. But the governor of Iowa was a man exhibiting the qualities of which plutocrats make their tools. He seemed to think the army a mob of lawless vagabonds, and ordered out the state militia to repel them. The railroads were united against the suffering men and the governor could not have acted more obediently toward them, nor more brutally toward this army of hungry and weary human beings, had he been a railroad employee, subject to absolute orders.

The army was driven from Council Bluffs and its members mercilessly herded like cattle in some fair grounds four miles from town. There they were guarded by the militia as if all were the inmates of some convict camp. There came on a chilling rain and then—in this supposably civilized country"—and here Sam's voice rang out with honest indignation—"occurred scenes unworthy of the race or of the age! I have read of how convicts doomed to the Siberian mines are sometimes treated by the brutal guards in charge of them, and now I understand their sufferings! There was an amphitheater and there were sheds upon the grounds. On that terrible night of April 17, we were gaunt and weak with hunger, for the Council Bluff authorities had refused us food, and with the beginning of the rain it became bitterly cold. We started 'for the amphitheater and sheds. Father, it is hard to believe, but the soldiers stopped us! They herded us, father, actually herded

us there on the open field, all night long. The rain
turned to sleet and came down without interruption on
the fourteen hundred men, nearly all scantily clothed
and many with their bare feet on the ground!

"There were the sheds within a hundred yards of
us," he said, as he raised his arm as if indicating the
direction, "and we were not allowed to go to them for
shelter. Finally weariness caused the men to sink
down upon the chilly, muddy ground, and the sleep of
exhaustion came to the relief of some. But it was
murder! One poor fellow died during the night. He
had joined us at Reno. He was on his way to Philadelphia, trying to make his way back to his mother,
a widow. He had suffered from a bad cold for several
days. He was one of the first to lie down on the ground
that night, and I was standing near him." Sam had
ceased his nervous moving about, and was standing in
front of his father and brother.

"He called me to him," he continued, "in a hoarse
whisper, and I saw by the color of his face that he had
a high fever. He no longer felt the cold—he would
never feel the cold again. I got down by him on my
knees, for, as I said, he could only whisper, and tried
to catch all he said:

"'I was cold, so cold,' he whispered, 'but I'm all
right now. I'm warm again. Why, I even slept a
little while just now, and dreamed I was home again
with my mother. It was good. But I know I shall
never see her! I can feel it somehow. I'm burning
and I'm weak, awfully weak. I don't know your name,
but I've noticed you, and I like your face and I want
you to do something for me if you will. Please say
you will.'"

Sam paused for a moment, while tears came into his eyes again at the recollection.

"Of course I promised, and the poor young fellow began his hoarse whispering again, though the task became harder for him with every word: 'I want you to take this,' he said, 'and give it to my mother in Philadelphia,' and he managed to get a little package with an address upon it from one of his pockets (and that package I have seen to it has since reached its address), 'and then she'll know that I always kept straight anyhow and only had hard luck. You'll do it, won't you? Oh, I wish I could see her!'

"I promised him again," said Sam, "and it brightened him up a little, but he was dying. I lifted his head out of the mud and slush and so held him. He tried to speak again, but could not. His breath came harder and harder, and finally he gave just a slight gasp and ceased breathing altogether. He lay there in the mud, dead, with the cold rain coming down on his white face,—murdered by the authority which had denied him the shelter close at hand! That was in Iowa, in the United States of America, father! What do you think of it?"

The old man's face had grown very stern during the recital; the eyes of Jack were blazing.

"It was murder, as you say," was the father's only response. "Murder by the tools of a sentiment existing in this country that is unexplainable."

Sam resumed: "You know, of course, pretty well what followed. The mayor of Omaha exerted himself again, and the working men of both cities had resolved to act as well. The next morning"—and now Sam grew intensely dramatic in his utterance—"when we heard the cheers of six thousand men, brawny mechanics from the workshops of Omaha, crowding across the bridge that spans the Missouri river, coming to our rescue, I knew that the God of humanity still moved hearts in the breasts of men. In that one moment of inspiring welcome wafted to us on the breeze, cold and wet to the skin as I was, blood, life-giving blood, rushed through my ateries and veins, and warmth and life came back. I looked around at my companions. Their cheeks were pale and their lips were white, but it was the tremor of excitement that comes with news that fills the soul—that greeting that came on the air, dying down but rising again, louder and louder as it came nearer—it was music to our ears, and the song it sang was the brotherhood of man. The soldiers were withdrawn, and the forward journey of the army began."

The excitement of the moment before now seemed to have left the narrator, and he spoke in a calmer tone.

"It was here that I first met Frame. He had come from Los Angeles, and had overtaken us at Council Bluffs. His knowledge as a newspaper man sometimes enabled him to get passes on the railroads. For some reason he took a fancy to me and wanted me for a companion, and he secured transportation on the Burlington Railroad for us to Chicago. I reported to General Kelley and was' excused, and we arrived in Chicago in time to start from there with Randall's army."

And then stopping suddenly, he asked: "Do either of you know what has become of Annie Lindgren, our nurse, Jack?" turning to his brother. "The woman who nursed us when we were little?"

"When she and her husband left us they went to Chicago," said Jack, "and we have not heard from her for a year or more."

"I went to look for her in Chicago," continued Sam, and then added: "She is dead. Crushed to death in a scramble for bread. An account of her death was published in the Chicago papers at the time. I went to a newspaper office and looked it up." And drawing from his pocket a *Chicago News*, of January 23, 1894, he read from that paper to his amazed father and brother, while they sat as if paralyzed, the following:

Crushed to death by a hungry mob battling for food in the county agent's office, Mrs. Annie Lindgren's body lies in the little bare parlor at 66 Marion place.

Literally stricken down and the life crushed from her frail body in a struggle for bread, death came as a relief to the hungry and unhappy woman. Her husband sits beside the plain coffin which the county agent furnished and the mob still battles for places in the long line before the county agent's window. That one frail form is not missed.

It was 1 o'clock yesterday afternoon when Mr. and Mrs. Lindgren entered the county agent's office to ask for assistance. Neither had eaten anything for two days, and the pale, sick woman leaned heavily on the arm of her husband. Within the room a mob of men, women and children literally fought for places in the line before the windows. Every few moments a rush from behind would break the line, and those pushed out of their places would fight to regain them to save the long wait for food which going to the end would necessitate.

Mrs. Lindgren, weak and sick, shrank back in alarm, but food must be had, and she led her weak husband to a chair near the wall while she wearily took his place at the end of the line. Slowly those in front presented their tickets and moved away, slowly the line moved forward. Suddenly there was a rush from the rear, the center of the line bowed out and those nearest the wall fought stubbornly to save themselves from being crushed. Above the other voices sounded a woman's scream. Then the police pushed their way through the crowd to where Mrs. Lindgren lay crushed and motionless upon the floor. She had been carried down in the rush and her frail hold on life was almost broken.

Tenderly and hastily she was raised and borne to an ambulance. Her half-frantic husband followed and the wagon was quickly driven to the cheerless home, 66 Marion place. There the county physician made a careful examination of the woman and found that her left hip was crushed and that the resultant internal injuries were serious.

For hours the husband sat watching his wife's life ebb away until late last night, when death brought her relief from her suffering. Meanwhile the county agent's office had sent food and fuel to the little home, where three children shivered around their mother's dead body.

The county will bury Mrs. Lindgren and care for the family.

Mrs. Lindgren was 56 years of age and her husband is about 75. He has been out of employment for several months, but up to yesterday the family had asked no assistance from the county agent. When the injured woman was removed to her home by the 28th precinct ambulance, the officers made an examination of the two small rooms in which the family lived and they found not even a crust of bread. The wagon was returned to the county agent's office and a supply of meat, bread, provisions, etc., and a load of coal were at once sent out. Dr. Quail of 52 Fowler street called at the house and attended the injured woman until she died last night.

County Agent Happel says that the accident is due wholly to the lack of room to receive the crowds that call at his office.

"We have from 1,200 to 1,500 people to wait on every day," said he. "We have been criticised for not allowing them all to crowd into the office at once and we threw open the doors, with this result. We have but five police officers to handle this crowd and many of them, half starved and wild with hunger, cannot be controlled at all. I don't believe the entire police force could keep the crowd that gather here orderly and in line. They are packed in the office like sardines and the only thing I can say about Mrs. Lindgren's case is that she got in the jam and was crushed. Others have been injured in the same manner, but fortunately her case is the only one that has resulted seriously or fatally. Things have come to such a pass that we must have more room or close the office altogether. The county board should secure larger quarters at once."

The inquest on the remains of Mrs. Lindgren is being held this afternoon at the home, 66 Marion place.

"My God, my God!" exclaimed the father, "why did she not let us know her condition?" while Jack wiped the tears from his eyes, and said nothing.

"Father," said Sam, "it is not to one's family or intimates left behind, that one applies for assistance. Pride prevents that. The self-consciousness of shame at the inability to succeed in the struggle of life, is a barrier that closes communication with home and friends."

"And you left Chicago—go on, Sam," said Jack, with his form stiff and rigid in the chair in which he sat, and his face looking as cold and white as marble.

"Frame had tried hard but failed to get passes in Chicago, so we started with the Chicago contingent. All went well until we reached La Porte, Indiana, and there, in that pomposity-beridden town, occurred a specimen of official tyranny, blundering, and ineffectual malice which would have been still harder to endure, but for its ludicrous aspects and the real alarm of the Justice Shallows and prosperous Pecksniffs in office. We had not even reached the place and were marching in the middle of the country highway, when a force of police and deputy sheriffs from the town, headed by a mayor who seemed about equally scared and vengeful, met us, arrested all our officers and detained the rest of us under guard in the suburbs.

"Well," and here Sam could not help smiling at the recollection, though speaking with feeling, "we were held there while Mayor Scott, Judge Norris and other good and loyal millionaire citizens," speaking with bitter sarcasm, "put their heads together to study out what charge they could make against us.

"It must have been an imposing sitting. After an all night's session in the office of the States Attorney, they filed a complaint against General Randall and his officers, charging them with conspiracy to steal 10,000 loaves of bread of the value of to wit: $500. This is what they calculated the people of Indiana would give us while passing through that region, and that this bread would not be given to us unless we were there; therefore the conspiracy! The teachings of the lowly Nazarene to 'give to the hungry,' was to be interpreted; 'if a man be hungry and asks you for bread, give him a stone.' When the cases came up for trial in the big court room of their new court-house with Judge Norris on the bench, and the court-house full of people, one half sympathizing with us, and the other half believing we were anarchists, the news some way got to the judge that our attorneys were going to subpoena the whole army as witnesses, and as this would bring

them all into town,—just what they did not want,—
and put them on pay at $2 a day, he hurriedly con-
sulted the state's attorney and dismissed the cases.

"As Randall and his officers," continued Sam, "had
been arrested in the middle of the road, and had not
committed the slightest infraction of the law, the general wanted to vindicate himself and his men to the
citizens of La Porte, and the Opera House was engaged
for him to speak in that night.   Would you believe it,
Jack," and Sam now faced his brother, "Judge Norris
and Mayor Scott, both, like yourself, sworn to support
the constitution—that *magna charta* of American liberty, that gives to us the priceless principle of *free
speech*—with threats used on the owner of the Opera
House prevented that individual from opening the
doors after he had agreed to do so!" And now Sam grew
eloquent again as he exclaimed:

"If Columbia were typified by a living woman, and
could have seen our trials and hardship, and the treatment accorded us by the officers of the law in this extraordinary town, she would have either wept in despair or have drawn the sword with which she is
sometimes represented.   No scene of tyranny and
oppression was ever enacted in Russia more destructive of the rightful liberties of the citizen than occurred
at La Porte, and was so pronounced by the five
Chicago reporters who warmly shook the hands of our
officers, and assured them of their sympathy.

"There isn't much more to tell," Sam added. "Frame
was full of resources and stumbled upon a railroad conductor for whom he had once done a service and who
was in sympathy with us. He carried us for the length
of his run and assisted us in making further progress.

At Pittsburg, we fell in with Carroll, who was on his way to join the regular Coxey army, and we three of us come on that night together. Both my friends had many acquaintances among the politicians here and we got along well enough until I stumbled upon you in the hotel—for which I thank God—"and his eyes become moist again.

There was a knock at the door, followed by Frame and Carroll entering the room.

Excitement was plainly visible on their faces. They came to announce that Coxey, Brown and Jones, "Faith, Hope and Charity," as Carroll put it, were all in jail, and they wanted a lawyer whose heart was as big as a "Colorado potato" to defend them, and they were after Jack Melwyn for that purpose.

And after some talk in which Frame and Carroll took a large part, and which served to set all to laughing, and to forget the sadness of the reunion, they left the room, to go to the District jail.

CHAPTER XX.

As the summer wore on Rogasner's mind ran principally on his love affair. He gave very little attention to the banking business. The bank served as a blind to mask his real designs in Washington. It came natural in the family of which he was a descendent to be a banker, and to so organize and set the checks and balances as to make this business run with success. He gave very little of his time to it, and though the president, his name did not appear on the letter heads.

The bank had no foreign connections; doing all of its outside business through the New York Bank of which his brother Edward was in charge. Everything was avoided that would draw attention to or disclose the identity of Victor Rogasner, and nothing had yet occurred to embarrass him in his operations, the success of which, aside from his love affair, was his sole ambition and the cause of his being in the United States.

His plans in this respect were all meeting with success, and public sentiment had been moulded until it was scarcely necessary to do much more than had been done to hold the authorities at Washington to the opinion that silver should not be rehabilitated.

And yet he was sleepless in his energy. The bankers and money lenders in the United States had become his allies and were exerting a powerful influence, but there were many things they did not think of, and while keeping himself informed as to their work, he was constantly doing something to mould public sentiment or otherwise strengthen his position.

About the time of the investment of English capital in·the breweries of this country, he had caused the purchase, through agents sent direct by Baron Rothe to the United States, of a majority of the stock of several metropolitan newspapers, selecting the ones that would most probably suggest the policy of political parties, and other papers. These purchases were made through bankers and other capitalists, in whose names the ostensible ownership remained.

He had bought up nearly all the "ready print" houses in the large cities through agents, and had installed Englishmen in part or altogether as managers and employees of these. establishments.

About ninety-five per cent of the newspapers in this country use ready print matter. This is news or interesting reading matter put into type in these houses, and then stereotypes are made from this type, and are sent out at so much a column to hundreds or thousands of newspapers, to appear almost simultaneously in their pages. The competition in journalism resulting from the hard times made this practice of using plate matter by publishers a necessity.

The ready print houses are mostly the judges of the character of matter furnished; hence it afforded an excellent opportunity to spread educational matter to discredit silver or to befog the public mind on the financial subject. It was an opportunity Rogasner had early seen in his campaign against the United States, and he was constantly strengthening this branch of his service.

On a day in June, 1894, a time we now invite the reader to look in upon this English diplomat, he was just finishing a letter to one of his agents on a Metropolitan paper in Chicago, asking him to increase the quantity of special matter in the Sunday edition of that paper, on the news and other interesting reading matter from Europe, when his ,brother came into the office, having just arrived from New York.

"Why, Edward, old boy, I'm glad to see you," said the English agent, looking up.

The brothers cordially shook each other's hand. Edward was smaller and did not much resemble his brother, but was a shrewd money-maker and a good business man.

"I wanted to get away from business, so thought I would run down and see you," said the younger brother.

"Always glad to see you," returned Victor, "especially so, since I am chafing from playing the American for so long a time."

The conversation soon turned on the drift business affairs were taking in the United States, and the probable events of the near future. The elder brother recounted the invincible campaign he had made, and dwelt with pride on many of the maneuvers conducted by his masterly hand.

"How soon do you expect serious results?" asked Edward.

"That will depend on the extent of the suffering among the people," replied the hard-hearted conspirator. "It is now very general and extensive, but I do not look for serious business till seventy per cent of the people are in actual distress. When thirty per cent of the people are starving there is no danger, nor forty nor fifty, but when it reaches seventy, the match will be lit and the magazine will explode."

"Well," asked Edward, 'is it now forty, fifty, or what do you estimate it?"

"It is not far from the bubbling point," replied the elder brother. And then continuing, he said:

"The Coxey movement will soon play out; then something else will come. The riots in the mining sections will continue in a state of incipient rebellion, ready to blaze up afresh with each new disturbance. Something startling is now almost sure to happen every ninety days—the steam gauge is sizzling, and the pressure is increasing all the time. Each new outbreak will be accompanied with increased excitement. The approaching election, however, will tend to allay disturbances by centering the public mind on the campaign. After that, everything will go from bad to worse very rapidly."

"Isn't it astonishing to you," said Edward, "that the people do not see what is the matter?"

"No," replied his brother. "Some of them do, but not enough to make an impression. Not one man in one thousand understands that under a redemption money system, the commercial value of the redemption money fixes the purchasing power of all other money. What seems so plain to you and me, is all mud to the people. Money is to them an intricate and abstruse science, they get a wrong notion and go off with it, and that neutralizes such elements' influence.

"Then, too, Edward," he said, as he continued, "you must think of this—the human mind cannot grasp more than one subject at a time. Look at the tens of thousands of people who belong to the Salvation army —they see only one thing—that's sin. They go through the streets beating their drums, carrying on an imaginary war against Satan; to them that is the one panacea to make the world happy; they will never even study the monetary question, let alone understand it. Now the Salvation army illustrates a majority of the people—it is either tariff, single taxation, socialism, nationalism, prohibition, or some other *ition* or *ism* the want of which, in their minds, is responsible for these times; and this excludes the possibility from their minds of understanding us."

Rogasner paused a moment and then began again:

"We are shooting from ambush, and are perfectly safe. Money moves the world. If every one were just, currency systems would be equitably adjusted; but the people can never be perfect so long as they are without a just monetary system. The latter must come first, then all the other schemes are possible. Money is the protoplasm of society. Without it, civilization is impossible, crime increases, and barbarism is the result. We are now living in a half state of barbarism—standing armies—wars, and man living in a state of constant warfare on his brother man—all this is because the monetary system is not right. Perfect the monetary system and you have made it possible to perfect civilization.

"Money is the blood of civilization," he continued. "If it is corrupted or congested, there will be sores and eruptions; if the circulation is perfect the whole body and surface of civilization may glow with health. Next to milk at our mother's breast, money is the first thing we need; and it is the last thing required when we die—to pay the undertaker's bill. Money enters into every organism of society. It can be used to keep society in its present maudlin condition, or it can be used to perfect civilization.

"But perfect civilization," he went on, as he lit a cigar and handed one to his brother, "cannot come first; the perfect monetary system must precede it. You must produce the conditions for perfect civilization, before such civilization itself can exist. You cannot put a roof on a house till the walls are up. You can not have an ideal civilization until you have money —vital organic matter—adjusted to the needs of society. It must be adjusted to flow without impediment among all the people."

"But," said the younger brother inquiringly, "if all the money in the world were divided up evenly among the people, a few would soon have most of it?"

"My dear brother, you do not understand me, or comprehend the scope of my thoughts," was the reply. "Once plagues were regarded as certain to come, and that nothing would prevent them. We do not so reason now. Removing the dirt has removed the plagues; vaccination prevents smallpox. Nor has the cause for money piling up been removed—if it were that would cease.

"If the money of the world were divided equally at the present time," he continued, "the world would be attuned to a happy chord while the condition lasted— a suggestion of the happy time to come, if it were permanent. Now what are some of the causes that prevent the establishment of these equitable conditions? In our country we have fixed incomes established by law. Many thousands drawing incomes—annuities attached to titles—without any compensation or return to the people who pay these large sums.

"But it is not necessary to talk about titled incomes," he said, as he leaned toward his desk and took up a pencil, and made some figures on a piece of paper. "There is supposed to be $1,600,000,000 of money in the United States, all told. Suppose that were divided equally among the people. There is over $2,000,000,000 to be paid by the many each year to the few, who have incomes built up under a law that recognizes money lending. This $2,000,000,000 is interest. It is just as effectual in taking money away from the people, as if it were titled incomes to the few fixed by law. And it is just as permanent—they can never pay the principal. Thus the people are paying fixed incomes to the amount of four times the cost of running the government. These debts will be perpetuated. By this means the many and producing classes are hewers of wood and drawers of water for the few or non-producing class. They pay annually more money to the few who have interest incomes, than the total stock of money in their country."

"How much are the debts of this country?" queried his brother.

"From a close study," said Rogasner, "I have recently given to partial reports of the United States census bureau, and other data, it is close to $40,000,-000,000."

"Is it so much as that?"

"Yes. The railroad bonded debt is over one eighth of this amount. The sum I have named includes interest-bearing debts of all kind. The assessed value of all the property in the United States is a fraction over $24,000,000,000. These debts of $40,000,000,000 embrace national, corporate, municipal and private indebtedness. An average rate of interest of six per cent per annum on this sum is, as you see, over $2,000,-000,000. It comes from the masses and goes to the money centers—to the money lenders. It is a constant stream from the people to the few, and saps the business vitality of whole communities. The machinery of law is adjusted to enforce these obligations—the courts render judgments and the sheriffs collect the executions. With 1600 million in money, they are expected to pay 40,000 million in debts, when it is not sufficient, if all were paid on the same day, to pay the annual interest. This condition has come about in the last twenty years. The remonetization of silver would now come too late; a greater evil has grown up in the meantime," and he smiled. "If there were no laws for the collection of debts, this anomalous situation would not have arisen."

"Why, Victor! you astonish me!" exclaimed Edward. "Not at what you say, but that you, one of our family, should show a prejudice against our business; besides, you know that this is only one of many advantages which the few have, and it is an honestly acquired advantage; it is an honest business to lend money. Are you weakening in the purpose for which you came here?"

"My boy," returned the elder man, "don't imagine for a moment that I have relinquished the object for which I came to this country. I shall sink this accursed nation; tear it into threads, and leave it bleeding and disrupted, if for no other purpose than to demonstrate the power of our money; but since I have been engaged

in this work I have learned a great deal. The horo-
scope of my financial knowledge was once limited, but
now it embraces the world.

"To return," he continued, rising and pacing the
floor, "suppose it were not possible for people to have
fixed incomes settled on their families by law or by
allowing the blood of civilization to be trafficked in—
money, this blood of civilization would flow among the
people, giving life to their industries. This tremendous
drain upon their resources would be removed; they
would embellish their homes and cares would be removed that now wrinkle their foreheads.

"Edward, do you know," he said, stopping and facing his brother, "that it takes men of our race to detect
this error in our civilization? Jesus Christ saw it, and
I have here memoranda that will direct you to what
he said on this subject," and Rogasner walked over to
his desk as he said this, and pulled out from a drawer
a paper containing the following and handed it to his
brother:

THE BIBLE ON MONEY LENDING.

Ex.   c 22,   v 25.
Lev.   c 25,   v 36, 37.
Deut.   c 23,   v 19.
Neh.   c 5,   v 7,   10
Ps.   c 15,   v 5.
Prov.   c 28,   v 8.
Jer.   c 15,   v 10.
Ezek.   c 18,   v 8,   17,   13.
Ezek.   c 22,   v 12.
Mat.   c 21,   v 12,   13.
Luke.   c 19,   v 45,   46.

And then he went on as he stood addressing the
younger man:

"The diversion of money from its natural function as a medium for the exchange of property, to one of hoarding and loaning it out, has littered the cycles of history with the wreck of nations. It destroyed the empires of the Medes and Persians, the Assyrians, the Babylonians and Phœnicians. With it, Sparta and Athens drank up the sustenance of Greece, and then fell themselves a prey to the anarchy it drew down upon their heads. Rome, strong and mighty when her people were prosperous, disintegrated and fell as a nation when the few became the owners of nearly all the property in the Roman empire through this same system. She not only fell when a republic, but again when an empire, and again and again, and each time the cause can be traced to usury—the accumulation of money through the interest system.

"You will find in Roman history," he continued, as he again commenced to walk to and fro, "at about the time of Christ, when they were going through one of their periodical reorganizations of the government, that the people demanded the repudiation of all debts, and they compromised with the creditor class by crediting all interest previously paid on the principal, and giving the debtors three years in which to pay the balance; but they continued the system, of money lending.

"The same system of trafficking in the blood of civilization brought on the French Revolution, and up to the very moment when that terrible deluge of blood began, the capitalists believed that the strong arm of the law was a sufficient protection. The great danger now to England is the secession of our colonies; but a standing army in Australia and New Zealand, and a few sepoys shot from cannon in India will probably hold these people in subjection.   Canada is not yet deeply in debt and there will be no present trouble there.

"The United States," he continued, "has drank from the cup of poison deeply, and these asses in Wall Street who make a commission on each transaction have facilitated the ravages of the disease. It is amusing to read what they say about gold exports. Can't they see that it is to pay interest on over $5,000,000,000 of their securities held in Europe? Such a set of fools as are running this government could not be bred in a family like ours." And he stopped and smiled at his brother as he made this last remark complimentary to their great house.

And then continuing, for he was now doing all the talking, he said:

"It will soon come. We have not long to wait. Inside of a few years it will be either a monarchy or a revolution with total disintegration of the American republic."

"I was interested," broke in Edward, "in what you were saying about the possibilities of a perfect civilization. I would like to hear why you think it is practical if fixed incomes were abolished."

The younger brother recognized in the elder a master mind, such as had only been thrown to the surface in ages, and he wished to further draw him out.

Here was a man who had inherited remarkable ability as a financier, and who had now for over twenty-one years specially studied the use and power of money. While using it for evil, he had also studied its counter advantages. In the hands of this unscrupulous man money had been a power for evil enveloping a nation —all this, with the attendant circumstances and discussions, made a school for him, superior by far to that in which any young man was ever before tutored. At his age now, he was ahead of his preceptor,. Baron Rothe, and could see the effects of money on society in a more comprehensive way than had ever occurred to the Baron.

"Yes," he said, in answer to his brother's request, "in a country like the United States the abolition of the right to deal and traffic in money would be the beginning of the grandest civilization the world ever · saw. But it is not all that is necessary—man's disposition has run so long upon the desire to accumulate wealth that some other things would have to be looked after, to hasten the rejuvenation of the human race."

"Well, what are they?" interposed Edward.

"First abolish debts," replied the sage brother. "Put in the constitution that there shall be no law for the collection of voluntary debts thereafter contracted. Next increase the amount of money *per capita* to the amount of money and credits now necessary to carry on business. If I had the other side of the case, as the lawyers say, that is what I would do first."

"If there were no law for the collection of debts, there would be no money lending," said his brother.

"That is scarcely a correct assumption. Money loaning would continue, but with a higher standard of morals. What is called commercial honesty would be replaced by commercial honor—a far greater thing. The dishonest man could not do business. There would be transient debts, but they could never grow into the magnitude of a national evil; the life-blood of a people could not be sapped."

"But it would destroy our business?"

"I wasn't talking about our business; I was talking about a perfect civilization."

"How could any business be conducted without enforcing obligations?" asked Edward.

"I only mentioned voluntary debts," was the reply. "The intention would be to break up money lending, and the practice of people going in debt. If I paid you for a horse and you failed to deliver it, the law would force you to do so, or respond in money—that would not be a voluntary debt."

"How about damages?"

"Damages for wrongs inflicted would not be a voluntary debt."

"Suppose a merchant," asked Edward, "should order of his importer a bill of goods, and it was not convenient to send the money, as he would not know in advance the amount to send, with such a law the importer would not fill the order until he had received the money."

"Yes, he would," the elder brother replied, "if he had confidence in the customer, and the amount not large. A man who did not pay such a debt would be black-listed; he would never get credit elsewhere— a reputation would be worth something—it would tend to make all men honorable. You must remember I have provided for enough money to do business on, and large purchases could be paid for at the time. To break up the credit system would be a benefaction. It cannot be done now, because there is not enough money. Under the conditions I mention, money would have no other function than the exchange of property —its legitimate function. It is a moral crime to divert it from that use. This law would make it impossible."

"Then morally we are criminals?"

"We deal with society as we find it. At present we are using this advantage for peaceable conquest, that it may redound to the benefit of our nation."

"Under such a system as you mention," asked the New York banker, "how could speculation be carried on?"

"It would be materially checked," was the reply. "Therein is a great advantage to society. A man could not buy a large tract of land by paying part down and getting cred t as to the remainder, expecting to sell a part or all the property in time to meet the deferred payment. All bu:iness would be conducted upon legit· imate lines for cash; there would be no plunging except upon actual payments of money. People would turn their attention to the sciences and arts, to literature, refinement, the graces and self-improvement. Money would no longer be used as a power to oppress. Debts would be virtually unknown."

"As you know," he said, now stopping and looking at his brother, who was still sitting an attentive listener, "it was 1,600 years after the birth of Christ before man discovered the circulation of the blood. We have not yet discovered how to make the blood of commerce and civilization."

"A man could not rise rapidly in wealth under your system," said the younger brother.

"A perfect civilizat.on does not contemplate a man acquiring so much more than his proportion of the lands and goods of this world," returned the elder brother.

"It would put a check on ambition and energy," was the next objection.

"Is that the only field for ambition and energy?"

asked the other. Then, continuing, said: "Ambition and energy would find fields enough in which to compete for excellence and merit—fine homes, the best cattle, the fastest horses, culture and a thousand other things. Rapidly acquired wealth would be rare, and heirs would dissipate or divide it up. The founders of this government provided against estates *entail*, but they did not foresee the accumulation of vast fortunes and the corruptions to ensue from the system of law they adopted. No—civilization is environed by laws that retard and work its ruin."

"Then you believe that if there were no such thing as debts, or the right to accumulate money by loaning it, civilization would be benefited?" asked Edward.

"Most assuredly," was the answer. "There can be no general prosperity among the people till money—the medium of exchange—the blood of commerce—is protected from being trafficked in as you would other property. Let it have its legitimate function only and it will flow uninterruptedly in the channels of trade. And there should be a normal quantity. Where credit is now used, money should be in sufficient quantity to take its place."

"How could you get your new money in circulation?" asked the younger of the two men.

"With public improvements. If it was here in the United States, this were being done, I would build canals. One across the State of Michigan—connect the lakes with the Mississippi river—a ship canal connecting the ocean with the lakes, and have the ocean vessels land at the wharf of Duluth, 1,500 miles in the interior. I would build one, two or three double or four track railroads across the continent—make reservoirs

in the arid regions, and have innumerable canals conducting the water for irrigation over millions of acres
of land. This would put the money in circulation. It
would put it in circulation among the people who most
need it—among the poor people, and there would be
no system of laws such as now exist, to take it away
from them.

"As it is now," he continued, taking a seat on the
corner of a flat top desk, "the people of this country
are paying a daily average of $5,000,000 in inter-
est on debts built up under the present system. This
money is going where? To money centers; to the
East; to England, the money center of the world. Do
you wonder at the lack of prosperity under such a system? If leeches covered your body and were sucking
your blood, could you long be healthy? If you were tied
naked to a tree in a mosquito swamp you would not
expect to be very cheerful. As leeches and mosquitoes
would be to your blood, so are debts and money lending to the blood of civilization."

"And demonetization of silver?" said Edward inquiringly.

"Hastened the culmination of these disasters," replied
the money philosopher. "It made falling prices covering an era of twenty-one years,—that are still falling
—so that all debts when contracted, must be paid at
the time they come due, by the sacrifice of more property than would have been necessary at the time the
debts were contracted. What would have come to
these people in the way of disaster in fifty or a hundred years, will now come to them in 25 years."

"How do you account for the prosperity that came
periodically to Colorado and other sections during the

—·

last twenty-one years?" asked his brother, who had made a visit to the state named.

"They got drunk on borrowed money, and were aided by a sudden flow of money for investment," was the reply.

Victor Rogasner now summoned his butler and directed him to bring a certain rare wine from the cellar.

Here was one of the most remarkable men in the world; on the subject he was discussing, the most remarkable. He had studied money and monetary systems from a vantage point probably never before occupied by a mortal man. Statesmen! with crude notions of finance, busily engaged in looking after the loaves and fishes of office, were as pigmies in knowledge, compared with this man, whose hand for twenty-one years had been shaping the destinies of the nation. To his perception the world lay before him as a map, and the effect of financial laws upon its geography and its civilization was as the A, B, C's to him.

Was it possible that he was about to reverse his policy and throw his great influence on the side of human happiness? If the reader have such idea, the first remark he made after the wine was set before them and the butler had withdrawn, will dispel the hope.

"This is a pretty picture you have drawn, Victor; am I to suppose that you are about to turn philanthropist, and work for its realization?" asked the younger brother.

"Not for an instant," the elder brother exclaimed. "I have neither the taste nor desire. Mankind is devoid of gratitude; what is seemingly such, is selfish·

ness fawning in anticipation of further favors. The one who would do this, must be a man who loves to work for the benefit of mankind. I do not. Besides, it is not the work of one man. If it ever comes, it will be with a combination of elements and circumstances. It will require a great upheaval, such as turn foundations over and rend empires. Then if the right man ride upon the war cloud, in whose soul there is no element of dross, and to whose imagination it has been given to comprehend what is now infinite, his hand will guide the destinies of a people from semi-barbarism into civilization.

"It is only possible here in the United States," he added after a pause.

"Why only here in the United States?" asked his brother.

"Free schools—general education," was the laconic reply. And then he added:

"It is not possible anywhere else in the world. The constitution of this country guarantees the right of every citizen to bear arms—it may come at the point of the sword."

"Why was that put in their constitution?" asked Edward.

"The founders of this government," replied his brother, "who framed the constitution under which it was to exist, did not regard a government worth preserving that was in danger from its own citizens. They thought only of the dangers that might threaten the liberties of the people through corruption and despotism and provided for them the right to bear arms, that they might repel assaults upon their liberties. For the same reason a small standing army only is maintained in this country; the theory is, that a nation that cannot be held together by love, ought not to be pinned together by bayonets. It is different with us in Europe."

"But," said Edward, "should the people revolt in this country as you are now expecting they will do, will not drastic measures be resorted to and the people be repressed?"

"That depends," he replied, "upon the time, the opportunity, and the men who lead in the revolution. The chances are that it will end in monarchy, with the people slaves to the money power. But should it come over a contested election and have a leader fruitful in resources, comprehensive in details, honest, firm and patriotic—a statesman and a warrior combined—whose declared and real intention is to preserve the Union till the regularly constituted authorities can be elected, it will succeed, and the government will be reformed in the interest of the people. What *we* want to see is its dismemberment into numerous governments, or a monarchy."

After discussing for some time the different forms a revolution in the United States might take, the younger brother said:

"Tell me something more about your perfect civilization. Men will get rich, even though money lending is stopped. What have you to say to that?"

"It is a different kind of wealth," he replied. "It is spasmodic, or the man acquiring the wealth is an active quantity in the business world— he gives employment to men. He is taking risks, and statistics show that ninety per cent of our speculators and business men in time fail, and their wealth dissolves.

"Not so," he continued, "with money lenders. They

seldom fail where their interest income is sufficient to
provide for their wants, unless they deliberately squan-
der it."

"Bankers fail, and they are money lenders," interjected Edward.

"That is not where individual effort controls its own
money.   In the case of banks it is where speculation,
or corruption of some officer diverts the money from
the business for which it was intended. Money lending
on well established business principles is absolutely
safe.   Here and there a debt may be lost, but it will
be the exception and will not affect the average success
of the business."

"And the result?" asked the brother.

"Is the establishment of incomes, in a non-produc-
tive business as dangerous to the prosperity of the people generally as incomes established by direct act of
Congress "

Continuing, he said:

"It is claimed that most people go into debt with
the same facility that a candle fly seeks the warmth
of a burning blaze. If this simile is true, it is also
true to say that both blazes scorch with equally fatal
effect. In the case of the people their apparent readiness to go in debt is on account of the scarcity of
money, or its unequal distribution."

"Then you think the accumulation of wealth is principally due to our system of laws, and not to well directed efforts?" was the next question from the attentive listener.

"Yes. Individual efforts, however, will acquire
more for one man than another or than his indolent
neighbor, but the general and permanent accumulation

of wealth is almost wholly due to a system of laws that recognizes the right to deal in the blood of civilization as a subject of commerce. In the first instance it will not stay together—if quickly made it will be quickly spent—and heirs divide it, or it is again risked in other business enterprises. In the latter instance we see its effect in a class of idle young men who are not able to spend their incomes, and whose only lesson, well learned, is not to encroach upon the principal.

"Suppose," he continued as he took a seat facing his brother, "four men were to sit down to a table to play a game of poker, and the money in the party were equally distributed, say $100 to each man, and there were a hole in the middle of the table, and the rules of the game required a dollar to be put in this hole out of each 'jack pot'. It would only be a question of time till there was no money left with the four men. England is drawing from the people of this country in the way of interest about 250 millions each year. We are giving back nothing for it. What is not being done by us is being accomplished by the money lenders in this country. We interest-gatherers are the hole in the middle of the table."

"You should remember," said Edward, "that these people parted with their principal."

"Yes," was the reply, "and they are entitled to their principal back, and would be also to their interest indefinitely, the same as one would be entitled to the hire for the use of a horse till it was returned, if it were not for the destructive results of such a system. In the case of the horse a useful property is being employed. In the case where money is borrowed, a useful agency intended for a purpose, is trafficked in, in a manner to destroy and divert it from the purpose for which it was intended.

"Experience and statistics teach," he 'continued, "that the net profits of general business and production are less than three per cent, while the average profits from money lending are six per cent. One eats the other up. The man engaged in an active and useful industry will meet with losses or reverses—a failure of crops or other misfortunes. Not so with the money lender who holds a mortgage on a farm or factory—his interest is accruing day and night and does not stop accumulating on account of any misfortune or disaster. M. Jannet quotes the elaborate calculation of an ingenious author to show that 100 francs, accumulating at 5 per cent compound interest for seven centuries, would be sufficient to buy the whole surface of the globe, both land and water, at the rate of 1,000,000 francs (£40,000) the hectare. This constant uninterrupted trafficking in the money of a nation, will ruin the prosperity of any government in the world, and is destructive of civilization."

"What else would you do," asked the visiting brother, "after you had provided against the interest system?"

"That depends," was the reply, "on the shape matters took after the new system went into effect, but there is a great deal in suggestions now being made by reformers. Among them is the principle of single taxation. This New Yorker, Henry George, thinks the millennium will come when all revenues are collected from lands. He is wrong there. But wherein the principle he teaches is valuable, is, that taxation is a powerful weapon in the hands of the people to break up and destroy monopolies, whether it be land or anything else. In the interest of the people I should use that weapon."

"But," interposed his brother, "the constitution of the United States says taxation shall be equal."

"Then enforce the constitution," replied the other. "It is a farce anyhow as now enforced on that subject. The rich evade taxation and control the assessors. The poor under the present sytem pay most of the taxes. And herein we see the corrupting influences of wealth. I would make it impossible for any man to be very wealthy. I would set a limit on a man's wealth. You must break the human mind loose from *greed*,useless wealth,before you can turn it in the direction of the magnificent in civilization."

And as he said this he got up, poured out a drink of wine, and passed the decanter over to his brother.

"How is that possible?" asked the younger man.

"Tax a man to death whenever his wealth exceeds a certain amount," was the reply.

"You would find that very unpopular," was the retort.

"That depends on how we look at it," said the diplomat. "If selfishness is to have full rein; if greed for gain is the highest and most laudable ambition, and to give it full sway is in the best interest of civilization, then put no check lines upon it. The stronger it gets the more it will demand. It will commit crimes both inside and outside the law. Like Alexander standing with the bloody sword of conquest in his hand praying for more nations to destroy and rob, it will satiate its thirst for wealth only when there is no more to be obtained.

"Now let me paint the other picture," he continued,

as he walked slowly up and down the room. "Suppose wealth were generally diffused among the people, and every one knew that there was a limit to it. Not being in the hands of a few, wealth would be more generally distributed. There would be correspondingly more people in prosperous circumstances. That would mean more general happiness. The thirst and hunger for wealth would be in a manner allayed. The feverish pursuit of millions would have ceased. People who now think of nothing but money making, would turn their attention to something else.

"Go with me on the street," he said, suddenly stopping and facing his brother, "and look at each individual that passes us. What are each and all of them thinking about? Money making—how they are to make a living—what is to become of a certain financial scheme—all their minds are running on money. If it chance to be a boy passing by, he can scent a dime a square away. If it be a girl, you will generally see her careworn hurrying to or from her employment, a slave to the present industrial system. Life is a burden to the great mass of people from morning till night. They live on hope. Life is a competition for money, and it is hard to get. Our business system is adjusted like a spider web and we are the spiders. The people are the flies.

"Under the system my plan foreshadows," he continued, as he again began to pace the floor, "the people would turn their attention more to other things. Each new invention would be used to lessen the number of hours in a day's work, instead of throwing men out of employment as it does now. The human race would be improved. The mad struggle for gold would cease.

The hand of human intelligence would have re ;hed forth and dropped into the boiling caldron of gr. ed a dissolvent converting its contents into a cool and life-giving draught, where all could quench their thirst. Our art studios would again be filled with the finest paintings; sculptured marble would be fashioned into forms vying with those of Greece and Rome in their palmy days; civilization would take on a new hue; the secret laws of nature would feed the genius of the inventor, and happiness would take the place of sorrow. But let us drop this subject; it interests me only as the rubber ball floating in the air interests the child. It is a plaything for my thoughts, just as I find pleasure in the opposite thoughts, which amuse me much more. How do you enjoy New York?"

He had stopped and dismissed the subject, in a summary way that meant that he did not wish to return to it.

Rogasner's views thus expressed to his brother, were without reserve, and revealed his true thoughts. He was accustomed to be reserved, and to others he conversed with frequently advanced opinions that he did not honestly entertain.

Freeman was the only exception to this rule, aside from his brother. His secretary had become such a part of his life, and had acquired such a knowledge of his secret mission that he at times found relief in the candid disclosure of his views to this business companion.

On one occasion while the great railroad strike in the summer of 1894 was in progress, these two were discussing the probable results, when Freeman asked his employer if he thought it meant immediate revolution, when the latter replied:

"No, I do not; the time is not yet ripe, unless some hot headed leader who thinks the people are as advanced as he is, should start it; and yet," he said after pausing a moment, "I have thought in the last twenty-four hours that Mr. Cleveland thinks so."

"Why do you think that?" asked the private secretary cautiously.

"It is the first occasion," was the reply, "in times of peace in the history of this constitutional republic, when the federal army has been turned against the people. It is claimed in this country that the States are sovereign principalities, each endowed with the power of local self-government, which includes, of course, the right to exercise police power over its own citizens—protection for its people from being shot down by imported soldiers, unless the governor inform the president that he is unable to handle the insurrection. The governor did not ask for assistance, and when the president was rapidly massing the national troops at Chicago the governor made a vigorous but vain protest. A precedent was made for future action. There will be less protesting the second time. Why he did this—he, the head of a party that has always been tenacious in its interpretation of this principle in the constitution, has set me thinking, Freeman," and he smiled, as if there were more meaning in his words than they expressed on their face.

"And where do your thoughts lead to?" modestly inquired the secretary

"There are some things, Freeman, I will not discuss even with you." As Rogasner said this he was standing by the window and was playing with a tassel pendant of the heavy damask curtain. "In this country," he continued, "it is said that nine women out of ten place an exorbitant value upon a title or crown;" he paused a moment and then added, "I wonder what proportion of the men attach a value to them."

"Do you find many people in this country who do not believe in the ability of the people to govern themselves?" asked Freeman.

"Yes. That is common," replied the English diplomat. He then added, "The number that think so is now growing very rapidly—it is principally among the rich who want protection from the masses."

"Is it not a surprise to you" asked his secretary, "that Mr. Cleveland does not understand the cause of these troubles?"

"No," said Rogasner. "He was the attorney of men who trained his mind on this subject, and since he has been in office he has had neither time nor inclination to study it. Like a common mortal, he has been set one way and has stayed that way."

"But," interposed Freeman, "he was out of office four years."

"Why, my dear sir," was the reply, "he lived in New York City during that four years; and men who live in cities do not study—their minds once made up, they seldom if ever change them—great statesmen have invariably come from the country. Mr. Cleveland was busy during those four years with his law practice and other large business in which he was interested."

This financier—this man who had mastered political economy—was right; men who live in cities and spend much of their time going and coming to their place of business, who live among artificial surroundings,

among the hubbub and hurry of business, may become
great experts in their professions or trades, but they
can never become statesmen.

There is something profound, yet simple but broad
in that knowledge that comprehends the scope and
science of government and can adjust the equities of
men. A man who presides over the destinies of a
country should be one of nature's children; he should
have walked in its shaded lanes, suffered beneath the
burning suns, worked with the toiling masses; a student of nature as well as books; inspired to be just
and to deeds of greatness by a country mother, and
with thoughts as broad as the view upon the Western
plains. He has grown up most thoughtful and far-see-
ing, who has not had his attention and thought diverted
from what is greatest by the petty and narrow incidents of city life, diverted so, from childhood into
manhood and after. No contracted circles bound his
fancies or his reasoning. As the country makes the
body better than that developed in the city, so also,
even in a greater degree, it does the mind and soul. It
is man-making.

On another occasion when discussing with his secretary the probability of the people overthrowing
the present conditions by the use of the ballot, he
said: .

"That will hardly succeed; there is not one chance
in ten that it can."

"Why so?" asked his secretary, and to this he replied:

"The power of money sets public sentiment, and
when pressed sorely it uses its last but most effective weapon -it arouses prejudice against those whom

it seeks to destroy. The people trying to change existing conditions are in the attitude of reformers. If
they inaugurate a political movement, naturally the
anarchists, socialists and oppressed of all kinds flock
to it. It is then easy to accuse them all of being anarchists, and their intemperate utterances can be used
to make the people so believe. Prejudice is a feeling
the easiest to be aroused in the human breast."

"You think, then, that would defeat any reform movement?" asked Freeman.

"Yes," said Rogasner, "the people do not hold responsible the political party that makes anarchists.
They hold responsible the political party the anarchists
affiliate with. If people learned anything from experience or history," he continued, "you could not play
upon human nature, and always get the same tune out
of it.'

And with this remark he walked over to the book-
case and took down from the shelf a copy of Swinton's
"Outline of the World's History," and opening it at
page 195, said to Freeman: "I want to give you an
example of how reformers are talked about in their
time, in any age.

"Nero and his followers at one time," he said, glancing at the book, "had destroyed by fire a large part of
the city of Rome, and while it burned, that dissolute
emperor played upon his lyre. Upon coming out of
his drunkenness and realizing the situation, he decided
to use it as he had other matters, to the prejudice of
the Christians, who were reformers at that time, and,"
continued Rogasner, looking at his secretary, "I want
to read you this extract Swinton copies from an ancient
history by Tacitus."

And Rogasner read aloud, commenting as he read:

"'With this view, that is to divert suspicion, Nero inflicted the most exquisite tortures on these men who, under the vulgar appellation of Christians, were already branded with deserved infamy.'

"Mind you this historian says *vulgar appellation.* The word 'christian' was an epithet, or word with which to express contempt, and they were *'branded with deserved infamy.'* Now mark you he says *deserved* infamy. The historian so thought.

"'They derived their name and origin from one CHRIST, who in the reign of Tiberius had suffered death by the sentence of the procurator Pontius Pilate. For a while this dire superstition was checked; but it again burst forth, and not only spread itself over Judea, the first seat of this mischievous sect, but was even introduced into Rome, the common asylum which receives and protects whatever is impure, whatever is atrocious.'

"Do you observe *'impure'* and *'atrocious?'* These reformers were *impure* and *atrocious.*" And then he read on:

"'The confessions of those who were seized, discovered a great multitude of their accomplices and they were all convicted, not so much for the crime of setting fire to the city, as for their hatred of human-kind.'

"*Hatred of humankind,*" he repeated as he raised his eyes from the book and smiled, as he thought how easy it was for capital to make the people think how dangerous were the reformers of the present day, and then continued reading:

"'Some were nailed on crosses, others sewn up in the skins of wild beasts and exposed to the fury of dogs; others, again, smeared over with combustible materials, were used as torches to illuminate the darkness of the night.'

"On another occasion the emperor posted a proclamation warning the people against these dangerous reformers, and here is what happened," he said, as his eyes fell again on the history in his hand:

" 'Scarcely was' the proclamation posted up, when a Christian of noble rank tore it to pieces. For this he was roasted to death.'

"We are more refined," he went on speaking, as he put the book back in its place on the shelf, "in our treatment of reformers in this day. We call them 'cranks', 'calamity howlers', 'anarchists', and that settles it. Human nature is prone to be conservative, and prejudices are easily aroused against those who would change the present conditions. The people of the United States are optimistic. They like to speak well of their country, their state, city and neighborhood, and are hopeful of the future. This trait in their character will cause them to decry the attempt of reformers to point out the evil in our present system, and they will thus assist in perpetuating their own bondage.

"No, we are safe," he continued; "the power of money will scatter the people, and array one set of them against the other. The attempt of the present reformers will come to grief, as the world has learned nothing, and human nature is the same now as it ever was."

CHAPTER XXI.

The idea of having Melwyn for a rival had annoyed Rogasner no little, and he had planned to remove him from his path so far as it would be prudent to go in the use of money. The night after the Atweld ball he had sent one of his agents' to investigate that congressman's financial condition and social secrets if any. The only vulnerable point he could discover was a mortgage about to fall due. He had caused it to be purchased through the Chicago agent of whom we have before spoken, and to be so contrived as to keep his name out of the transaction.

This mortgage was now being foreclosed, and had already served to take young Melwyn away from Washington for some three weeks, and would probably tend to harass and worry him. He felt confident that with the use of money such as was at his command, he could prevent the reëlection of his rival, and that would remove him permanently from Washington life.

He had concluded not to stop in his cruelty, with the affairs of the son alone, and later had, through another agent, purchased the $100,000 mortgage owed by Mr. Melwyn, Sr., and had also caused foreclosure proceedings to be instituted on it. The note given in this case was what is known as a "judgment note;" that is, it was a note with a power of attorney attached, authorizing the attorney named to confess a judgment on the note when due and not paid, and this had been done.

All the property of Mr. Melwyn, Sr., was advertised for sale, and the old man had returned to the scenes of his former business triumphs, heart-broken and in despair.

It was in the month of July, a few days after the sale of all the Melwyn property in New Jersey, which constituted all the accumulations and saving of a life-time, that Jack Melwyn received a telegram from his sister in Jersey City: "Father is very sick; come at once."

He took Sam, who was still in Washington, with him, and left for the old home on the first train they could catch.

Arriving there, they found their father very feeble, his white and pinched face and white hair giving him the appearance of one already dead.

He was lying on a bed in the room where their mother had died the year before. It had been a sitting room for them when children, and had been familiarly known as "mother's room."

Here they had been "rocked" when babies, and had learned to stand on their feet the first time when pulling themselves up, probably by their mother's dress as she had sat sewing in front of the comfortable old grate fire. Every spot in that room was familiar to them both. The cracks in the plastering, the broken place in the grate, the figures in the carpet, a notch in the window casing cut by one of them when a boy, were all there as of old, and brought back effectively the memory of their boyhood days.

It touched a tenderer spot with Sam than it did with

Jack. He had not seen his mother for several years before she died, and had only learned of her death months after. He had been a devoted son, and it had grieved him ever since when he thought of her, to think that he was not there when the time came for her to leave them forever, and he blamed himself for having severed communication with home.

Poor Sam! The conflicting emotions of duty neglected, and the absent one, the mother of his little babe in the far off California grave, brought a lump to his throat and tears to his eyes. He tried to suppress his emotions as he sat down on the bed and spoke to his father, but the feeling of a thousand sad memories was too much for him, and he arose, and went out into the hall and upstairs into what had been the "boys' room."

Here he found everything pretty much as when he left it. Their mother had purposely kept it so, as she had told him once in a letter. He fell across the bed and cried aloud, the memories of a lifetime crowding into the moment, and he was moved by the thoughts of his mother gone and father going, and the desolate sadness that seemed to be around him and to fill his soul.

There was no thought of himself or his present condition that entered into his feeling, and it was more of his mother than his father that he was now thinking. The strong man shook with each emotion passing in waves through his mind, as he thought of his dead mother, dying in his absence, and of many little incidents in his life so closely connected with her motherly kindness and care.

They were noble tears. It spoke the true character

and nobleness of the son. Where is the man, if he be truly a man of character, who has not shed tears over the death of his mother? The greatest chasm to which man comes in his unfinished journey along the trail of life, that yawning abyss which only the soul can explore, is at the death of his mother. It is then that he sees childhood gone upon the one hand and old age coming upon the other, and recognizes that he is but a part of a principle, and only an atom in the wheel of evolution whirling through the cycles of time and space.

They learned from their sister, that their father had gone around Jersey City and New York to numerous brokers, seeking a loan to take up the old note that had merged into a judgment, but failing everywhere, he came home the night before the sale and had gone to bed, and had not been out of his room since.

The doctor said it was a breaking down of the system, with derangement of the kidneys, and death might be expected at any time.

The father was rational, and in talking with his children, toward the last, grew calm. They were all present when he died, and death came rather unexpectedly. He had asked Jack to prop the pillows up behind him, and when this was done, in a low but clear voice he told them he knew he was going to die, with no fear of death showing in his manner. And as he went on he said:

"You will give up the old place in a few days, for it is ours no longer. Jack, look after them," looking toward his two other children, "until the times get better and Sam gets employment. Sam, get your wife to Lincoln. Jack," and he turned his eyes toward his eldest son, "can't Sam get something to do there? And Lucy," looking at his daughter, "you could teach school.   When I am gone, if I can see what is going on in the world, I hope to see you all together at Lincoln, where Jack has made a name and has many friends. You can then assist each other, and the world will not feel so cold to you."

As he spoke the last few words his face twitched, and he threw his head back. A shudder seemed to pass over him and he was falling off the pillows as Jack threw his right arm under his head, attempting to lift him back where he had been, when looking into his father's eyes he discovered that death had come suddenly.

They arranged a pillow and laid his head upon it, and each in turn kissed his brow, and went into the next room, while some friendly neighbors who were in the house took charge of the remains.

The funeral over, Sam and Lucy started for Lincoln with money for their expenses furnished by their brother, where Sam would stay with Jack's partner in the law office until other employment could be obtained, and the sister would look for something to do. Jack returned to his post of duty at Washington, and from there the next day forwarded letters to Sam to be sent to his wife that would secure her transportation to Lincoln, with money to pay her other expenses.

Our young congressman's heart was sad. His father dead, following in a short year his mother, and his country in distress. For, understand, he was a patriot. No blast of trumpet, and clang of steeled helmet or saber, were necessary in his case, as is usual with men, to arouse his patriotism and zeal, and his thoughts now were of his nation.

Scarcely a day passed that he did not think of Grace Vivian as well, and now he thought how much greater comfort than he had ever felt before, it would be if he had her for wife and companion.

Then he could face the world with all its trials, and it would make him a Hercules in the defense of the principles he espoused. He had not seen her except at a distance since before he went to Lincoln in May and was absent so long.

He firmly believed that she was engaged to be married to his rival, and that no interference of his would in any way affect her choice.

CHAPTER XXII

·And how were affairs progressing with the adroit Englishman? As already related, he had obtained Senator Arnold's permission to seek the hand of his fair ward, and he had been waiting for a favorable opportunity to express his devotion and ask her consent to a union in marriage.

It was in the early days of August that the opportunity came, and he felt the occasion auspicious for the all important declaration he was about to make.

They had returned from a ride, to find dinner about to be served. Rogasner received a pressing invitation to remain, one which he accepted gladly, anticipating the opportunity which might come to him. Miss Vivian, he was delighted to observe, was in the best of spirits. She had enjoyed the ride and, dinner over, was conversing in the drawing-room with her suitor. He had never seen her in a mood more buoyant or companionable. He was full of hope.

They were sitting in the deep embrasure of a window and there had been silence for a time, when he resolved to stake all upon the issue of the moment. He took one of her hands in his, and though she made an impulsive movement to withdraw it, he but clasped it more firmly:

"I must speak, Miss Vivian," he said—and his voice, usually so well-controlled, trembled—"I must speak, and you must listen to me. You know I love you;

you could not but have recognized it. **Will you be
my wife?"**

The girl uttered no word. She appeared surprised
by the suddenness of it all, and the look in her eyes
was one more of alarm than one suggesting any answering sentiment. Rogasner was encouraged even by the
silence. Unaccustomed to defeat, there had been no
time when he had not counted her as practically his,
but there had been a shade of uncertainty. Now, once
embarked in the test of his powers, his confidence returned. There came upon him, too, an awful desire
of possession. The woman was looking her loveliest,
and fairer creature exists not upon earth than a beautiful young American woman. She was a splendid
creature as she sat there in all the bloom of her per-
fections, such an one as would in all ages have brought
heroes to her feet to win the love that Rogasner
sought. The man's eyes blazed with the fire of his race
in the old days, the fire that came when David gazed
upon Bathsheba, or when the eyes o Jacob first rested
on Rachel at the well. It had but b n smouldering
through the centuries. He broke forth impetuously,
half fiercely:

"You belong to me. We are fitted for each other.
We supplement each other, and I love you madly.
There is involved no question of relative wealth or
social position—you know that. Be mine!" And the
look upon his face was one half pleading, half triumphant.

The girl had sat as if dazed during this outburst.
Then she snatched her hand away and leaned back,
still silent. It was a moment or two before she recovered herself, but when she did so, she was self-
poised and all dignity. She spoke calmly:

"You will believe me," she said, "when I tell you I had not expected this. Perhaps I have been careless. I had thought we were warm friends; that was all. You are mistaken as to the relationship. I admire you. You are a very gifted man, but I do not love you. I could not talk to you as I am talking now if I loved you. It would be all different—somehow I know that. Let us forget all about what has passed. Surely we can be good friends still."

The student of human nature would have been deeply interested in the changing expression upon Rogasner's face as Miss Vivian spoke. With her first word the look of triumph had faded away and one of profound surprise had taken its place. Was he, *he*, to be rejected? He would not admit it. With her concluding words came greater desire than ever and desperate resolve. He would gain her somehow! He renewed his declaration. He even pleaded—a new thing for him—but he could not change her decision. She was not th ʾ ɪghtless of expression; on the contrary, she was most ..ısiderate. She treated him with the greatest defer ..ıce and made it evident that she felt a sympathy for him, but she would not sacrifice herself on that account. The only expression he secured upon which to base a hope was when he asked that if she changed her mind she would inform him. She answered that she would.

Rarely lacking tact in the gravest emergency was this man of the world, and even in this moment of the greatest humiliation of his life his sense of what was to his best interest did not desert him. His face expressed but sadness and respect, though inwardly he was a volcano. He withdrew even gracefully, with but the utterance of a hope that he had not displeased her beyond redemption. Half an hour later he was in his own office, pacing the floor and a different man. A baffled, enraged, and desperate man was this. As on the occasion when the fate of the great Bill in which he was so interested hung in the balance, he resorted to the brandy bottle until his face flushed and new plans came to his brain and hopefulness again, as the stimulant affected him.

"I'll have her yet," he almost snarled. "Am I, I who have accomplished so much, who have changed the very destinies of a nation, to be thwarted in my choice of a woman to be closest of all to me? Bah! the idea is absurd! Those who surround her are puppets with whom I have played already, and she, beautiful as she is, greatly as she affects even me, is but a human being, but a woman with, necessarily, all a woman's dreams and hopes and ambitions. I will find a way or make one. She belongs to me and I will have her!"

He paused in his walk, threw himself into an armchair, leaned his head upon a hand, and remained motionless for a time, absorbed in swift thought. That subtle brain was working at high pressure. Suddenly he leaped to his feet, his face indicating a new resolve. He drank of the brandy again and resumed his restless pacing. He was all alone and he thought aloud. The utterance of his decision, the sound of the words to him, for the moment, seemed a stronger enunciation of his fixed purpose.

"A first attempt is nothing. I have attempted many things and have not succeeded the first time, but always in the end. Where one device fails another

succeeds. 'She is a woman, therefore to be won,'"
and he laughed at the quotation. "Why not play the
strongest card? The stake is worth it. Why not tell
her who I really am? She knows me but as the successful Washington banker and the accomplished gentleman. She shall know more. She shall know that in
winning me when my true rank can be made known,
she gains a place which will make her the envy of
every petty title-hunter in the capital. She will appreciate the prospect at its value. She is a woman!"

Firmly fixed in his resolve, Rogasner but waited a
fitting opportunity for his second assault upon this
charming citadel. It did not come at once, nor did he
seek to hasten it. He was too adroit for that. He
knew that after the scene which had occurred there
must be a respite before a relationship with the proper
tone could be established. He did not discontinue his
visits to the Senator's residence, nor did he abate one
jot in courteous attention to Miss Vivian. He was a
trifle reserved, it may be, but thoughtful and attentive,
and she could not but admire what she deemed his
manly resignation. A sentiment of pity grew up toward
him, and she resolved to show him that if she could
not return his love she could be at least an appreciative and earnest friend. Gradually the old companionship was reëstablished. This was what Rogasner
had counted on. And, one day, after some time had
passed, came his second opportunity.

Oddly enough, they had been riding again and he
had remained to dinner. The circumstances attendant
upon the former declaration were almost duplicated
and what had occurred on that occasion must, neces
sarily, Rogasner knew, be in Miss Vivian's mind. She

was not repellent though, and, as they chatted together in the drawing-room, he almost fancied that she
might already be regretting her decision. Suddenly he
arose and stood upright. before her, and it must be
said of him that, rascal as he was, he looked very
much a man.

"You do not expect it, I know," he said, and there
was no tremor to his voice this time, "but I may not
have been altogether fair with you when I asked you
to be my wife. You did not understand it all, and I
should have told you. I am going to tell you now.
Miss Vivian—Grace—I hope, I believe, that when you
have listened to me now you will give me a different
answer." And his face glowed as he spoke.

She did not answer. She was scarcely less astonished than on the former occasion. He did not notice
that; he was too assured and too absorbed. He went
on impetuously:

"You have thought of me but as a banker here, but
as one of the social group with no connections beyond
those of the ordinary American. It is different; it is
altogether different. Were my real status known all
the title-hunters in Washington would be fluttering
about me. I come of one of the oldest and proudest
and wealthiest of European families. In fact the oldest and wealthiest in the world. Our millions aid in
controlling the affairs of nations. In influence, of all the
titled families of Europe, we are next to the crowned
heads. I am one of that family. There is nothing
American about me. I am here on a mission national,
even international in its importance. A title will be
mine for the asking on my return to Europe. I will
in time be a baron. I shall not remain here. I shall

return to occupy the position which is mine, as it will be yours. You will occupy a castle, if you wish. You will be presented at court. You will rank, among the proudest, as you will be the most beautiful of the fair American women who have left this country to become the ornaments of an older and better civilization. You will be the envy of all whom you know. That is what I offer you. That is what I should have told you before, but for my foolish confidence. Grace—darling, say now that you will come to me, that you will be mine. Or say that now, since the mask to my identity is removed, you will let me woo you with renewed confidence!" and he stood with gleaming eyes and reached out his arms toward her.

Upon the girl's face as he spoke had come the index of varying emotions. Surprise had given way to sheer amazement, and as at last she fully comprehended the bent of his appeal, and the full nature of the declaration and argument upon which he relied so confidently, the look changed to one of fervent womanly indignation. She sprang to her feet and shrank backward as he advanced toward her. Her face, usually so gentle, was full of resolution. Her soft eyes flashed. There was ɔ ˉ﹄g to her voice as she answered him.

"And so, sir, I have been mistaken? What I supposed was manly acceptance of a situation which cannot change was but an adroit patience exercised until the time should come for a purely commercial offer! You thought to buy me—you thought that, regardless of love, I would accept you because you could offer me unlimited wealth and an exalted position! I do not doubt your word, sir. I do not imagine you would be guilty of a misstatement as to what you have to offer, but that does not matter. You sneer at America and talk of a better civilization of which you say I may be made an ornament. I am proud of being an American woman and I am content with this civilization of which you speak so lightly! It may be barbarous, but I am content. And—you will pardon me, sir—but I fear your usual tact has deserted you to-day. Did you imagine that such a proposition, such comment, could incline toward you a woman with self-respect or with that regard for her own country and its institutions which a woman should feel not less than a man? I am proud of my country! You have made a grave mistake. And—you will pardon me again—but I feel it will be better if we see no more of each other to-day!"

She swept from the room with a flushed face, leaving Rogasner staring at her as she departed. He was for the moment stunned and then as a full realization of what had been the outcome of his intended coup, came upon him an oath burst from his lips.

"And even this shall not be the end!" he muttered as he left the house.

CHAPTER XXIII.

To say that Rogasner was humiliated by his latest defeat would be to express but feebly the sentiment which now animated him. Unaccustomed to failure, the object he sought had but increased in value in his eyes, and his love for Grace was now inflamed into an absorbing passion. Mingled with his desire of possession was a feeling of keen resentment, but that was swallowed up and lost in the deeper wave of emotion. His infatuation had become of the sort which brooks no resistance, and he chafed and raged like a balked wild beast. His feeling did not, however, show upon the surface. A strong man, a 'trained one, and of indomitable spirit, was this lover in pursuit. He had not abandoned the chase. He had but reached that frame of mind when he would adopt almost any course giving promise of success. His ordinarily soft method of policy was cast to the winds. He had one more means to utilize, though, before resorting to an extreme measure.

He had determined to enlist the services of Senator Arnold in his behalf, to induce that astute gentleman to exert himself to the utmost in influencing his ward and bring about the result Rogasner so ardently desired. He realized that he had marred his chances seriously by his latest attempt, but he counted again upon the effect of time in softening any resentment Miss Vivian might feel toward him. After all, it was because of love of her that he had committed such a gross blunder, and what woman cannot forgive a man for loving her? He consoled himself into a degree of hopefulness again, and then visited the capitol and sent his card in to the Senator. He was received in one of the committee rooms. An appointment was made, on the plea of matter of importance to be discussed, and the next day the men met in Rogasner's private office. Freeman was sent away on business that would keep him absent for some time, and precautions were taken for securing the utmost privacy during the interview.

The Senator was curious but not at all excited over what was to come, and when he learned for what it was that his call had been requested, his interest did not visibly increase. He may have surmised that it was in connection with his wooing that Rogasner wished to see him, for there were few shrewder or more observing men than Senator Arnold. Rogasner told his story.

Very little was concealed by the arch-diplomat, though he did not relate all that he had said at his last meeting with the young lady. That would have revealed some things that he did not wish the Senator to know—at least not yet. But he told of his first proposal and his rejection, and in a general way, of the failure of his second attempt. He was not bitter in any of his comments. He softened the aspect of the case by an assertion that he believed the young lady was well inclined toward him and that it required but a little effort to turn the scale in his interest.

"Then," said the Senator, "as I understand it, you wish me to exert my influence in your favor?"

"Such an interest in my behalf would be most grate-

fully appreciated and is what I most earnestly desire,"
was the response.

"I will not do it," was the crusty answer. "Grace
will select her own husband, and I shall not interfere."

The lover did not lose his temper. He had resolved
that on this occasion every impulse should be curbed
and that no error on his part should be committed because of anger. He made what was partly an argument and partly an appeal. He spoke temperately and
persuasively—and to do him justice, he spoke well—but
with no effect. A passive verdict had been practically
rendered in advance. The Senator undoubtedly preferred Rogasner to any other suitor for the hand of his
ward, but, as a matter of fact, he was at heart opposed
to all. He was insanely peevish and jealous concern-
ing the fair girl who was such a light in his home, and
did not relish the idea of giving her to any one. He
had, of late, grown exceedingly selfish in this respect.
He did not want her taken out of his life. As the
housewife becomes attached to the canary bird, or any
other pet, until it seems almost a necessary thing for
happiness, so had this grim old politician learned to
prize the girl who made the home so cheerful, who
rendered him less solitary, and who was a solace and
a comfort to him.

A father would have wished to see his daughter happily married and a promising future assured for her,
but the Senator was devoid of this fatherly instinct.
His practice had not been in the line of self-sacrifice.
He thought first of himself, and was firmly convinced
that it was an injustice to him personally that his
ward should think of leaving him. The great law of
nature did not count. He was petulant in the consider-

ation of it all. That a suitor should have the assurance to ask his aid in promoting his own discomfort seemed to him preposterous. He was careless of his demeanor and said peremptorily that he did not care to discuss the subject further. The fact that he was receiving $25,000 a year from the man Rogasner represented, either did not occur to him, or if so, it did not seem to have any weight. The man he left did not, a moment later, look like the one whom the Senator had addressed. All the demon in Rogasner's nature was finally aroused.

His urbanity had disappeared, and after his usual habit when alone after a disappointment, he again gave full rein to his passions.

"D—n him!" he said. "This vulgar American politician, this spawn of some farm or some little town of his crude country, treats me as arrogantly as if he were my equal—no, by—! as if, if he were my superior! I should have ordered him from the place. But I need him. I will have him, too! He doesn't know it, the pompous old fool, but he belongs to me. He shall have one more chance, just one, and then, if he fails to do as I wish, he shall learn what will spoil his rest. He must come to terms!" And Rogasner laughed as he leaned back in his chair. He felt every confidence in the effect of the Senator's influence on his ward, and of his own ultimate control of the old politician he had not a doubt. There remained in his hands a weapon he had resolved to use. The act would be a dastardly one, but that did not affect him.

The plotting man took no further step for some days. He brooded over his disappointment and pondered over every detail of the plan he was resolved to carry out.

Every move he was about to make was fixed in his
mind and then he made another engagement with the
American statesmān.   This time the interview was to
take place in the Senator's own house, and on the
next Friday evening.   Thursday Rogasner's brother
Edward arrived from New York.   On the same evening they had a meeting in the former's private office.

Rogasner had awaited his brother's coming eagerly.
Under other circumstances, with schemes of the ordinary nature on hand, he would have cared little for his
presence.   Even now, he had no idea of gaining any
assistance or even a suggestion of value, but he had
reached that condition of mind which comes after a tense
nervous strain, when to impart one's secrets to another
who may be trusted implicitly is a relief and a rejuvenation to a man, a safety valve which allows the escape
of pent-up emotions and tends toward securing a normal phase again.   He was resolved to tell his brother
everything.   It would be something to have an ally
at heart, even though not in the field.

There were cigars and wine, the doors were looked
to carefully and the brothers sat down in easy chairs
together.   "You do not look as well as when I saw
you last, Victor," said Edward.   "You're working too
hard on your great enterprise."   '

The elder brother laughed.   "It is something else,"
he answered.   "The fact is, Edward, I've been demon-
strating that, in one way at least, I am as other men
are, and I'm going to tell you about it.   I am going
to be married, but there are some problems to be
solved first.   It will be rather a relief, 1 imagine, to
unbosom myself."

The interest of Edward was aroused at once.   "I've

supposed," he said, "that you were a little too internal
in your living, a little too much absorbed in the accomplishment of an end to care much for women—except as occasional playthings. May I ask upon whom
you have looked so approvingly?"

"Yes; there'll be no reservation. You've never met
her. She is a Miss Vivian, the ward of Senator
Arnold."

The face of the younger man fell a little: "An American and a Christian?" he queried.

"Yes."

"Are there not women of our own race and faith
beautiful enough and with all grace of mind and body
to fit them for any man? What has become of our
fair Russian of whom you once wrote me?"

"Do not speak of her. We do not always regulate
our fancies. This is the one woman I want, and the
one I will have! Besides, what matters it?" he continued almost fiercely. "Did not our ancestors, even on
Arabian plains, take whatever women of whatever race
most pleased their fancy? Nor did they hesitate at
means. Who knows the blood of Bathsheba? Uriah
was doubtless some mercenary from anywhere, such as
often made up the forces of the time, and yet she suited
David, and a mercenary more or less counted but little. As for the blood, it is soon lost in that current
which has changed but little with the ages."

Edward laughed. "Well, as you say, I imagine it
does not matter greatly. Our family pays little attention to the letter of the Mosaic law, anyhow. We are
adaptable. But as to the obstacles? Tell me about
them."

Rogasner flicked the ashes from the end of his

cigar and leaned back smilingly in his chair. "The first," he said, and there was triumph in his voice, which was raised as he spoke, "was a fellow named Melwyn. He is already disposed of!"

And in that triumphant leer, in raising his voice at just that moment, Victor Rogasner committed a more fatal error than could have been previously placed to his account in all his more than twenty years of scheming effort, in all his plotting and planning at the capital!

Kathleen, the girl whom Melwyn had once rescued from the assault of a street ruffian, had never forgotten the episode nor the man who had done her such a service and had conducted himself toward her in her distress as thoughtfully and courteously as if she were the wife of a cabinet minister. She had recognized the young congressman upon the street, had learned his name, and her gratitude had not decreased when she became acquainted with his standing. For Rogasner, her employer, she had never learned to feel any particular regard—her race and his were too far apart— and he himself scarcely knew of her existence—but she was a trim, deft servant, neat to look upon and faithful in the performance of her duties, and the housekeeper was suited with her. She had become a fixture in the establishment. As Rogasner spoke she was passing along the hallway beside the rooms and his words reached her ears distinctly. "Melwyn!" She paused without thinking.

"An' what is it they be doin' wid Mr. Melwyn?" she whispered to herself, and then—let Kathleen be forgiven —she lingered to hear more. She was very close to the keyhole and every word of the subsequent conversation was audible to her. Perfectly honest was Kathleen; she would not for the world have been guilty of what she thought was very wrong, but her sense of honor, socially and technically, had never been cultivated. She but did impulsively what she thought was right. In this instance she did not think at all.

As the girl listened, a look of alarm succeeded that of perplexity upon her face. She crouched more closely to the door. Her ear was close to the keyhole. For more than an hour she remained there motionless, then rose silently and fled to her attic room.

What Kathleen had heard was well calculated to alarm her. There had been no hesitation, no reservation on Rogasner's part as he talked with his brother. He fairly rioted in the abandon of free utterance of what was in his heart and on his mind. He told of Melwyn's first appearance as an apparent lover of Miss Vivian, and of his own consequent disquietude. Then, gloatingly, he told of how his strong, silent force had been exerted to crush a rival, how his vindictiveness had extended to all members of that rival's family. He spoke of the wreck of Melwyn, senior, and there was no trace of regret when he told of how the helpless old man had died after the shock of his bankruptcy. "Money is the power, money is the thing, Edward!" he almost shouted. "They got in my way and I utilized the strongest agency there is in the world. The fate of that family is sealed. I will crush them out, root and branch!"

He went into details regarding the purchase of the mortgage threatening the elder son; of his intention to defeat his reëlection, and explained fully his designs for making the young man's ruin as complete as had been that of the father. Here he spoke gleefully. "He is done for, absolutely done for," he said; "he cannot meet that mortgage and his affairs will be so affected that he must disappear from Washington. He is absolutely out of the way. Miss Vivian imagines that he has neglected her, and he is under the impression that she has forgotten him, as doubtless she has."

Edward commented musingly: "You're not a man to interfere with safely, Victor. You remove obstacles ruthlessly enough."

"Yes," assented Rogasner calmly, "I do. But there is more to come." And he then told of the present necessity for Senator Arnold's aid and his resolve to have that assistance at all hazards. "I'll not go into details about that," he said, "but I have a ring in that arrogant person's nose by which I can lead him when the time comes. He'll feel the tautening of the rope very soon now."

When the brothers separated the elder was in a mood which was almost jubilant. The unburdening had relieved him. He was all confidence.

The girl, Kathleen, had missed no word. Intelligent enough to comprehend the meaning of everything, she was in a tremor of the greatest excitement. All the emotion of her impulsive race was aroused within her. She tossed upon her bed in anxiety and perplexity, but before morning the resolution was taken. She cared not for consequences. She would seek Mr. Melwyn and Miss Vivian and tell them all. They must be warned. How to find them was the poor girl's chief source of perplexity. But she was determined.

It was still early morning when Kathleen, having obtained leave of absence from the housekeeper on a plea of the illness of her mother, emerged from the Rogasner establishment.

CHAPTER XXIV.

It was a puzzled girl who emerged upon the avenue from Rogasner's home. There are a great many congressmen in Washington during the session, all conspicuosity is lost and the places of residence of nine congressmen out of ten are unknown to any save their personal friends. It is true there is a congressional directory, but Kathleen did not know there was such a publication in existence. She relied solely on personal inquiry, and her first step was to find a cousin who was employed about the capital. He had gone out when she reached his home, but she waited patiently. That she would find Congressman Melwyn somehow, in some way, she was fully resolved. Her cousin returned at about ten o'clock, and she told him what she wanted. The big, good-natured Irishman laughed:

"An' is it a congressman ye're afther, my dear?" said he. "Well, he could have no betther swateheart. Or is it a bill ye do be wishin' introjooced, Kathleen?"

But Kathleen was in too anxious a mood for chaffing, and begged her cousin to get her the information she sought as soon as possible, as she had a message to deliver. The task was an easy one for the man, and the girl set out for Melwyn's boarding place, on Capitol Hill.

There was no difficulty in finding the residence to which she had been directed, but Kathleen found that

finding the congressman himself was quite another'
thing. He had gone out, they said, and would not return
until six o'clock in the evening. She might find him
at the House later in the day—but Kathleen, ignorant
of methods, would as soon have thought of strolling in
unannounced on the Pope as of invading the capitol
and trying to reach a congressman upon the floor.
She was in despair, for a time, but reflection suggested
another course to her. She would see Miss Vivian
first! Perhaps, she reasoned, that would have been the
better way after all, and she started for Senator Arnold's residence.

There were no further geographical difficulties in
the way of the impulsive girl. Everybody in Washington knew where Senator Arnold lived, and she was
very soon ringing the door-bell timidly, almost tempted
to run away now that she was so close to the ordeal
she had taken upon herself. How would Miss Vivian
receive her? Was she not a foolish girl on a very foolish errand? Then came a thought of all the cruelty
and wickedness of what she had overheard, and she
was resolute again. The old colored man, Abe, came.
to the door.

Kathleen explained hesitatingly that she wished to
see Miss Vivian, and declined to say upon what business. Old Abe, whose quick eye and long experience
enabled him to distinguish caste at a glance, rolled
his eyes wonderingly. He said nothing, however, after
his first question, and, leaving the girl standing in the
hall, sought his mistress. She was not a little puzzled
at receiving a call of such a nature at such an hour in
the day, but her curiosity was aroused and she di.
rected that the girl be shown up to her apartments.

With her heart in her mouth, Kathleen entered the sumptuous room, where a soft perfume pervaded the air and where the appointments were more luxurious than she had ever seen before. The living center-piece of it all was adapted to such surroundings. She stood in the middle of the apartment, a creature very fair to look upon, her flowing morning gown draping gracefully a perfect figure, and the lace at her throat suggesting in its physical way no more softness and purity than did the expression of her gentle face. She received her timid visitor with all kindness and asked her, in such manner as to relieve her embarrassment as much as possible, the object of her visit.

Then came to poor Kathleen the hardest trial of her simple life. She blushed furiously. She did not know how to begin. Becoming desperate in her strait, at last, she broke forth recklessly:

"O, miss, it's lots I have to tell you. It's you, you know—you and Mr. Melwyn—and what they said, miss! Oh, it's awful!"

To say that Grace was bewildered would be but utilizing a mild form of words to express her condition after this droll outburst. Was the girl insane? No. there was no chance of that, she could see plainly enough as she looked into the honest creature's troubled but intelligent face. But about Melwyn—about herself —coupled together, too—and the blood rushed to her own cheeks and her heart beat tumultuously at the thought. She was a unnerved, almost, as the young woman before her. But curiosity and anxiety exerted themselves in her aid and she recovered her composure. She addressed Kathleen soothingly:

"Don't be disturbed," she said. "Tell me all about it, just quietly and slowly."

Thus encouraged, Kathleen regained her wits and her composure. She could talk well enough, this bright Irish girl, when all herself, and she told her story graphically. She began at the beginning. She told how a gentleman had once rescued her from an unpleasant situation, and how subsequently she had recognized him and learned his name. And then, concealing nothing, she told how she was led to listen at the door and what she heard. She remembered every sentence spoken and repeated it with wonderful accuracy. As she progressed a degree of excitement possessed her and she spoke with a certain dramatic effect; not merely the words she had heard, but their very spirit was reproduced in the recital. The astonished listener saw the whole scene reënacted before her eyes. She could imagine the leering triumph on the face of Rogasner as he spoke of his immediate plans, and his look of satisfaction when he told of the destruction of the father and then—in his opinion—inevitable crushing of the son. She saw herself, *herself*, the central figure, the aim and end of all this plotting and wickedness—and she shuddered at the thought. And then scarcely less revolting came the knowledge that her guardian, he whom from earliest childhood she had been taught to love and respect, he for whom despite his hardness she felt a genuine affection was, if Rogasner's boasting were justified, somehow in this man's power. It was horrible! And, above all, was the woman's feeling for the one she now knew she loved. He had not abandoned her, but had borne nobly what he thought her own abandonment of him. He had been hurt, because of her, through those he most loved, and was the target of deadly animosity himself—all because of her! The tears came into her eyes, her bosom heaved, and as Kathleen completed her story the servant was the more calm of the two women. But that was only a condition of the moment. A spirited American girl was this, one with force and character and brains and a conscience, and one who could act in behalf of one dear to her. She arose to her feet with a sudden resolution showing itself in every feature.

"God bless you!" she said; "you have acted courageously and nobly, and I shall be grateful to you all my life! But you must give me reason to be more grateful to you still. You must find Mr. Melwyn for me—at once—to-day! Will you not do that for me?"

"I'll do anything for you, miss, anything—you've been so good to me—and you understood. I don't blame Mr. Melwyn for loving you, indeed I don't, and I'll help you all I can."

The blush which came to Grace Vivian's cheek at the girl's ingenuous answer was quite as deep as the flush of excitement which had a few moments before preceded it, but she did not forget her immediate object.

"You must do this," she said. "Listen carefully to what I now say. Find Mr. Melwyn and tell him from me—no, take him this note," and she sat down at a little escritoire and wrote:

"My Dear Mr. Melwyn:—Something very astonishing, something very important to you—and to others —has just been learned by me. I wish to see you at the earliest possible moment. May I not ask that you will grant my request, and, furthermore, will you not permit me to ask a strange thing of you, that you enter at the side gate to the grounds at just nine o'clock this evening? Old Abe will meet you at the gate and bring you to me,

"This is a strange note, I know—but I know, too, that you will understand that there is occasion for it. There has been much wickedness on the part of some, and there has been delusion and misapprehension on the part of—others.   ·

"GRACE VIVIAN."

She gave the note to Kathleen.   "You will probably find Mr. Melwyn at six o'clock, the hour when they told you he dined," she explained.   "Give him this note and answer any questions he may ask you. Tell him all you have told me and tell him of your visit here to-day.   And that is all.   I am very grateful, I want to say that again.   And I will be your friend always."

Very proud and elated was Kathleen as she left the house.   She had no occasion now to regret her impetuous course.   She knew that she had done what was right, and she now felt assured that in putting upon their guard those whose happiness was imperiled she had probably accomplished a great good.   Promptly at six o'clock she was at the house on Capitol Hill, and was soon in the presence of Jack Melwyn.   She gave him the note.

As his eyes fell upon the handwriting there was more happiness apparent in the young congressman's face than had shone there for months before. His hand trembled a little as he opened the missive, and as he devoured its contents his heart was uplifted in a way he had thought it would never be again. He could read between the lines and he knew, upon the moment, that his love was no longer hopeless. No such woman as Grace Vivian would write such a note to a man to whom she was indifferent. But the mystery of it all puzzled him. There was occasion for it, of that he was well assured, for he knew his love's fine sense and judgment, but he could not comprehend it. He turned to Kathleen.

"Tell your mistress," he said,—for he did not rec· ognize the girl—"that her request shall be complied with,"—but Kathleen stood hesitating.

"If you please, sir," she explained, "I have something to tell. She—Miss Vivian—told me to tell you all I had told her."

Needless to say that she was taken into the parlor of the house, that she was ·seated and asked to say what she wished. Had she not come from Grace?

But the man was not prepared to hear what was related to him. It stunned him. To such a nature as his the whole fell story was something monstrous, and as the account proceeded he recognized its absolute truth. A thousand confirmatory circumstances occurred to him each moment. He recognized that he—and Grace as well—had been victims of one of the foulest of plots. He recognized sinister influences for which he had been unable to account. His face grew hard and his teeth were set, and when the girl had ·con·cluded her story he sat for a few moments silent. But he was a new man. He recognized his foe now and was ready for the issue. It would be no longer a fight unfair and under cover. He could take care of himself. But what of it all—in the midst of his great happiness? She loved him! The world was a good one, after all. How could it be otherwise when She loved him?

He turned to Kathleen. "You have been very good," he said. "Why did you do it all?"

And Kathleen, thus fairly cornered, had to explain with flushed face and much hesitation the connection between his own act in rescuing her once upon a time and her present course. Melwyn recognized then that to be a simple gentleman with duties toward all is sometimes profitable!

And at nine o'clock that night, Jack Melwyn stood at the side entrance to the grounds attached to the residence of Senator Arnold.

Old Abe was at the gate and even in the dusk could be distinguished by the gleam of his teeth as he grinned on a broad scale in recognition and welcome of the visitor.

"Come in, sah, come right in, sah," he said as he opened the gate. "De young lady hab given dereckshums fur to conduck you to de back drawin'-room froo de side entrance," and he led the way with vast dignity.

The house was reached and entered, and a moment later Melwyn was shown into the drawing-room by the old negro.

CHAPTER XXV.

Rogasner's confidence did not desert him after the relieving conversation with his brother. His condition was now normal, with the possible addition of a new element of sternness and cruelty in his resolves. He was even buoyant in his anticipations and smiled grimly as he thought of the coming meeting with Senator Arnold, and of the manner in which he would humiliate and crush the overweening American while at the same time forcing him to become an instrument in the attainment of his own desires. The reflection was delicious to him, the race instinct which, ages ago, made the victorious Israelites "harrow" the conquered now manifesting itself again. He was eager for the interview.

So easily confident, so pleasantly interested was Rogasner in all that was to come that on that Friday night of such consequence to him, he dressed himself with more than usual care, though to surpass his ordinary daintiness in this respect was difficult. There was a vague idea in his mind that his love affair might culminate at once after his talk with the Senator, and that he would return from the senatorial residence a man engaged to be married to the one woman in the world to him. He was a gentleman of the world, attractive in every way, as he emerged from his home to take a carriage for the Senator's residence. A very handsome man was Rogasner, as are almost always those of his race in whom the pronounced promontories of face are softened by occasional inter-breeding with the Gentiles in time past, and to the expression of whom has come that refinement which follows education. A close, earnest look into his eyes by some keen physiognomist might have revealed the slumbering devil there, the grasping, conscienceless devil, but that could not be visible to any save the few initiated in the world. Even the driver of his carriage looked upon him admiringly—and one's servant is the harshest critic.

The drive occupied but a few moments. The city of magnificent distances, has no magnificent distances as regards reaching the most aristocratic residence district starting from near the corner of Fourteenth Street and the avenue. There was but the patter of hoofs and the roll of wheels for ten minutes and then Rogasner was being ushered into Senator Arnold's drawing-room. He did not have long to wait. The Senator came in, placid and courteous. In his own mind he had divined the object of Rogasner's visit. "It will be but a repetition of his last effort to secure my aid," he grumbled to himself. "I will pack him away again. It is absurd—the whole business. I will not be bothered."

His demeanor was, nevertheless, courtly and even cordial as he greeted his visitor, for this successful American politician had during the schooling of long trimming years learned to act with more unconscious cleverness than could many a successful man upon the stage. "I'm glad to see you, Rogasner," he said. "You've been to dinner of course and smoked? So have I. We'll just sit down here together and talk over comfortably whatever it is that you want to see me about."

Rogasner uttered the proper perfunctory sentence in the way of thanks and the two sat down. The Senator rose again.

"I imagine it may be some personal matter you may wish to discuss, and as Grace may come in I'll close the folding doors. Now, my friend, go ahead."

In every sentence, in every phrase, in every word of the Senator's expression was a burden of easy, self-confident, uninterested patronage. Rogasner smiling, imitating the altogether respectful, half-hopeful, half-appealing younger man, was beneath the surface raging, impatient and vindictive. But his iron will made him self-contained and politic. He was what would have been rather a pleasant picture to a casual observer as he answered the old politician:

"Senator, I am grateful to you,—grateful for the manner in which you talk to me. I dare say—no, I'll not say that I more than guess, I know that you have divined the object of my visit. Of course it relates to what in every man's life at one time becomes to him what is life's gravest matter. It is about Miss Vivian. I want to say to you, now, and again, that I have come here to talk with you—more openly and fully than I have done yet—and to ask you to aid me, to ask you to influence her, if possible, in my behalf. That is why I am here to-night. You may or you may not approve of it all. There are questions to be asked and answered. But questions—we will begin all anew—generally follow a proposition. My proposition is that I want to marry your ward. She has refused me, but I think that your influence cast in the scale would in-

duce her to accept me. I mean no perfunctory influence but a real one, the utmost you can exert. Now,
am I the man you want your ward to marry, if she
marry at all? I know that you know enough of me to
say 'yes.' You know that I am rich and you know that
I am not a fool. Senator Arnold, I ask you to see
your ward on this matter. I ask you to do for me what
you would do in getting a great bill through. I want
you to give Grace to me. You can do it."

Rogasner paused and looked at the Senator curiously,
expectantly and—despite all his shrewd concession of
air—almost defiantly and commandingly. The Senator
noted not at all the vague ownership ring to the man's
voice, nor the confident and forceful look in his dark
eyes. He was—this shrewd politician of decades of
experience—but a blind thing fumbling with what was
before him. Rogasner understood all this.

Senator Arnold's air as he responded was what could
be described as the patronizingly—irritatingly—dignified.

"I like you, Rogasner," he began, "but it seems to
me you have strayed a little out of boundaries. You
have forgotten the obligations of others"—and here he
assumed an expression which would have done credit
to a moderately established saint—"you have forgotten
the obligation I owe this ward of mine. She is a very
intelligent young woman. She is capable, if any
woman be so, of choosing for herself. She is, naturally,
not merely an object of my solicitude and care and
love, but, as she has developed, of my respect. I have
every confidence in her judgment and I have resolved to
leave the choice of a husband to her absolutely and entirely. She will know best. And so, Rogasner, my

friend, I cannot interfere without abandoning my decision, which is backed by the best reasoning. 1 will not interfere. I will not talk to Grace at all upon the subject you have mentioned. You must fight your own battle, and win if you can."

The Senator leaned back in his chair, tolerably well pleased with his own presentation of his attitude, and looked at Rogasner inquiringly. That individual, for a moment or two, said never a word.

A full minute had passed when the swarthy, handsome man rose from the easy chair in which he had been sitting, and walked once or twice up and down the room. The Senator looked at him in astonishment. It was not merely Rogasner's sudden freak of walking that had startled and puzzled the other man. Rogasner's face had changed. It was pale now. And, not only was the man's face pallid, but the skin seemed tightened over it and the blood gone from it. It was a tense, hard face, but it had none of the desperate hopelessness which shows in faces ordinarily—so strained of tissue. It was a triumphant face with all its nervousness and hardness. He spoke, and his voice was like the sound which comes from some machine, some machine which cuts or saws or grinds:

"I will not say, Senator, that I had anticipated such response to my appeal to you. I have counted it as among the possibilities, but I had not thought you could be so foolish."

The Senator leaped to his feet. "Foolish?" he repeated in amazement. "What do you mean?" And he stood excited, angry and inquiring.

Rogasner turned in his walk and looked the other man sternly in the face: "I mean," he said, "just what

my words might imply. I meant that I did not imagine that you could be so foolish as to imperil your
own welfare, your own prospects, all that an ambitious
man holds most dear, by refusing me.

Senator Arnold fairly gasped in his astonishment
and contemptuous indignation. "Imperil my prospects?
Do you know what you are talking about? Are you
insane?"

Rogasner laughed: "No, I don't think I'm insane.
But I may be a trifle excited and the blood may have
flowed to my brain a trifle more rapidly in consequence. And of course the effect of it all has been to
make me think rapidly. And one of the things it has
caused to occur to me is that a bribed man—a man
occupying a high and trusted position under a republic,
yet bribed to aid in its destruction—should not talk of
morals nor of honor nor of obligations of any kind."
His tone was a sneer in itself. He paused a moment
or two, then continued: "Such a man as this should
accept all that comes to him, morally or ethically, and
deal with it in a practical way." He looked at his
stunned auditor in a way which was as patronizing as
the Senator himself had ever used toward a powerless
constituent. "And, Senator, I want you to help me
with your ward."

It is hard to describe how the Senator, this potent
representative of a great state, looked or acted at that
particular moment He did not yet realize all that the
man before him knew, nor all that the man could do.
Yet there was something in Rogasner's manner which
impressed him absolutely with the knowledge that he
must be careful. He recovered himself with an effort.
"I do not quite understand," he said with an air of

what was almost placidity "Just put your case. You have formulated what is the gravest charge you could have made. What do you mean?"

Rogasner stood easily and carelessly and altogether at ease in the drawing-room of this senator of the United States. As he spoke his voice was vibrant, clear and controlled. "What I mean," he said, "is this: It is but a simple statement of fact and of a part of the natural sequence of a certain bargain made years ago. What I know—what I can prove—is my capital, my strength as I stand here now talking to you. This is what I know, this is what I have to tell you. This is the anchor, the intrenchment, the palisade of my being here—of the foundation of which I talk to you now. I know—I have proofs aside from the confidence of my relative, Baron Rothe, that since the year 1869 you have received the sum of $25,000 annually for the practical betrayal of your country's interests. I know it. You know it! Do you want all the American world to know it?"

The grim face of the hard, strong American had paled as the dark man had spoken. He did not need to hear the end of a sentence—this one among the most keenly perceptive men of a perceptive race and nation—to recognize its full significance. He knew, at that instant, at that moment—at whatever indicates the narrowest limit of time in which the brain can act,—that he was in Rogasner's power! His face took on the look which appertains to those who have paid the debt we owe to nature and who—so far as the body is concerned—lie motionless and stolid. His face was that of one who has been hurt suddenly, grievously, by something falling, who has been stunned and does not recognize things, who, thus hurt, has little sense, yet may distinguish a sinister influence, and who has yet the instinct of fight, who is yet a reasoner and who sees the quality and the chances of every struggling against odds. He felt that this man knew all about him. There was no occasion for going into details. He was startled; he was foolish and selfish in his alarm; he was not strong.

He leaned back in the chair he had taken, he tried to preserve a semblance of outward dignity and force. Rogasner, watching him, but laughed noiselessly. Finally the Senator spoke: "Tell me just what you know," he said. "Tell me the simple truth of it. Then we will deal together."

It was rather a surprise to Rogasner, this attitude of the Senator. With all his acuteness he had never, as they put it, "figured upon" the attitude and force of a man, a keen American politician, absolutely at bay. But Rogasner had his own campaign outlined most clearly. He could at least express a cruel determination.

The American and the man from an older world were face to face at last in an issue of moment to both of them. The one was easy, self-possessed, and relentless; the other was alarmed, inquiring, yet courageous in his way, and one who would be as ruthless with an advantage as the other. So they stood.

Strangely enough, it was the Senator who first broke the silence and asked what the outcome would be. "Well," he said, "what are you going to do about it?"

The hard man of the world, the one with the advantage, was perplexed for the moment, but it was necessary that he should answer the question. Then occurred a scene which was dramatic.

"This is it," he said. "This is the situation. I am going to put it to you very simply, and you will pardon me if it be a trifle harsh. I have occasion for your services. I want your influence with your ward. I have asked for it before and have been refused. Persuasion has failed, and now I propose to utilize another factor. It is a very pretty factor in its way—it is called force!"

He clasped his hands behind his back and took a turn across the room, laughing inwardly still; then he resumed:

"The utilization of that force, Senator, is this way: You are a traitor to your country and a receiver of bribes! You have been in receipt of $25,000 a year for many years, which sum, amounting in the aggregate to over five hundred thousand dollars, has been furnished you by an English syndicate of which Baron Rothe is the head and for which your influence has been cast in favor of such financial legislation as would most grievously affect the country of which you are a citizen. An exposure of the facts would result in dragging you down to an infamy almost without parallel. You know that what I am saying is the simple, absolute truth, but you have not known that I was familiar with all the circumstances. I have the proofs, absolute, unimpeachable and unquestionable proofs in my possession! Unless you accede to my proposition —one which it seems to me you should have acceded to without compelling this dernier resort—I propose to drag you down from your petty pedestal! I propose to ruin you utterly, to make your name one which shall be a gibe in the newspapers and a synonym for all that is sleek and base and despicable! You have now

my simple program outlined. It *is* simple, isn't it?
What are *you* going to do about it?"

The Senator had fallen back into the chair, his
hands resting upon each arm of the seat and his head
thrown back against the cushioned rest, his face as
pale as death. But he was not yet conquered.

"You cannot afford to do it?" he uttered in a timid,
frightened, and inquiring tone.

"You deceive yourself," replied Rogasner, and the
cruelty of his tone and manner grew doubly cold and
cruel. "We need you no longer. Our purpose is accomplished; your country is ruined, and no power on
earth can save it. The undoing of the wrong your
hand inflicted will now come too late. The miserable
and degraded situation in which your government is
now placed, can be left to its own people. They will
eat each other up. We can toss you into the drift-
wood of your country's wreckage, and they will tear
you to pieces, literally, limb from limb."

The Senator was crushed. He appeared almost like
a man stricken with paralysis, as he caught the full
force, the gist of Rogasner's utterance. His face paled
and his fingers twitched nervously upon the leather
beneath them. It was curious about his hands. They
seemed for a moment no part of the man. They were
working wildly and independently apart from him. So
had some sudden, queer affliction of the nerves affected
them. It was pitiable! It was dreadful in every way!
It was the cold-blooded murder of what had been a
manhood. Before Rogasner, shrinking back in the
chair, was the corpse of pride and arrogance and all
confidence. Mortal terror showed in his face. It was
a face from which the blood had retreated in shame

and agony. The man looked twenty years older than
he did when the two had entered the room.   His eyes
opened and shut, he was fumbling mentally with something like the instinct of some dumb brute, seeking
egress from a pitfall. The shock had, for the moment,
affected his brain. There came but slowly back to his
countenance the look of intelligence and reflectiveness,
as he became a reasoning being again. But the look
of mortal terror was still upon him.

An artist who delights in painting the greater ones
of the cat family, who puts upon the canvas tigers and
panthers and the sleek yellow lion of our Rocky Mountains, would have been in an ecstasy of delight could
he have looked upon Rogasner then. Of human sympathy, there was no more indicated, than is shown by
any one of the great cats when it has made its first
stroke, and toys with its benumbed prey before the
death scene. He was not exactly smiling—he was
leering, and he was as happy as Nero was in the death
agonies of his mother. The Hebrew was "harrowing"
again.

The man in the chair suddenly recovered himself,
leaped to his feet and advanced toward the other, his
face still white and fearful, his hands stretched forward, and just at that moment there came upon both
men the subtle knowledge that there was another person in the room. There, standing before them near
the folding doors between the drawing rooms—the
folding doors which moved without a sound—stood
Grace Vivian! She had heard what had passed.

It was worth seeing—what happened then.

She had heard it all. She had been afforded time
for reasoning and comprehension of it all. The first

great shock of the revelation of her guardian's perfidy
had come, and her mind had compassed its sequence.
Not firmer was the face of Rogasner himself than that
of the girl who had entered the room. Her face was
absolutely transformed. She stood there a Judith!
She seemed like some angel with a sword!

While waiting for her appointed interview withMel-
wyn, Grace had entered the rear parlor. She knew that
Rogasner was in the house and was then with her
guardian in the front parlor. It was with no real intention of listening that she seated herself on a sofa
near the folding doors, for her thoughts were of the
young congressman, and she was anxiously awaiting
his coming.

But she now heard the voices of the two men, and
heard plainly their words as they grew louder—the
whole pitiless story—and as it concerned her, her future and disposal, she continued to listen. At last
impelled by a feeling she could not control, she threw
back the doors and entered the room.

She spoke slowly, easily and distinctly. This young
woman had become self-poised and strong.

"I do not know what to say. I do not know how to
express what is in my mind. Everything, somehow,
seems like a blank to me and something horrible. I,
just a girl, stand before you two men and for both of
you I feel a contempt that is beyond description! I,
just a girl, know very well that both of you, despite
your great ability and experience, are less worthy
of respect than the servant who waited upon us at dinner. I don't know what to say. Senator—Mr. Arnold
—I have respected you so much! I have loved you
so much, and yet behind you lay this hidden, despicable

thing all the time!   Did I not know that there were good people in the world it seems to me that I should want to die now, this minute."

She paused for a moment, and then there came a beautiful hardness upon her face as she continued:

"As for the other man, the man who stands there near you, I have something to say and it seems to me that it is a duty to say it.   He wants me to be his wife. He has sought to force you to become an agent in help ing to obtain his ends.   I know the whole story of it. I know how he has gloated over this prospective course of his which has culminated to-night.   I know all about it.   It doesn't matter how, but I know it.   How can I express my contempt for this creature?   He has intelligence, wonderful intelligence—I know that—but he is a distorted thing mentally and morally.   He is wicked.   He is offensive.

"Mr. Rogasner," and here she turned and faced the man fairly, not defiantly but as some judge might face a culprit, "Mr. Rogasner, this I have to say to you. You are very shrewd.   You are very wise in your way, the commercial way, inbred through generations.   The politic, scheming, devious way inbred through generations also.   You are as repulsive to me as anything that could exist.   Of course, you understand that I do not want to ever see you again, in all my life.

"All your plotting," and now her voice rose, "against me, falls harmless, and my life is to be uncontaminated by further association with so corrupt and vile a thing as you are.   Would that others had escaped your cruelty as I.   You are no friend to me, or my countrymen; we will gladly see you return to the country that gave birth to so impure a monster.   If my country weep because of what you have accomplished, her daughters will wipe away the tears, and her sons will right the wrongs you have inflicted. As to this man," and now she faced toward the American traitor, and spoke as if speaking to herself, or to her country, "guardian of mine no longer, how could he be? What monstrous deed is this he has done, that when he's charged with its commission, he admits the charge to be just, and cringes' and deals with his accuser? Recipient of a fortune, great sums of money —and this house—" and now her eyes glanced around the room, "where I have made my home, possibly purchased and paid for with the price of his honor—"

While she spoke both men had recoiled and resumed their seats. The Senator appeared to be trying to fend off something, he turned his face, and in his feelings seemed to cringe, to creep and crawl as if a nightmare possessed him.

Rogasner sat sullen. He was not cowed, he was the heartless, conscienceless man as ever. He arose and was walking toward her, for what purpose it is not known.

She was not looking in that direction. Now, something else had occurred. The man for whom she had sent, the young congressman from Nebraska, had been ushered into the house and into the drawing-room—as has already been related, by the trusted old negro servant. Here came one of the coincidences that affect the current of our lives. Melwyn had entered the drawing-room but a moment after Grace had opened the doors separating that from the room in front. He could not but hear, could not but see, and what he saw at that particular moment was Rogasner advancing upon the woman who was his, the one whom he knew was his because of the letter she had written to him.

Rogasner may have only intended to forcefully present a defense, or tauntingly express his vindictiveness instead of gracefully retiring from a contest he now realized was hopelessly lost; but no matter what he intended, at that moment Melwyn, the typical American man, the man whose whole heart responded to the love of this lovely woman, and who was now fully informed and conscious of the true character of the man he now looked upon for the first time since the death of his father—with an impulse born of the instant, sprang forward—this young western giant, and taking Rogasner by the throat, first drew him forward, and then with "you villain," threw him with a force that sent the Englishman against the floor at the farther side of the room. Then he turned and the eyes of the two lovers met. They knew that each belonged to the other; they met for the first time knowing this, and under circumstances that formed a crisis in the life of the woman—at a time when she was sorely tried, and when she, this orphan, needed the love of some true friend—and no love is greater support than the love of a strong man—instinctively, promptly, his arm encircled her waist, and he drew her toward him, and as she looked up into his face, her loving eyes spoke back the love they saw in his, and then followed what is the natural impulse of two human beings loving each other, and in such position physically, their lips met,—the instinct of a contact of nerve centers—that test of impulsive love, came upon them both at once.

Nothing more happened. How could anything more

take place? There was an end and an adjudication of
all that was between this quartet of human beings.
Grace took the arm of Melwyn, and with him went into
the rear drawing-room, while old Abe, who had just
come in, at a motion from his young mistress, closed
the folding doors. What need to tell of what happened
in either drawing-room after this? Pledged lovers in
one apartment, two men of brains, exposed in their
weakness and wickedness, in another! That was all.
What the lovers said all the world may guess at. The
two men in the other room were henceforth harmless.

CHAPTER XXVI.

It is not easy to tell of what were the emotions and what were the thoughts of Rogasner as he left the Arnold mansion. Here was a man, a passionate, strong man, who had seen the fondest hope of his life, the one end and aim of his present ambition, blighted suddenly and irredeemably. Here was a man with nothing to live for—at least in the estimation of the moment. His great life's work's plan was known and he was crippled there, and might possibly be published to the world. His love was bestowed where, he knew at last, it could not be returned. He was a shriveled, frost-bitten thing and he knew it. He staggered as he left the cab to enter his place of abode. He was not the Rogasner who had left the house an hour or two before.

He entered his office, and, as he opened the door, was surprised by the blaze of light. The place was occupied. Jeanne Soutleffsky, the fair Jewess who had been his agent in so many instances, was there to welcome him.

She stood there a being certainly fair to look upon. She might have been Rebecca solicitous over Ivanhoe, so earnest, so good and gracious and beautiful and of all faithfulness was she. She stood there as the mentally stricken man came into the room. She rose to meet him.

The story of this beautiful woman has not yet been

told, and its telling should be properly a part of the
history of these events so fraught with an importance
in the real inner history of the man. She was of gentle
blood. This is the story of Jeanne Soutleffsky and
Rogasner. He was an attaché of an embassy to St.
Petersburg, a young man well connected, with enormous
wealth behind him, with the brains he showed in later
life, and with all tact and impressiveness. He had met
the young Jewess at one of the many *fetes* to which his
official place gave him admission, had been fascinated
by her, had wooed her, and after many months had won
her, won her beyond all redemption, won her so that
henceforth she belonged to him.

Then came the shift which is the regular part of
English diplomatic politics. The young man, sup-
ported by unlimited money, was yet but a slave to a
regime, and must follow the course marked out for
those of his class. He was ordered to Constantinople,
and then the ordeal of parting from the fair Russian
Jewess came. It was an ordeal through which neither of
them passed properly. Each of them showed weakness
and human nature. They decided not to part. Each
of them had money, and money affects the course of
many lovers. There were reasons, so he said at least,
why he could not marry her at the time, but she was
recklessly broad-minded, desperate, a woman worth the
loving. She had abundant means and no connections
that could not be severed easily, and she said to him
that one spot upon this round world was the same to
her as another, if he, this particular man, was hers,
hers absolutely.

She would endure the climate of some tropic region.
She would endure anything for the sake of being with

him. Cultivated, a brilliant woman of the world was
this, but a woman of the world with a love that had
absorbed and grasped her totally. She loved him—
and by the way, for a woman with the desperado instinct in her, he was a man well worth the loving—
and she had been with him in Washington through all
these years, relieved only by an occasional trip to St.
Petersburg and back.

He had promised to marry her on the happening of
an event on which hinged the consent of his uncle,
Baron Rothe, and at one time claimed to her that the
passage of the bill she assisted on, would secure the
desired result. In this he had played her false.

She had been his tactful adviser in all social equa-
tions, and she had been to him whatever it is that a
woman's instinct may supply to a scheming man who
sometimes gropes and doubts and turns for aid to that
which to the fighting male animal seems almost like ·
an inspiration given. She had been as close to him
as woman may come to man. Yet she had been neglected, forgotten, and she knew it. She alone had been
watchful from the beginning. She alone for months
had been aware of his love for Grace and of its possible termination. She had watched each phase of the
love story, watched it angrily, furiously, despairingly,
yet ever self-contained and faithful. When Rogasner
entered the room, and she saw him pallid, wavering
and shivering, she knew that his adventitious love
affair had failed, and that so far as love, pure love
was concerned, he belonged to her completely.

She rose as he entered, and her face was a poem, a
great epic poem of the grand old Jewish race. It was

a face in which shone all love, all resolve, and all self-sacrifice. It was a face for which such a look from which, a man little broader than Rogasner would have chanced his life. The man came into the room staggering still; he looked at her and his eyes brightened. *There* was help, *there* was relief. He looked at her appealingly and then sank backward into a chair. Still he looked at her and his eyes had a volume in them. She looked at him. She looked at him again in amazement, and then in alarm. She appealed to him to tell her what was wrong, to put it into words, but he did not answer.

Then this woman, this woman with a woman's love and instincts, and strength in an emergency, moved forward to learn physically what was wrong with the man whom she so loved. She asked him, she talked to him, and he answered but vaguely and blunderingly. She felt of his limbs, she felt of his arms and of his legs, and she, acute woman of the world, knew what had happened before he knew of it himself.

What had happened was this: This man, this man with nerves tense, overstrained and exhausted, had attempted more than the human machinery could bear unscathed. This man had unconsciously brought upon himself a crisis which could not possibly in his case have been avoided. The tautness of all things had told upon him and he had broken down—that is what kills so many men at Washington—a hopeless invalid, hopeless for all time, hopeless for all time within the limit of a human life. He had received a sudden paralytic stroke, the effect of a tense mental strain unrelieved for years; and there he was just a cripple, a hopeless, human wreck. A paralytic sat there in an easy chair gazing up with dimmed fishy eyes at the woman, the dark-eyed, tempestuous-natured—but faithful and loving woman who had clung to his fortunes. Perhaps his eyes were opened then, who can tell? She, this woman, this splendid Russo-Jewess woman, saw the whole thing in a moment, and she did not falter. It may be there was something almost triumphant in her look; she knew that this wreckage was all hers with none to interfere.

In the city of Philadelphia is a house in which are certain relics and records, and, may be, a photograph or a portrait or two—probably the term "daguerreotype would be better, since the picture of the one represented could have been taken only at the time when the sun's services in making faces were but halfway comprehended—if there be such a portrait as is here suggested—and if there be the story of her life—the legend still clings around the Rebecca whom Walter Scott made so lovable in Ivanhoe.

The man's eyes were opened then. He saw this helpless wreck, figment of a man who but an hour or two before had been so strong; he saw more than had come to his mental eyesight in all the years that had passed in his active life. He saw what is worth the living for. He saw how great are some things and how little are other things. He saw that of all there is in this world some one woman's perfect love is the greatest, and, even to a strong man, the most protecting and helpful force.

There came to the mind of this shrewd trickster a great revulsion, and a great cleansing. That physical effect which is almost death, had taught him the lesson which men learn but slowly. He, this paralytic, had seen per force of nature what there is—what thousands of men should see earlier—and he could reason, this ruthless man, this mental desperado, and he knew that he was helpless for the future—he could feel it in his substances and he knew it. And he knew, too, that for him there was no solace for all the future, save as might come from the tender lovingness of some one woman, and there was but one woman, the one he had so wronged and who was now beside him and ministering to him.

Why tell further in detail the story of this man—this extraordinary man? What happened, was but what must have happened anyhow. The woman took him away to England to a great Sanitarium, and there she is watching him, guarding him, attending and being all to him, as a woman may be still. That is the story of Rogasner and the Jewess, Jeanne Soutleffsky.

CHAPTER XXVII.

Grace left the house of Senator Arnold the next day never to return, accompanied by her old family servant, Abe, and went to the Arlington Hotel.

The next day Congress adjourned, and on the following day Melwyn and Grace were married in a private parlor of the hotel, and left the same night for Lincoln. Kathleen and old Abe accompanied them.

Senator Arnold sought recuperation, broken and decrepit in appearance, at a quiet summer resort, and is in mortal dread of publicity being given to his nefarious connections with the English conspiracy against his country.

Freeman remains in Washington, awaiting instructions from Baron Rothe.

Frame and Carroll may be seen now most any day in Washington in the hotel lobbies, at some legation, or at the political headquarters, and say they are going to return to the West only when it can be truthfully said that the "stars and stripes" wave over the "land of the free and the home of the brave."

That this book should record a nation's shame, is not the fault of him who chronicles it, but of the characters who have written it in the history of his country. To redeem that country and give back to its citizens the priceless boon of a free government should now be the earnest and zealous duty of every patriotic American.

Is the story overdrawn? This may be the question of many. Take the case of Annie Lindgren, the old nurse of the Melwyn family, dying crushed to death in a frantic attempt to obtain bread, in a city where as this is written, the elevators are filled with grain, and the railway tracks are blocked with loaded cars. Here the optimist may think the imagination was drawn upon. The reply is that even here, all was confined to the simple truth, and that the account was but taken from a Chicago newspaper, where it appeared when it was current news. It requires a great cataclysm such as now shakes the nation, to have produced the instance, or to have made it possible of belief; and yet it is only one among thousands of such cases of suffering, diffe ing only in degree.

Those living in affluence or comfortable circumstances, who have not yet joined the great majority who live in want or stand in dread of the to-morrow, are as a rule, indifferent or conscience-deadened, and to them the case of Annie Lindgren will be a thought of to-day, to be gone to-morrow. If the story of her suffering and death could be written in letters of blood on the blue sky, there to remain by day and by night, the good mothers and fathers, and brothers and sisters of this republic would stand with blanched faces, as they read the scroll, and not one would rest contented till the possibility of its recurrence was removed from our civilization.

The awful responsibility is upon the present generation. They should take up and solve the problem that is ours to deal with. Let us meet it bravely and as wisely as we may be able, and let no prejudice embarrass us. To the one who would deride our cry of

alarm, let us answer: To the man in the still hour
of the night, who discovers a house on fire, whose un-
suspecting and sleeping inmates know not their danger, the first instinct of duty is to rescue them from
their peril. To the man standing in the Conemaugh
valley who was first to see the break in the dam and the
rush of waters that swept down upon the doomed city
of Johnstown, the instinct was that of the hero, as
he dashed down the pike in that long race that day
with death, giving the alarm to the thousands whose
lives he saved. In either instance to hesitate would
have been the act of a dastard. Let all who wish to
defend the present conditions, and the characters pro-
ducing them, do so if that be their choice. Their
position is not an enviable one. Their species existed at
the period of our revolutionary struggles, and again on
both sides, in the struggle between the North and
South; but history fails to mention them individually,
and only collectively to record their existence as a
class.

To those who would have their children inherit
a higher state of civilization than exists at the present,
and whose ambition is onward and upward, there is a
higher sentiment in life than ever comes to the inert
and selfish.

If the reader regard lightly the story of suffering,
and of a people's great wrong, then the reply is, in
the language of a revolutionary sire:

"If you have not suffered, if you have not gone hungry, then you are no judge of those who have."

Of the business man who has done business on a
falling market for twenty-one years, it is asked that
he reflect upon the financial problem, and examine it

with a view to solving the cause of this decline in prices.

To the citizen generally, the study of history as it bears upon the perpetuity of government and promotion of civilization, is recommended, and, above all, it is urged that he take an interest in elections. Each citizen is a stockholder in the great corporation of government, and he should study intelligently the policy he would advocate by his voce. It is also to be wished that he should not be satisfied with the relatively crude development of the present, but should look to the future for a higher and better civilization.

And as a parting reminder, in this age when the few are accumulating the wealth of the country, and the many—the masses—the yeomanry of the land—in whose keeping in times of national peril, is the life of the Republic, are growing poorer, let us remember the trite quotation:

"Ill fares the land, to hastening ills a prey,
Where wealth accumulates and men decay."

On the 29th day of September, 1894, there sailed on the steamer Paris from Liverpool a representative of the foreign syndicate to take Rogasner's place.

THE END.